THE DAY I DISAPPEARED

ALSO BY BRANDI REEDS

Trespassing

Third Party

THE DAY I DISAPPEARED

A THRILLER

BRANDI REEDS

LAKE UNION
PUBLISHING

This is a work of fiction. Names, characters, organizations, places, events, and incidents are either products of the author's imagination or are used fictitiously.

Published by Lake Union Publishing, Seattle

www.apub.com

ISBN-13: 9781542006552
ISBN-10: 1542006554

Cover design by Shasti O'Leary Soudant

Printed in the United States of America

For Madelaine and Samantha,
who taught me the will to survive,
& Joshua, who gave me another reason.

Many Years Ago

He checked on Amy one last time before he went out to the shore to cast a line.

She was asleep.

Her white-blonde curls spilled over the pillowcase, and her pink lips puckered, like someone had tied them into a perfect bow. The white cotton nightgown draped over her pudgy thigh, exposing her ruffled-bottom panties.

He straightened her nightgown to cover her, pulled the quilt over his little sister's sleeping body, and tucked her favorite doll into her embrace.

"I'm going fishing for a while," he whispered. "I'll be right outside, on the pier. Call me if you need me."

She sighed in response.

He kissed her on the forehead, then headed out of her room and into the hallway.

One last look.

She'd rolled over; her nightgown rode up her thigh, again exposing her ruffled panties, and she'd shoved the quilt halfway off the bed.

She'd be okay. It was a warm night.

He descended the old pine staircase, skipping the third to last step, which creaked something awful. Always careful not to wake Amy. Since the day she was born, that lesson had been drilled into him. *Don't wake the baby. Don't wake the baby.*

She was almost five now, but he still heard Mom's voice in his ear whenever his sister was asleep.

Don't wake the baby.

When he dimmed the stairwell light and looked out the enormous window facing the lake, a sense of calm washed over him.

He loved it up at the lake. Such a break from the city and its noise—constant sirens, unstoppable movement. Here, fireflies danced in the navy sky, their yellow lights blinking, as if beckoning to him in Morse code.

He stepped onto the porch, where he'd leaned a fishing pole, and after one last glance up the staircase to ensure Amy remained asleep, he headed toward the pier.

He cast out line after line but got no nibbles. He reeled in the line, looking up at the crescent moon. Fish should be biting this time of year, this time of night, under a moon like this.

He took to the shore, cast into the reedy waters under the willow trees.

He got a few steps farther from the property line with every cast. Always, before moving down the shoreline, he glanced back at the house to make sure Amy's light remained off.

The fish were biting here, thrashing on the line, battling against his will.

He caught, released. Caught, released.

Let them live another day.

One last cast, and he'd head back to the house.

He looked back toward Amy's window only to find he'd ventured farther down the shore than he'd realized. He couldn't see the house.

His mother and father would be back from the church potluck soon, and he'd promised them he'd take care of Amy.

And he had. She'd been fine every night he'd gone fishing after putting her to bed.

What if she awakened? Mom would ask. *What if she needed you and you weren't there?*

He and Amy had a plan, in that case. She'd stand at the door and call to him. He'd reel in and come.

Their little secret.

But . . .

He'd never strayed this far from the pier before.

If she'd called, would he have heard?

He reeled in a little faster, a niggling doubt in the back of his mind.

Had she called him?

Had he been too busy casting a line to notice?

He packed up his bait and tackle and ran, barely paying attention to the rocks and brush that could trip him up in the dark. Until he got in sight of the house.

The light in Amy's room . . . it was *on.*

"Amy?" He dropped his tackle box and ran faster. Now he could see that the front door was open. She'd come outside. "Amy!"

He spun around and around, searching for her, but the night was so dark, the brush along the shore too thick.

"Amy!"

His heartbeat clouded his ears. He tore into the house, taking the stairs two at a time until he was at her bedroom door.

Her bed was empty. Only her favorite doll occupied the space.

He felt sick, as if at any second he'd turn out his dinner.

He threw open doors, checked closets. "Amy!" She had to be somewhere.

But she was nowhere.

Gone.

He heard the crunch of tires against the gravel drive. Their parents were home.

Frantically, he peered into every crevice—behind the toilets, inside kitchen cabinets, under couches and under the creaking step, which he, in utter desperation, pried up with his bare hands.

Tears blurred his vision, and his breath became a series of huffs and coughs. "Amy," he wheezed. "Where are you?"

"Son."

He turned to face his parents, the old pine stair board in his bloodied hands.

"What are you doing?" his father asked.

"Amy." He wiped a waterfall of tears from his eyes and saw the horror dawn on his mother's face.

"No, no, no—" She hopped over the open stair and scurried up the remaining steps. "Amy?"

"What's happened, son?"

"Amy!" Mom's voice shook the house. "No!"

The truth settled over the house like a fine dust. There was no escaping it: she was gone.

In a daze, numb from his core to his extremities, he witnessed his parents' pursuit of his little sister.

Father was screaming now, only inches from his face. Later, he could only imagine the words his father might have said; the ringing in his ears overpowered all other sound.

The ringing morphed into Amy's pretty little voice singing nursery rhymes. *One, two. Buckle my shoe . . .*

The house filled with police officers.

The night sky flashed red and blue.

Where is she, son? Where is she?

What did you do to her?

Who did you let into the house?

Who had access to her?

It was days before they found her, ensnared in the underbrush off the shore, her bloated body drifting on the current until the divers freed her from the weedy tethers. Her blue lips. The blank look in her eyes. Her porcelain skin turned greenish-black and scratched and marred by the underbrush.

She wasn't his sister anymore.

The taste of her absence was bitter, like the blood from his split lip after Father struck him with a closed fist.

Your fault.

Guilt emanated from his flesh like the ever-ripening stink of fresh fish and mosquito repellent in which he'd been stewing since the night she disappeared. The stench clung to him long after Father shoved him into the shower and slammed his body against the tiled wall.

Even the pain was numb.

He collapsed into the tub, the water beating onto his clothed body along with fist after fist after fist.

Keep it coming, Dad. Keep hitting me.

When the officers pulled Father off him, he still felt the pummeling force of his father's rage.

Time was a requiem in Amy's honor. The wiggling little tooth in her mouth she'd never lose. The dresses she'd never wear. The boys she'd never kiss. The years she wouldn't be able to live. Time was nothing if not memories, and in those frenetic moments, time stopped.

Her room remained untouched, like a shrine.

The yellow tape the police had put up in the hours after her disappearance stretched across the doorway—a boundary.

From the hallway, he stared at the things inside the room, and suddenly, Amy was among them, lying in bed, just where he'd left her.

Relief swept through him.

He ducked under the caution tape and crawled into bed next to her. He took her warm, soft body into his arms. "I'll never leave again," he promised. "Never."

But when he brushed her hair from her forehead, glassy eyes stared back at him—the same blank expression he'd seen when they pulled his sister from the lake.

He scrambled off the bed, screaming.

The body he'd held was no longer warm . . . it was cold, hard plastic.

Amy's favorite doll.

It lay where Amy should be, staring up at him with a smirk on its face.

Laughing at him.

CHAPTER 1
HOLLY

June 5

I was only four years old when it happened, and at that age, how many of us remember anything concrete? I remember things before it happened. I remember right after. I remember the bread, so to speak, just not the peanut butter and jelly.

It's like one of those time lapses in a movie, when the picture fades to black, and when it comes back to life, words scrawl across the screen: *three months later.*

One minute, I was jumping rope at the park with Katherine Hershey, my lifelong best friend, whom I lovingly call Kitten.

And just a breath later it was suddenly dark outside, and much colder. I was nestled in my father's embrace, his large hand cradling my head: *Daddy loves you. I'm so sorry, Holly-Dolly. You're all right now, you're all right.*

Of course I was all right. I was with my father. Why wouldn't I be okay?

I tongued a bloody nub in my lower gum—I'd lost my first tooth. I remember the taste of it, the pulpy texture of it. But when did it happen? When did I lose it?

"My arm hurts." That's all I said. And there was a reason for the pain. During my absence, I'd sustained some sort of injury on my arm. A jagged laceration.

I still have the scar, a small arrow-shaped mark about two inches long, just north of my elbow on my forearm.

It seemed, even in my young mind, an excessive reason for Dad's gushing. I didn't know until much later—years later—the reason for my father's emotional display, the reason I had no memory of meeting the tooth fairy, of the leaves turning that year, of my fifth birthday: I'd been gone. Presumed dead, the victim of some sicko preying on little girls.

I'm told the first three days are the most crucial in a kidnapping investigation. I was gone for more than three months.

A witnessed stranger abduction, they called it.

"It was a long time ago," I say to Lake County detective Jason Guidry. From my position on the balcony of this high-rise condo, I glance through the patio doors at the party going on without me, then out at Lake Michigan, sparkling in the distance. I wonder how he got my cell phone number and why anyone from the police department is calling now after all this time. "I was a kid. I'm not sure I can offer any new information."

"I'm not necessarily looking for *new* information. Just want to go over the basics. The reports are . . ." I hear the rustling of papers through the line. "They're lacking in organization, shall we say, and as I was just assigned to your case—"

"I didn't know *anyone* was still working the case. Alan Kohlbrook is in jail. I mean, the case is solved, right?"

"There've been some new developments."

"What kind of developments?"

"A few months ago, a lawyer received some sort of manifesto in the mail, for starters. He says it's proof of Kohlbrook's innocence and decided to represent him. There's talk of an exoneration."

"Meaning he'd be out?" Uneasiness courses through me when I consider that the man convicted of holding me hostage could soon be walking the streets.

"If this lawyer gets the leverage he's aiming for, it'll be all over the news in a few days. We thought you should hear it from us first."

"You're saying he might be *freed*."

"It's a long shot, but you understand it would be helpful to talk to you about it."

"Of course. But I'm sort of in the middle of something right now." *Something* is Kitten and Eliot's bridal shower—a *couples'* bridal shower (*ugh*), which I'm attending solo. "And it was so long ago."

More than twenty years, to be exact. It's like it happened to someone else, or like I was kidnapped in a play. I experienced it, obviously, but it's so distant, so far gone. "I don't remember anything." I sip my bourbon on the rocks and set the glass on the railing.

I slipped outside to take the call. This place is in the Edgewater neighborhood of Chicago and belongs to a pair of Kitten's friends, the Joneses everyone's trying to keep up with. Despite my ducking out so as not to disrupt the celebration, I can practically feel Kitten's dagger eyes slicing me through the sliding glass door.

"I understand," Guidry says. "But I'd still like to talk to you. How's tomorrow morning?"

"I'm supposed to work tomorrow, and I could use the overtime, so—"

"Tell me what time works for you." There's such urgency in his voice that my fingertips tingle.

After a moment, I ask, "Is this an emergency? Did something happen?"

"Not *urgent*, you understand, but important." He sighs. "Look, Miss Gebhardt. You're here, alive and well, and Alan Kohlbrook is in prison. But we've got another case with similarities—"

"A copycat?"

"I don't know yet. But you were recovered. Not every child is. Anything you tell me could help out on this other case."

"Wait a minute. Are you saying there's a copycat kidnapper out there? Or are you saying that Kohlbrook might *not* be the one who took me?"

"Well . . . I guess that's why I'd like to talk to you. To determine."

A tornado of nerves roars in my gut. It happened again. Another little girl was snatched away. I fight the urge to fly out of this party, if only to google *missing girl, Lake County, Illinois.* "I haven't had to think about any of this in a long time, you understand."

"Mm-hmm."

"I might not be of help."

"Yet you might be."

"Is tomorrow afternoon all right? We only put in half days on Saturdays, and I should be home by one. Or do we have to meet sooner?"

"Tomorrow works. Your residence?" He rattles off the address of my parents' acreage, adding *and a half* to denote the long, winding drive to the converted barn in which I live. This guy knows everything.

"It's a ways off the road," I tell him. "Keep going. The drive dead-ends at my place." I glance at the party carrying on inside. Kitten, arms crossed over her chest, taps her toes—as if to say, *I'm waiting.*

"See you then, Detective." I hang up and instantly search for news about a missing child. A rash of headlines pops up about a runaway teen found last month. I go back, click on the next item, and a moment later, I'm staring at the face of a five-year-old girl.

Blonde, just like I used to be.

Blue eyes.

Just like me.

But I came back alive, and this girl—

Her name is Skyler Jane Kipniss. She's from a tiny town just outside Indianapolis, about a four-hour drive from my place, and she's been missing for more than two months now—seventy-nine days. But unfortunately, lots of girls go missing, and this one isn't even from around here. Maybe Guidry is just grasping at straws.

I exit out of my browser just as the balcony door slides open.

"Derrion Sterling, I presume?" Kitten's lips curl into a pucker, as if she just sucked on a lemon. She nods at my phone. This is Kitten in defensive mode, claws out, wanting to protect me from a guy she thinks is no good.

"You think I'd duck out of your party to take a call from *him*? Wow. Thanks for the vote of confidence, Kitten."

"If the shoe fits . . ."

Sterling and I ended our relationship nearly two months ago, but he was supposed to accompany me tonight. We're still stuck on a well-worn path between his place and mine. Back and forth, waiting at the same traffic signals—stop, go.

Go to work, come home.

Meet for a drink.

Drink too much.

Argue.

Reconcile. Usually in bed.

Wake up alone.

Go to work . . .

I can't help it. What's good between us is very, very good. He once parlayed a discussion about peanut butter fudge into an impromptu weekend boat trip to Mackinac Island, for Chrissake.

It's like he knows me. I don't have to talk about what happened when I was a kid because he remembers when it happened. He and his friends came to Lake Bluff from Chicago to help canvass the neighborhood to look for me. The day we met, he looked at me a little too long and said, "Ah. I'm in the midst of a survivor."

It isn't as if no one had ever called me that before. But people tiptoe around my past, and I liked that he didn't. The open and honest attitude didn't last, though.

There are days he comes to my place after a week on the road, collapses on my sofa, and doesn't pay me—or his dog, whom he often straps me with during his absence—any mind. I understand that his job as a research analyst for an online news outlet can be stressful. In the world of cutthroat digital competition, being first to the finish line is everything. If someone else reports something adjacent to what he's been tracking down, his entire week could be for naught. So he tends to shut down sometimes. His silences can be icy, but what are you going to do? You take the bad with the good. I learned that from my parents.

Kitten says I'm getting too old for this pattern, and she's probably right. But she's also judging me from the glow of having found "the one." Not everyone is as lucky.

"So what's so important that you had to take a call in the middle of Eliot's toast?" she says.

I retrieve the glass I set on the railing and raise it. "Cheers?" I shrug and offer a smile.

"Honey." The claws retract, and Kitten takes a step closer and puts a hand on my shoulder. "Everything okay with your mom?"

Still holding the glass, I twist the ring I'm wearing on my left pinkie. It's my mom's ring, a twin setting of her birthstone and mine—a gift my father gave her when I was born. I've been wearing it for nearly two months now, ever since the accident, which occurred, coincidentally, just after Sterling and I broke up. "No change, as far as I know."

"So that wasn't the hospital."

"No . . ." I wish I'd thought to lie to her. She might forgive me if I'd left the party to receive news about my mother's condition. But there's been no change. My mother is still unresponsive, despite signs of brain activity.

"Fucking Sterling!" Kitten leans on her forearms against the balcony railing, balancing a glass of red wine in her left hand, months ago adorned with a sparkly thing I'm certain, knowing Kitten, is conflict-free. "Honestly, here we are at my *bridal shower*—"

The implication is there: I should've been hosting this party, being Kitten's maid of honor, but I dragged my feet.

"It's a day for focusing on the future," Kitten says. "And all you worry about is what happened in the past."

My past is more complicated than most, but contrary to what my best friend assumes, I've worked on letting it go. Suddenly, with the detective raising the discussion of my abduction, I feel vulnerable again. Off-balance.

"You should've severed all communication when you broke up with him," Kitten continues.

Oh. Kitten's not talking about my comprehensive past. She's talking about my past *with Sterling*.

"He blew you off tonight," she says, as if I don't already know. "*Again*. And you're letting it get in the way. I mean, are you even happy for me?"

Isn't it just like Kitten to assume the world revolves around her impending nuptials? "Of course I'm *happy for you*—"

"Holly." She grabs my wrist. "Do you ever want to be happy yourself?"

"I do, as a matter of fact." And that's why I have to get out of here.

This place, this party, these *people* . . .

I miss the days when it was just Kitten and me, and maybe her brother, Matt, if he happened to be on leave from the army, hanging out at the Moonbeam bar, betting on darts and shooting pool. I'm not going to say Kitten changed when she hooked up with Eliot, but she tends to prefer places of higher culture these days. She slipped into the role of a white-collar fiancée as if through a buttered sleeve.

But I don't fit in here with Kitten's new confederates—everyone she met at college, at her new job, and after that fateful night when Eliot swept her off her feet. I don't do well with new people, period, let alone this clan of metrosexuals, all of whom dress in business casual and work from nine to five. It's stifling to be standing here, feeling as if I don't have a thing in common with anyone else in the room.

"Look." Kitten nudges me, her gaze aimed at the blue line in the distance where Lake Michigan meets the sky. In the distance, Chicago's skyscrapers cut shapes into the dusk. Home is only twenty minutes north of here, but it feels as if it's worlds away.

I lean against the railing alongside her.

"Do you remember when we were about thirteen and your dad and my mom took us camping in Montana?"

Instantly, the image of an endless sky flashes in my memory. Even now, all these years later, it nearly takes my breath away.

Neither of us spoke during that first sunset. Kitten put her arm around me, I rested my head against her shoulder, and we sat in bewildered awe as the last rays of the sun dripped down the horizon. It was then we decided the world was enormous. We vowed never to let anything that happened in or around our tiny burg shake us. While girls in high school fretted about this guy or that rumor, Kitten and I had an understanding of the bigger world.

"Keep your eye on the sky," Kitten says now, repeating the mantra of our teenage years. "Greener pastures. Bigger sunsets, remember?"

"Yeah. But I like Lake Bluff."

"You can like it and stay there and still remember how big the world is."

"I do."

"Stop using what happened as an excuse." In Kitten's mind, "what happened" happened to *us*, as she was the sole witness to my abduction. Our mothers were chatting on a nearby bench (my mom sipping on lemonade spiked with vodka), planning my surprise fifth birthday party, so the story goes, but they didn't see the guy snatch me. They didn't know I was gone until Kitten ran up to them, hysterical, with tears bursting from her eyes like twin geysers. "If I've moved past it, so can you. I'm starting to think you just don't want to."

Leave it to Kitten to boil the incident down to something I *choose* to fixate on. If she's over it, she assumes I could be, too. But here's the difference:

She remembers the horror of the moment the man grabbed me. She remembers the frustration everyone felt when they couldn't immediately locate me. She was sad and scared and lonely and having nightmares about the "shadowy man" who took me.

And suddenly, one day after I was recovered, she remembered this, too:

It was someone her parents knew.

Alan Kohlbrook. Handyman. Parishioner at the Hersheys' church.

He tried to take me, she'd told the police. *But I kicked him. Then he took Holly.*

The guilt affected her for years even after I was recovered.

Me? I don't remember much of anything that happened while I was gone, but that doesn't mean that whatever happened during the months I was held—*some*where with *some*one for *some* indeterminate purpose—didn't damage me.

After I was recovered, I attended my first therapy session. I drew pictures, talked, laughed. The shrink's verdict: *Holly is a well-adjusted, happy girl. Effects of the incident have yet to present. Monitor and continue therapy.*

Not said: *because effects will present eventually.*

"Stop using it as an excuse," Kitten repeats. "You're not the only one whose life changed that day."

Valid.

"Get your shit together," she says. "Working for your dad was supposed to be a summer job, right? And here you are all these years later—"

"I like my job."

"You're comfortable. You don't want to stir things up. Most women, let alone *college-educated* women, don't work construction, you know."

"All evidence to the contrary, seeing as *I* do." And I do it very well, thank you very much. "What I don't know is how most women wear these damn strappy, heeled sandals ninety-five percent of the time." I can't wait to take them off. This dress, too, was a bad decision. But the invitation said to wear purple, the signature color of Kitten's upcoming event, and I don't own anything even near purple, save the bridesmaid dress I was supposed to pick up last week. So I squeezed into the only purple thing I found in my mother's closet.

Kitten's talking about ripping off the Band-Aid and some other cliché advice women give when it comes to leaving no-good men behind. But I'm more interested in something I see beyond the sliding glass door.

"Be *present*," Kitten says. "Is that too much to ask?"

I focus on the object sitting inside on the fireplace mantel: a small pewter box. I zero in on it and imagine the way it might feel in my hands.

Cold and hard and heavy.

Kitten's words—something about her brother missing the party, about how the army never gets people home when they're supposed to—fade away. My next gulp of Jim Beam burns in my throat, my chest, my cheeks.

"And my dipshit father can't be bothered to be part of my life. I mean, I don't even think I'd recognize him if he walked up to me on the street! Who can say that about her dad? Thank *God* I have yours to rely on to walk me down the aisle—"

My fingers twitch.

A spinning sensation whirls in my head for a few seconds . . . as if I'm drunker than I thought I was. I can't help it. I need to hold that box.

"You have nothing else to say?"

I refocus on my best friend. "What?"

Kitten, straightening, takes a healthy sip of her wine. "Maybe by the actual wedding date, you'll put forth some effort. Get to know the rest of the bridal party. These girls are great, once you get to know them."

"I'm sure they are."

"Be social. Stop hiding on balconies."

"I'm not hiding." I blink hard to center myself, but the box keeps drawing my attention.

It's a smaller version of one I saw when I was a little girl. I don't remember where, but I remember reaching up on tiptoes to grasp the box. I can practically feel my fingers closing around the embossed treasure chest.

Just as quickly as I imagine the moment, it flickers away. I exhale a breath I didn't know I was holding.

I try to grasp the moment again, try to remember where I might have been when I saw the box. But honestly, I don't remember. It's like looking through a blurry window and trying to determine details of what's outside.

"Hel*lo*?"

I return my gaze to the guest of honor.

"Are you even *listening* to me?" Kitten asks.

"I—" I shut up.

"Oh, God, just go then. Burrow back into your barndominium at Casa Gebhardt."

"I'm fine."

"You need some tough love. Snap out of this funk, young lady." Kitten points a finger at me, but her smile belies her tough-girl act. "That's an order."

"I'm fine, Kitten. It's just that—"

"Oh, look. Mr. Wonderful finally got here."

Through the glass, I see the late arrival. Derrion Sterling stands near the fireplace, with one hand in a pocket, the other raising a glass to a circle of bridesmaids.

"Maybe *now* you'll come in." She slides open the door and disappears into the crowd of milling party guests. "Eliot? Holly needs another drink."

Really, I don't.

The only thing I need is to get home.

Maybe I should've told Kitten it was a detective who called and that he wants to talk to me about my abduction.

Maybe she would've given me a break if she knew another girl had been taken.

Now that thoughts of the twenty-years-old incident are rising in my head, I feel almost sick.

As Guidry reminded me, I came home—I'm luckier than most. The Lake County Police Department inexplicably found me in the same park from which I'd been taken. I don't even know why the abduction haunts me when I have virtually no memory of those three months.

No recollection.

And try as I might, I can't conjure the circumstances surrounding that box.

I throw back the rest of the bourbon swilling in the bottom of my glass and head inside.

The box on the mantel—magnetic—pulls me in.

I can't help myself. I have to touch it.

Cecily

Beep. Beep. Beep.

The constant sound of the heart monitor is like an alarm going off.

I'm up, I want to scream. *Turn off the alarm already.*

But there's a disconnect.

I can't put a voice to my thoughts these days any more than I can fling a hand at the alarm clock to silence the damn thing.

Enough's enough.

I'm ready to wake up.

I've come to think of this cold, antiseptic space as purgatory, where souls come to ponder their errors before they die.

And I've made a few hundred doozies, haven't I?

I've been thinking about those mistakes a lot these days. What else do I have to do? And I've come to realize that, in a way, I was destined to fail. When people think the worst of you, it's only too easy to deliver.

Imagine a well-groomed young father dropping his daughter off at kindergarten. Her face is smudged with remnants of breakfast. Her clothes are rumpled, and her hair is heavily snarled and pulled back into a crooked ponytail.

And Dad forgot about her snack. *Shoot.*

The young mothers in the drop-off circle dig in their bags for a spare package of crackers to help.

Bless him. He's trying so hard.

Now, imagine it's Mother dropping the child on the curb in such condition.

Someone else has to offer up a snack for her kid, lest the poor child go hungry. Eyes roll. They'll help, but for the sake of the child. Not for the negligent mother.

Bad mom.

If no one says it, everyone's thinking it.

Sigh.

What can you do? It's the way of the world.

We hold women to a different standard.

And I know this better than anyone.

Just a few seconds was all it took. Just a small distraction.

And the next I knew, Holly was plucked from sight.

They all descended on me—cops, neighbors, my own husband, who shook me by the shoulders and demanded answers:

Who took her?

Where is she?

Why wouldn't I give up the location?

Why wouldn't I cooperate?

Why wouldn't I tell the police what I knew so they could bring her home?

I'd been drinking that day.

I had secrets I wouldn't divulge.

And the fact that Holly turned up one day, out of the blue, as if she'd simply been dusted off and put back on a shelf after someone found her discarded beneath the bed.

She came back to us untouched, if you know what I mean, which was something no one expected. After seventy-two hours, the police (although they wouldn't explicitly say so) didn't expect her to come home alive, and when she did, they suspected whoever had taken her had kept her for one sick purpose.

Virtually unharmed, there she sat at the top of the slide in the very park from which she'd been taken, in a pristine white nightgown, with crystalline snow falling all around her. The eighth of January. Her homecoming.

I often wonder . . . If Trevor had been with her at the park that day, casually sipping on a beer as she played, would the vultures have descended on him? Would the neighbors have eyed my husband sideways, avoided him at the market, and whispered theories behind his back?

She knows where Holly is, I just know it!

Maybe if I hadn't disguised the alcohol in a sports bottle that day . . .

Maybe if I hadn't at first denied the vodka in my lemonade . . .

Maybe I would have been treated like a credible witness, like a mother who'd just experienced her worst nightmare.

Instead, I was a suspect.

And even after Holly came back to us, Trevor was always watching me. And even when we weren't talking about it, he was pondering the possibility I'd stashed her with Kohlbrook, perhaps as the first step in an inevitable divorce I've yet to file to this day, or perhaps as a measure against the one person who loves her as much as I do. The question passed over his lips once: *Would you hurt her if it meant you could hurt me, too?*

Those in the periphery, looking down their noses at me: *bad mom.* They don't wonder how I survived such a horrific ordeal. They wonder how I can live with myself.

How could I have been drinking just after noon when I was supposed to be playing supermom?

So I needed to take the edge off.

So I needed to numb myself to deal with the life I'd chosen to live.

So I'm one of those bad, negligent mothers who drops her kid at school without first wiping the chocolate frosting from her face (and yes, a chocolate cupcake sometimes sufficed as the first meal of the day if I didn't have milk for cereal, or even cereal itself). It doesn't come naturally to all of us, you know. We're not all meant to spend our lives performing puppet shows and building with blocks and coloring in books and singing nonsensical songs to entertain our offspring.

That doesn't mean I don't love my daughter.

On the contrary, I wish I'd spent more time assuring her that I do.

It's just like anything, I suppose: I should have done something when I could have.

When she was gone, I used to spend nights in her room, if only to feel close to her. I spoke to the walls, explained everything in her absence.

And now, the tables have turned.

I'm the one who's gone.

I'm trapped in a white room in my mind, where everything is orderly and antiseptic.

She visits. She speaks to me.

She's more honest with me than she's ever been.

Things weren't like this before the car I was driving tipped over the edge of that ravine on April 16.

I want to tell her about what happened when she was a little girl. I want to tell her about the day she was taken, and all the days leading up to it.

More than that, I want justice for her.

Most people will tell you justice was served when Alan Kohlbrook was locked away.

But I know things now that I didn't understand before I slipped into this white space.

Was justice served?

Far.

From.

It.

CHAPTER 2

HOLLY

June 5

"Holly, come on." Sterling follows me onto the elevator at the Edgewater high-rise. "You can't leave. I just got here."

"That's right." I push the lobby button. "*You* just got here. I've been here for hours."

"I'm sorry I was late. I got caught at work."

"I don't care. Honestly, I'm not mad. I just . . . look, we keep ending up in these situations. We decided to break it off. I'm getting too old for this game, and if *I'm* too old, you're *definitely* aging out."

"Age jokes. Funny."

When we met, I liked that he was in his midthirties. But now, he's edging closer to forty and still acting like he lives in a frat house. That's the thing about men in this city. They can't even begin to consider growing up until they're half-dead. "We broke up," I say again.

"I think that was a bad idea." He takes my hand, pulls me closer. "Let me at least get you home."

A breath before his lips touch mine, the elevator bell announces our arrival in the lobby. "I got an Uber." I step out.

"Holly." He's at my heels. "Mind if I join you?"

"I do, actually. I have an early day tomorrow." I get into the car awaiting me. "And if you wanted to spend time with me, you wouldn't have shown up at the *n*th hour, just in time to take me home."

"This isn't over."

I close the door on the rest of his argument, and the Uber pulls away.

My head is starting to ache.

Maybe I drank too much. My mother and I wouldn't have anything in common, if not for our love of bourbon. It's an acquired taste, one that burns like white embers. I drink it on the rocks. I sip slowly, and it warms me and helps me keep up with the social butterfly who is my best friend. But sometimes, when I get anxious in social situations, I drink a bit too much too quickly. While I never noticed it before her accident, now that I think about it, Mom did, too.

I hope Kitten doesn't think I left the party to catch up on lost time with Sterling. I'll never hear the end of it if she thinks I chose him over her. He's not exactly Kitten's type of people.

Lately, since Kitten started this new job in corporate America and paired up with Eliot, I guess I'm starting to wonder if *I'm* still her type of people. I don't care about meeting sales goals to earn incentive trips to the Bahamas, or company outings and team-building experiences. In my line of work, company outings take shape in the form of canned beer and a game of horseshoes at the park. I wonder if her new friends would even drink a mass-produced pilsner, let alone without a frosted glass.

My phone buzzes in my purse.

I dig it out to see a text from Sterling.

The words blur and seem to buzz and jiggle on the screen.

Whoa.

I mentally tabulate the number of drinks I had. One on the balcony. One inside, which I don't think I finished, after the toast. I was standing near the mantel, eyeing the pewter box to see if I could get the feeling to come back—it didn't.

Did someone bring me another drink after that?

Maybe.

In any case, I can't stop things from spinning before my eyes. I squint at my phone screen to make out Sterling's words:

Should I follow u?

Before I have a second to reply, he sends another:

We hardly had time to catch up.

I reply, thankful for autocorrect because my fingers aren't cooperating: Clean break. We agreed. Shouldn't have invited you tonight.

Sterling: What if I changed my mind?

I put my phone away. Leave it at that. Don't engage. Don't say something I might regret later. Because at the moment, all I really want to say is *come over and talk.*

But a minute later, he's texting again.

Miss u.

Make it up to u?

I turn off my ringer and shove my phone back into my purse. I can be strong. I can ignore him. I lean back against the seat. So comfortable. And with my eyes closed, the spinning ceases.

I could fall asleep, right here, right now.

But I shouldn't. I sit up and roll down the window. Maybe the fresh air will keep me up.

"Can you stop at the 7-Eleven?" I ask the driver.

Something tells me I'm going to need some Red Bull to get through the day tomorrow, and I might even need one to get through the rest of the ride home.

The driver pulls over.

Once out of the car, I yank on the hem of my dress so that it covers more thigh. A short Hispanic woman, as wide as she is tall, wobbles her way past me into the convenience store and holds the door when she realizes I'm coming in, too.

I follow her—these damn shoes—to the coolers, where she's already hemming and hawing over Ben & Jerry's. She's wearing a green, knit poncho over an ankle-length dress, black, printed with fuchsia hibiscus and green palms.

I have to go an entire aisle out of my way to get around her because she takes up most of the aisle, and through the fog in my head, I don't have it in me to say *excuse me*.

"I miss the Chocolate Cherry Garcia," she says when I arrive on the other side of her.

I don't reply. Maybe she'll stop talking if I don't engage.

"Perfect combination. Fruit's essential for good constitution, you know."

No such luck. I answer with a nondescript "Hmm?"

"Why don't they make it anymore?"

I glance at her, and the world shifts a degree or two off-kilter. I brace myself against the cooler. "Fruit?"

"Chocolate Cherry Garcia."

"It sounds good." I proceed to load a basket with energy drinks. I figure I'll need three, at least, for tomorrow. I toss in a fourth for good measure and grab a fifth, which I'll pop as soon as I pay for it.

"The thing about energy drinks," she says. "They make you feel more awake than you really are. Be careful."

She's obviously a mom. No one else would give unsolicited advice. "I will."

"Can you be a dear?" She points up at the far reaches of the cooler. "I can't reach the Tonight Dough."

I help. "One or two?"

"Oh, I couldn't possibly eat two."

"Live a little."

"You've convinced me." For the first time, she looks at me. Really looks at me. "Oh my."

An eerie chill races through my veins when *I* really look at *her*. It feels as if she's journeying into my brain when our gazes meet, as if her stare bores directly into the centers of my pupils.

"Do you see echoes of the past?" she asks.

The ice cream chills my palm, and I feel as if I'm swaying. There's something about her eyes.

"Echoes," she says again. "Of the past."

"Excuse me?"

"You feel them, I mean. Things that happened long ago. They're just out of reach, but they haunt you, these echoes."

"Echoes?" The pewter box flashes in my mind.

"I see them, feel them, when I look at you."

"Have a nice night." I drop the two pints of ice cream into her basket and turn toward the register.

"You used to be blonde."

The hair on the back of my neck stands at attention.

She's right. My hair isn't naturally as light as it used to be when I was a child. But a few months ago, desperate for a change, I started dyeing my hair, masking any sign of the golden tones with a chocolate brown Kitten calls "dramatic."

"There's a lovely energy about you," she says. "A strong determination. But you're conflicted about something. You disagreed with a man tonight."

I swallow over my shock and mutter, "Well . . . who hasn't?"

"I think you could use my help. You need direction. You're losing your balance."

"Oh, *that*. It's these shoes . . . I don't usually dress up." Flippant, yes. But my lack of direction, or even my slight inebriation, is none of this woman's business. "I'm fine, but thank you—"

"It's the way of the world. You helped me." She nods toward the ice cream in her basket. "I'll help you. I see something about you. A rose in your garden."

"Really, I'm fine." I take a step toward the register.

"There's something unsettled here. A murky spot on what might be bright and shiny one day. You need to cleanse that, and I'm an expert."

"I'm sure you are. It was nice meeting you." I turn and walk away, but I hear the drag of her steps, her chubby little feet in mules half a size too big.

"I see the number eleven when I look at you," she continues, even as I say hello to the cashier. "Does that number hold a special place for you? A birthday, perhaps? A lucky number?"

"I don't—"

"The number eleven signifies rebirth into a higher sense of knowing, a jump to a level more spiritual. Are you experiencing anything like that? An event, perhaps, that you're looking at differently? A readiness to face your past head-on?"

"Just trying to get through my best friend's wedding," I say and hope that's enough to satisfy her.

"There's a reason you stopped *here*, of all places, and there's a reason I happened to be here when you did. It's the echoes."

I pay for my Red Bull.

When I turn to go, she's offering a business card in her outstretched hand. "Please call."

I take it. "It was nice meeting you." I skirt around her and head back to my Uber.

Once inside, I glance at her card, which is lavender and plain. All it says, in block letters in a no-nonsense font, is:

PSYCHIC YANNETH

A phone number, handwritten, is scrawled beneath.

As my driver pulls away, I see she's watching me through the convenience store door.

CHAPTER 3
HOLLY

June 5

By the time the Uber takes me up the winding drive past my parents' house, I'm feeling a little better but still so, so tired. There's a light on in my old bedroom. Not the bedroom I had as a teenager, in the walk-out basement, but the bedroom of my childhood, the one I came home to after I was gone.

It stands in memoriam of the child I used to be: purple and green butterflies on the walls, a closet door in the fashion of a metal garden gate, and pictures of Kitten and me in matching outfits framed on the built-in bookcases astride a charming window seat.

Odd that my father would be in that room this time of night.

I imagine he's staring at the walls, chin propped on his hand, making plans for renovation. It's past time for Dad to update the space, which Mom refused to change, even when I was still living there. There's no better time to tackle the project, actually, as he and Mom argue over even paint colors, and if he starts a project now, while she's unable to offer input, there will be no fight.

Knowing Dad, he's probably already had a one-sided conversation with Mom about the renovation, if only to spark some sort of reaction from her.

I look now to the field that stretches between our house and the Hersheys' home, which Kitten's mother, Susan, put up for sale just before my mother's accident. With Matt wrapping a career in army fatigues and Kitten sporting a diamond on her left hand, it was time to downsize. Kitten helped her choose a condo in Chicago, not far from Eliot's place, so they'll be close to each other—but farther from me.

Whenever I think of what I want my relationship with Mom to be, I picture Kitten and Susan. Kitten's parents divorced shortly after I was recovered, and Susan, Kitten, and Matt became not only a team of three but an extension of our family. It'll be strange not to have them just across the field.

Everywhere I look, life is progressing around me. And I'm still here, like a toy train circling a track. Always moving but never going anywhere. I should have told Psychic Yanneth: I don't feel echoes of the past. I'm living in it.

I can't see the field in the dark of night, but I know that this time of year, the field is full of the wildflowers Kitten and I used to pick. I imagine the whisper of flowers bristling against one another as they sway in the breeze on their hearty stalks. I know every inch of this place, every scent, every sound.

It's home.

And maybe everyone is moving on without me, but I still feel satisfied here.

I get out of the Uber when it halts a few feet from the stairs that lead to my place above the barn, and I begin to ascend.

"Holly."

I startle when I hear the voice, but then Kitten's brother wanders into a beam of light shining from the apex of this big old structure. Matt's clothing belies his sister's claims that he was delayed returning from whatever overseas US Army base he was stationed at. He's clad in track pants and a royal-blue T-shirt boasting the logo of that other baseball team from the north side of the city.

He's officially discharged but still looks positively militant even in casual clothing. It must be the haircut.

The scar at the outside corner of his left eye, a souvenir from a car accident before Kitten and I were born, crinkles when he smiles.

As if on cue, the breeze picks up; along with it, the wildflower symphony.

I soften at the sight of him.

I can't help it. There's always going to be part of me that's hopelessly in love with Matt. When I was twelve, I decided I'd someday marry him, but Kitten quickly brought me down to earth. Logically, romantically, it would never work (you can't marry a guy who was there when you threw up blue-frosted birthday cake onto his mother's heirloom tablecloth), and legally, our coupling would have been challenging. He's nearly twelve years older than me, and by the time I was no longer jailbait, he was serving our country. I used to write him letters while he was away, always vowing to wait for him. He'd write back, and once I celebrated my twenty-first birthday, he even hinted at flirting back. But I sure wasn't waiting for a convenient time to try, and fail, at loving him.

"Kitten said you're delayed."

"I'll pay you to keep my secret," he says, grinning.

"You can't afford me."

"I seem to remember you could be bribed with chocolate."

"You remember correctly. But I'm no longer twelve."

"How about a drink?"

"Are you changing first?" I nod toward his T-shirt. "You've got a lot of nerve wearing that on this property."

"Your dad said the same thing." He chuckles. "But he's letting me stay here for a while, despite."

I think of the light on in my old bedroom. "He put you on the second floor."

Matt smiles. "Yeah, took me a while, but I finally found a way into your bed."

"You wish. The decor's gotta be giving you culture shock. Far cry from the barracks, aren't you, soldier?"

"Don't knock it. I like the lace-trimmed curtains. Besides, beggars can't be choosers. Mom's got a maze of boxes over there." He nods toward the Hersheys'. "I go home and she's going to make me clean out my old room."

"Your mom's packing up. End of an era."

"Yep. Leaving the ole homestead behind. Some things you never expect to change."

"Yeah."

"Like you and your natural blonde."

My cheeks warm, although I don't know if it's a compliment. I go to shove the key in the lock, but my fingers are numb, and the keys slip from my grasp. I catch them before they tumble to the ground. "Just thought it was time."

"Looks good."

"You know, Kitten really wanted you there."

Matt stuffs his hands in his pockets and looks up at me. "Just couldn't handle the thought of the festivities tonight."

"You and me both."

"This guy. Is he Kitten's usual type?"

I laugh and try again with the key. "What's her usual type?"

"You know. A chode."

"Come on up for a drink. We'll discuss." I probably shouldn't have offered, given I'm expected on-site early, but it's *Matt*, for God's sake.

There's something about Matt Hershey that makes me feel safe, secure. And maybe it was talking to the detective tonight, or meeting the psychic who was a bit too on the nose for comfort, but I feel raw, exposed. Vulnerable. I could use a little security about now.

"Sounds good to me," he says.

Cecily

The week before the kidnapping was fuzzy, marbled, and tripped up with alcohol and emotions.

"Did you see anyone at the park that morning? Or maybe earlier in the week?" Trevor pleaded with me to remember. "The police don't think this was a crime of opportunity. Someone focused on Holly. Someone knew you'd be there. Who?"

"I just. Don't. Know." I rubbed my temples and tried to remember, but the only things resurfacing were reminders of my own insecurities, my failings, my secrets. The things I didn't tell anyone about, even when pressed.

"What about hypnosis?" Trevor suggested. "Maybe something will come up, something you don't even know you know." Always, his eyes turned bluer with desperation. That shade of blue is hard to forget. It's etched into my memory like carvings on cave walls.

His hands gripped mine, locking me in that pleading blue gaze. "Try, okay? Hypnotherapy has worked on other cases."

If I agreed, would I tell all? Too much was at stake. With Holly gone, I couldn't afford to lose Trevor, too, and I knew as soon as he heard the secrets I'd been harboring, he'd have one foot out the door. But it wasn't all about me. If we expected to get her back, we had to work together. I couldn't compromise our unity just then.

When I began to shake my head, his grip tightened, and he gave my hands a sharp yank. "Isn't everything worth a try? When our daughter's life is at stake?"

Through tears, I looked him in the eye . . . and lied to him. "Okay. I'll do it. I'll try."

Within a few hours, I was in the office of Dr. Simone Parrish. There was no swaying watch on a chain for me to focus on, no black-and-white pinwheel spinning before my eyes, which I closed when she told me to.

"Sink deeper into the day," Parrish suggested. "Put yourself back there, in the park. Are you there?"

"Susan is with me."

"You're talking with Susan?"

"Yes."

"What are you talking about?"

"The birthday party." It's what I'd told the police. I didn't tell them the truth—that Susan had confided in me that her marriage was about to end.

"Tell me about the party."

"I can't."

"You can't tell me about the birthday party?"

"It's a surprise."

Later, when Trevor told Susan what I'd divulged in the session, she and I shared a glance.

I'd kept her secret, and in return, she kept mine: she never told anyone that I hadn't really been under hypnosis that day. If I had been, I wouldn't have lied about what we'd been talking about.

Ironic that my biggest rival had suddenly become my ally. I suppose, in times of distress, the enemy you know is preferable to the one you don't.

Parrish's questions kept coming:

What do you smell in the park? Is anyone smoking?

What do you hear?

Who else is in the park? What are they wearing?

What are you feeling? Are you vulnerable?

"I'm scared," I admitted in Parrish's office.

"What are you afraid of?"

"I'm not good at this. I can't keep the house clean. I can't manage healthy meals and holiday decorations, and if Holly comes back, I'll have to manage whatever she's been through. I can't. That's Susan. She's better. Holly and Trevor both deserve someone like her."

"Motherhood isn't a competition," Dr. Parrish said.

Nothing could be further from the truth. *Everything* was a competition. *Everything* was Susan versus me.

It still makes me want to scream.

Again, I try to fill my lungs with breath, with rage, with fear . . . with anything that will allow me to break out of this white room in my mind.

Trevor's here now. I feel his hand in mine. I smell the aftershave he splashes on his cheeks. A man's man. No place for Dolce & Gabbana in my husband's vanity.

"We got the toxicology report back." His voice is even and quiet. "You'd been drinking the day you drove over the edge of the ravine."

I sense his disappointment, which I'd like to address—really, I would. But there's something else there, too. The words he used . . . *You drove over the edge.*

Was that what happened?

"You'd been doing so well." He squeezes my hand. "What happened? You know I would've understood. Please, Cecily. Please tell me you didn't start drinking again and run over the edge because you were done with life."

The accusation hangs between us, and I'm not surprised he put it out there. Life's been hard. It wasn't supposed to be this way. The day we married, we made promises, but life gets in the way. Life helps you fail sometimes. But to think I would've been at the end of my rope . . . and *that's* why I had the accident?

I remember being upset. I remember thinking that things could have been so different. I even remember contemplating the edge of the ravine, but I wouldn't have purposely aimed for it.

Would I?

"Was there another car involved?" Trevor asks. "Were you forced over the edge? Or maybe, because you were drinking . . ."

I hadn't had a drink in twenty-three days before the accident, but too much happened, *too much*, and I lost my grip on sobriety. I want to explain it to Trevor. I think he'll understand.

First, there was the meeting with Paul Hershey I hadn't told Trevor about. None of us had seen him in nearly twenty years. He'd never come home for graduations or birthdays. He didn't show up the day Matt shipped out to Fort Knox for basic training or when Matt was deployed to Afghanistan. When he all but ignored the invitation to Kitten's engagement party, I left him a scathing message, which he also ignored for days.

But suddenly, my phone was ringing. He wanted to talk.

I'd planned to pick through a new haul at the Antiques Warehouse, and because it was raining, I'd borrowed Holly's SUV in case I found something to bring home that day. Otherwise, I might not have accepted the invitation, or maybe I would have insisted we meet elsewhere. But no one would know if I happened to drop in at the bar he'd suggested while I was cleverly disguised in a vehicle that wasn't mine; no one from AA would see my car parked outside the place. So I went in, if only to prove that I could do so and walk out sober.

Chalk another win up to Jim Beam.

By the time I walked in, Paul had already ordered for me: a shot of bourbon. Just a shot to calm my nerves. I didn't take it right away, but then he started talking, and I sipped. Then gulped. And then I ordered another.

What he admitted that day . . .

What was it? I can't remember now what had me so unmoored.

I remember that I tore out of the bar.

I had to tell Trevor. I had to call the police, who'd come to think of me as a nuisance. Every time I called with information: the dolls that were periodically left at the park, in the exact same spot where Holly had been taken from us; the messages that came through my email, which were just threatening enough to put me on edge but generic enough not to raise a flag . . .

Likely unrelated to the case, the police always said. *Probably someone digging through old news. You weren't exactly well liked, you know, when the story broke. But we'll make note of it. We'll stop the harassment if it continues.*

Words. Words mean nothing if they're not backed by action, and with Holly home and Kohlbrook in prison, my complaints weren't high on the cops' priority list.

Maybe they felt I deserved the harassment. What kind of mother doesn't cooperate with the investigation into her daughter's kidnapping? So they ultimately ignored me.

But what Paul told me . . . The police couldn't ignore *that.*

Whatever *that* was . . .

I was rushing home to tell Trev, to make the call.

The icy rain pelted the fogging windshield. It was just after seven, but the sun had already set, and the moon was waning. With the clouds and the storm, it was hard to see.

I approached the bend in the road.

For a fleeting moment, I thought about it: letting the secret die with me. Maybe it would be easier than living with it.

There was a large blue vehicle in the rearview mirror.

A white flash of light.

Then . . .

The next thing I remember is being trapped here, in my own head, the constant beep of the heart monitor in the periphery.

Beep.

Beep.

Beep.

Is Trevor right? Did I choose to end it all?

Was it an accident?

Or did someone, maybe whoever was driving that blue vehicle, want to end it for me?

Or did they want someone else dead?

I was driving Holly's SUV. Maybe someone wanted to finish what he started twenty years ago.

Maybe it's all, like it's always been, about the kidnapping.

CHAPTER 4

Holly

June 6

The image is fuzzy, like usual. Just out of reach.

A rectangular sign of sorts. A directional arrow, pointing the way to . . . something.

I try to focus, try to get a little closer, but—

The chiming of my phone jolts me from a deep sleep.

By rote, I silence the ringer so I can concentrate on what I almost saw in my dream. I close my eyes and try to conjure it. A sign. Rectangular. White, peeling paint.

These things always come to me when I'm sleeping, about to wake up, or sort of drunk, like the feelings that descended on me when I saw the pewter box last night. They're almost-memories. That's what I call them. They've plagued me since I was about nine or ten. My therapist suggests they're resurfacing details of something I experienced or saw while I was gone. She thinks I should try to focus on the images when they come to me, and write down everything I possibly can. Half a detail today could pair with another next week, and before you know it, I might piece together a clue.

But I can't remember anything concrete. Just a shape, a few letters. *P*, for sure.

The morning sun blinds me the moment I sit up in bed. Oh, God.

I rub my head at the temples and reach for my phone. I've missed two calls from Vellerman, the foreman on the construction site, and he's texted at least five times, too. Maybe more. I don't bother to count.

Overtime. Saturday morning crew. I should be there already.

Vellerman is one of Dad's newer foremen, and he's an absolute ass without a soul. He doesn't care if you have a good excuse, let alone a lame one. If you're late, in his book, you're a loser.

Fuck.

I text On my way, and spring out of bed.

My feet hit the floor, and my head . . . *yikes*. The pain is atrocious.

Deep breath. I didn't really drink that much last night, did I? I need food, that's all. And hydration. I meander to the kitchen and chug a glass of orange juice.

Details of last night start to trickle back to me. Clinking glasses. Toasting to . . . what? Freedom, maybe? Did I call Sterling back and tell him to come over? I must have, as evidenced by the two glasses on the coffee table. Empty highball glasses, empty promises. Despite his showing up severely late for Kitten's party, I probably dived into bed with him.

No wonder nothing ever changes. Like my father used to say to my mother, nothing changes if nothing changes.

I check my phone to see if I called Sterling, when a memory filters in. Matt. I look over my shoulder at my queen-size mattress. I don't think we would've crossed that line. But I remember the feel of his cheek against mine, his scooping me up from the sofa and carrying me to my room. Maybe he just helped me to bed. *Hopefully* that's all.

It's then I realize I'm wearing a shirt at least two sizes too big—about the size of a certain US soldier. And worse . . . it's royal blue. Inside out. And I'm pretty sure I feel the outline of a trademark *C* against my skin. I cringe and brave a look down.

"Oh, God!" I squirm and thrash and wiggle. I can't get the thing off fast enough. I've moved away from explosions more slowly.

But the fact remains: I was sleeping in Matt's shirt.

This can't be good.

Then again, at least I was clothed. I've got that going for me.

But I don't have time to dig deeper into the mystery of what happened last night. Something else is niggling in the back of my mind . . . something like a bad omen, or a premonition of impending doom.

The call from the detective, maybe. Another case like mine.

Of course I feel dreadful, considering *that*. And that strange encounter at the 7-Eleven.

Deep breath. Hit the reset button. I can't change what happened yesterday, but I can hope for better today. It's what Mom used to say whenever she'd wake up in the aftermath of a drunken episode. I used to think it was an excuse. But now I understand it more than I care to admit.

I find Psychic Yanneth's card and pitch it into the waste can, then turn on The Weather Channel for a glimpse of today's forecast, step over the purple torture device I wore to the party last night, and make my way back to the bathroom.

No time for a shower, but that's okay. We're aiming for a steamy eighty-nine degrees today. Bathing before work is pointless. I yank my tangled hair into a ponytail, scrape yesterday's mascara off the rims of my eyes, and toss on dirty work jeans, a sports bra, and a Sox T-shirt—extra juju, seeing as I was wearing the enemy logo all night long. I open a drawer for toothpaste.

My breath catches, and I quickly close the drawer again.

Tell me I didn't . . .

Abracadabra.

But it's still there when I open the drawer again.

The box I saw last night—the pewter one on the mantel—is nestled in the corner of the drawer.

I don't remember nicking it. I don't know why I would do such a thing . . . take something from one of Kitten's friends. Unfortunately, however, it happens. I once pocketed a button I found on the floor of a guy's apartment as a souvenir. For what? Good question. I've taken items to commemorate everything from great parties to great kisses—stones from the sidewalk, peelings of old paper from the walls, an autumn leaf tumbling across a lawn. But to take something like this? Something of actual value?

What was I thinking?

I pick it up cautiously, as if it might burn my fingers. Instantly, it feels as if I'm five years old, holding a forbidden object in my tiny hands.

I flip the clasp and open the lid.

A single dried rose petal rests at the bottom. Other than that, the box is empty, but a flash comes to me: a gold house key against a navy velvet bed and a lock of white-blonde hair, tied with a pink ribbon.

Hair the color of mine as a child.

The memory is so vivid, so real. I was doing something I wasn't supposed to do. Of that, I'm certain.

Even now, I practically feel the bite of an open-hand smack on my backside, the box being torn from my grasp.

My father never spanked me. My mother did occasionally.

I close my eyes and concentrate, try to imagine the box again. Try to put myself back there in time.

But I'm not a little girl anymore, and Mom's not here to scold me now even if I were. She's thirty-nine miles away, in a coma in the ICU at Loyola Medical.

Just thinking of her in that state, covered with wires and tubes, and counting the days she's been that way—fifty-one now—is enough to make my heart beat faster. I snap the box closed and stow it in my vanity.

Later.

I'll return it later to its owners.

I can't do it now. I'm already late for work.

I'll tell you later.

A voice from the past rises up.

Drink your juice.

I fixate on the pewter box, and I remember it again: *I'll tell you later. Drink your juice.*

A tingling sensation dances up my spine as more comes to me:

The stench of musty wood.

Mildewed carpet that should have been discarded after a flood.

The box snaps closed on my tiny fingers.

Drink your juice.

And something across the room:

White, ruffled panties.

A baby?

No, it's just a doll.

A doll posed on its side.

As soon as it comes to me, it's gone. I can't conjure the place, the details.

But I was there. I'm sure of it.

CHAPTER 5

Holly

June 6

"You think I care that half of you is Trevor Gebhardt's sperm?" Vellerman screams a string of profanity at me as I approach. He punctuates it: "Where the fuck have you been?"

I put up a hand, admitting I'm guilty as charged, and roll past the foreman to park my father's beat-up truck, which I've been driving since Mom totaled my Explorer.

I'm late to the site of my father's latest concept house by just more than an hour. My hands are shaking, as if I just traveled here from the Arctic Circle, even though it's hotter than the equator today. I'm hungover and discombobulated.

And the memory of the pewter box. Haunting. Yet just out of reach.

Just like Psychic Yanneth said it would be.

The crew is shouting commands at each other over the hum and pop of the tools of our trade; their words are blurred together, as if they're all talking underwater. It's hard to hear what they're saying over the noise, let alone over the static in my head. I shouldn't have tried to come to work today. I should've admitted I wasn't up to par and blown off the overtime. I'd take some lumps come Monday, sure, and Dad would have more proof that I'm not ready to be a foreman. But . . .

My hands are still shaking, and my heart rate is on a skyrocketing pace.

I won't be any good to anyone if I can't steady my grip. I inhale as slowly as I can manage and try to draw out the exhale as well. Inhale. Exhale. Inhale—

It's no use. I pop open the glove box and dig for the prescription bottle I've seen there. It's Mom's antianxiety medication. She never took it because she preferred to medicate with liquor, and there are labels all over this bottle: DO NOT MIX WITH ALCOHOL.

I bypass the warning (it's been hours since my last whiskey) and swallow half a dose—one pill instead of two. Inhale. Exhale.

After I've fastened my pouches at my hips, I start toward the pile of wood awaiting me. One of the guys shoulders past me, physically invading my space. "Thanks for showing up, *dickhead*."

I heard *that*.

"Well, well." Vellerman stands with arms folded and feet shoulder-width apart. "Look who decided to join us." He's wearing aviators, the kind with opalescent-type lenses reflecting an array of colors—sometimes green, sometimes gold, sometimes turquoise. They effectively hide the glare I'm certain he's shooting at me. "You got your nails done? Lipstick on? You're ready now?"

I'm neither wearing makeup nor sporting a manicure, but I mumble an apology—all I can do—and keep heading toward the house in progress. In my absence, the crew's been sheeting the second-floor deck. No wonder the guys are pissed. It's a task that gets easier with more people on it.

"I think it's time we took a break." Vellerman points at me. "You can keep on, though, seeing as you just got here."

I look from the stack of strand board to the studs before me as the entire crew meanders off the deck. I'll have to hike the four-by-eight-feet sheets of subfloor onto the second-floor joists, climb, and fasten them down. And repeat. It's a job for a team. For someone with less experience, it would be nearly impossible to tackle alone. But I'll have to manage. I was late. I guess I deserve this.

I yank on a pair of gloves and get to work.

I hoist a sheet and balance it like I'm Atlas holding up the world, carry it to the deck, and slide it up to the story above me, just *so*, so it stays up there.

I see on the edges of the lot what my colleagues are doing: they're sitting on their lunch pails, slurping on sodas, munching on sandwiches, and watching, as if I'm some sort of show.

Well, if a show is what they want . . .

Sweat pastes my T-shirt to my underarms and back, and my hair is already curling at my temples.

I pull my hammer from a loop in my belt, and I tack a few nails into a stud. Using the pins as footholds, I scale the wall and walk the joists and go to work with the pneumatic nailer someone abandoned up there. I skirt the sheet I just laid into position: *ka-chunk, ka-chunk, ka-chunk.*

Once the panel is secured to the deck, I swing down and repeat with another sheet of strand board.

If Vellerman thinks he can intimidate me, he ought to remember I grew up on sites like this one. One of my earliest memories is of toting small trim boards to Dad on my tricycle. Some happy times, going to work with Dad. Riding in circles, believing I was helping, when Dad was probably only doing everything in his power to keep me busy and out of his hair. But it did the trick. I learned what I needed to learn to get here.

I pause and look out at the four sheets of subfloor I installed while the rest of the crew snacked. It's good, clean work. No gaps. No bounce.

But it feels as if something is missing, like I forgot to do something. I mentally check through all the steps—did it, did it, did it.

I catch sight of a stray nail lying on the plywood.

Sites are full of debris like this. But this one calls to me. It's distracting. If I kick it down to the ground below me, I'll only be thinking about it *on the ground.* My fingers itch to pick it up.

I move toward it.

My eyes glaze over.

I bite off a glove and bring my now-sweaty fingers to my eyes to rub away the haze. But instead of things getting clearer, the world only grows into a blurrier, tilting mess.

I start to sway.

Things blacken at the periphery.

I shouldn't have taken that medication.

I pinch my eyes closed.

Blue irises flash in my mind. Far away—in time, in distance.

I crouch to the four-by-eight-foot sheet of strand board I just tacked down.

A skeleton of a floor spans beyond: just the frame of where floorboards would rest, if there were any, with a full view to the stairwell below, and fathoms beyond, into the basement. An acrid scent floats up from down there.

I concentrate.

Don't cross.

I hear the whispered plea, and a little girl, blonde, blue eyed, flashes in my mind.

She's in the dark.

I stumble.

I fall.

CHAPTER 6

Holly

June 6

Like a thousand volts of electricity cracking in the sky, suddenly everything's white and bright.

Before it even registers that I'm falling from the second story, I hook an arm around whatever I can snag. A second or two later, I've got my bearings back. I'm hanging between two joists, suspended between floors.

I look down into an abyss that is the basement. If I hadn't caught myself, I would have plummeted two stories.

Déjà vu.

I feel as if I've been in this position before, but I know for a fact that I've never slipped on a site.

I swing back up onto the deck, more gracefully than I anticipated, and regain my footing.

I already feel a tender spot on the rear of my right shoulder, where I must have banged it against a joist. I'll have a hell of a bruise, but it could've been much worse.

My heart is banging in my ears like a drum solo, and while I don't dare to look, I know the rest of the crew is on their feet. Some of them have probably resumed munching, now that they know I'm not plunging to my death. But either way, I'm on display.

I step down to a nail hold and climb halfway down the stud wall before jumping to the earth.

"Nice dismount!" one of the guys yells.

Vellerman's approaching.

My hand sears with pain, thanks to a mother of a splinter, about the size of a toothpick, embedded in my palm. I turn my back and fish in my pouches for a utility knife.

Unsheathe it.

Slice over the wood embedded in my hand and bite at it.

Yank the sliver free from my skin.

The metallic taste of blood lingers on my tongue, and I should probably tend to the gash in my hand, but I can't afford to miss even a beat.

I pull my dirty glove back over my fingers and imagine the infection already brewing there. But I pretend it doesn't bother me.

"You oughta have that looked at."

I look over my shoulder at the foreman. "I'm fine."

"Naw, I got orders," he says. "Guidelines."

Apparently, he ignores the one that prohibits my walking the walls as a single-man crew *and* the one that limits morning breaks to fifteen minutes; my team has been lolling at the fringes for nearly twenty now. "I'm fine." I roll my eyes, but it must not be enough of a reaction because he keeps talking.

"Next time, just say it's too much for you." He whistles to alert the rest of the crew. "Break's over." He claps twice. "Chop, chop! Let's help the little lady out."

God, this guy needs his clock cleaned.

By quitting time, my head is absolutely wringing with pain, and I'm practically drenched with sweat. It could be my imagination, but the scent of whiskey seems to emanate from my skin. I feel transparent, as if everyone on the crew knows I drank too much last night—like mother, like daughter, right?—and as if they assume that's why I fell.

My head is still cloudy. But of course it is. I imagine that's what medication like Mom's does to a person—calms you to the extent of idiocy.

I pack up my tools and pound the last Red Bull in my lunch cooler.

"What's going on with you today?"

I look over my shoulder to see Vellerman about three feet from me in his usual stance.

"Just not feeling well." I check the time. "And I have an appointment, so . . ."

At this rate, I'm going to be late to meet the detective. Looks like I'll be taking the shortcut home.

"Maybe you should see a doctor."

"If I didn't know better, I'd think you're concerned."

"I'm concerned about all my guys." He sniffs. "When it affects one of my sites."

"Well, I'm fine." I climb into my truck. "And so is your site."

"Is that right?" He leans a forearm on my open window.

There's a nasty scar on the back of his right hand. I don't know how I've never noticed it before. "How'd that happen?" As soon as I say it, I wish I knew how to shut up. Accidents happen all the time in this industry. It's none of my business. I blink up from the scar and reluctantly meet his gaze.

He grins and nods toward the scar on my left forearm. "Maybe we'll trade stories one day."

As if of its own volition, my arm whips down, out of view. "Mine's not all that interesting." Most people would disagree with that statement. A kid missing for three months and coming home seemingly unscathed, save for a mark on her arm and a lost tooth, is definitely not the norm.

Vellerman looks at me. "You know you're damn lucky you caught yourself."

My cheeks flush with embarrassment.

"I don't like that you were late," he says. "But the last thing I want is the boss man's daughter biting it on my watch."

"Let's pretend I'm not the boss's daughter. I'm just a worker bee."

"You and I both know that's not true."

There's something unsettling in the way he's lingering. "You know what?" I put the car in gear. "I really have to run. I'm going to be late." I hope the detective's not a punctual sort. "Have a nice weekend."

"You too." He backs away, but that stupid smile is still plastered to his face.

Maybe I shouldn't have said that, either. It seemed benign in my head, but sometimes these guys read into even the most basic niceties. Hell, some take a simple *hello* as a green light in this industry.

I roll away.

Vellerman remains rooted, arms crossed over his chest, eyes hidden behind those aviators. But he's smirking, as if he knows he's making me uncomfortable and he's enjoying it.

I shudder one last time as I drive over the hill and out of my dad's development.

My fingertips tingle. Must be the buzz from the energy drink.

Halfway home, Kitten's text tone rings out.

I'm not looking forward to reading her message. Call me paranoid, but I'm certain she's going to be inquiring about the box missing from her friends' mantel. How do I explain taking it when I don't remember doing it? And that's another issue altogether. If I don't recall doing something like that, I must have had more to drink than I realized, and I can't handle another of Kitten's lectures about alcoholism running in my family and responsible consumption, and blah blah blah. She may have a point, but I don't need to keep hearing it. I already know.

The *responsible thing to do* last night was to get out of there so I wouldn't drink too much, so I wouldn't end up in bed with Sterling. And I wasn't driving. My mother would've driven. I didn't. Proof enough that the inherited curse won't affect me the way it did Mom.

A mile or so later, Kitten's text tone sounds again. And again.

I silence the ringer. I can't think about the box now.

I have to take the shortcut home if I have any prayer of meeting the detective on time, and as such, I'm going to have to pass the scene of my mother's accident. I don't like to take this route. Every time I round the bend, I picture my SUV as it was when Dad and I arrived here after hearing the sirens.

And that's unsettling, too. Amid the whirring of distant sirens, Dad knocked on my door, handed me a jacket, and without a word, we left. It's as if he knew the ambulance we heard was coming for Mom, as if he knew what we'd find when we arrived at the scene.

I'd never believed in that sort of telepathic connection between lovers until that moment. In fact, I don't know that I really believed my parents loved each other at all until I saw the life drain from Dad's eyes when we saw her.

The SUV had ricocheted off the trunk of an ancient oak on the way down before hitting another tree head-on.

Mom was pinned inside the vehicle.

She lost consciousness in the ambulance on the way to the hospital and hasn't regained it since.

I slow down as I round the curve, and I grip the steering wheel a little. I try to put myself in my mother's position on the night of April 16, when the unseasonably cold rain turned to a bitter, wintry mix. Had she considered the weather and slowed as she approached? How aware had she been of her predicament the moment she tipped over the edge?

I look toward the bend and try to imagine it slick with freezing rain.

Something I see there nearly stops my breath.

It's a doll, posed on its side with ruffled panties exposed.

I pull over to the shoulder and take a minute to calm myself. "Okay. So the question is . . . did I remember a doll earlier today because I must have seen it here before?" Did the Uber driver take this route last night? I can't remember. "Or . . ." I think of Psychic Yanneth. "Did I have a premonition this morning?"

I know it's weird, but since my mother's accident, I occasionally talk to her—wherever and whenever the urge hits me. It's calming, in a sense, maybe because for the first time in my life I can say what's on my mind without having to hear her rebuttal.

I don't think I talked to her this much face-to-face.

"It must be a coincidence. It's the only explanation."

I imagine a young family driving down the road and a little girl tossing a doll out the window. Or maybe they'd stopped to admire the view—it *is* breathtaking—and the doll had been left behind accidentally. But the way it's positioned . . . I must have seen it before. It's too coincidental, and . . .

"I don't believe in premonitions," I say to my imaginary mother.

I know I'm already late, and I know I should let it go. But suddenly, I'm out of the truck and stomping across the road for a closer look.

The doll is about fifteen inches long. Blonde, like most dolls, with blue eyes. But this is no ordinary drugstore plastic toy. It's made of some sort of silicone, which feels like the skin of a real baby, and as such, its limbs can be posed.

It's eerie that a doll would be here now, the spot where Mom all but disappeared, because, as the story goes, there was a doll found at the park the day I disappeared. I remember playing with it, even though it was dirty and Mom told me to leave it alone. I wonder now if Kohlbrook lured me with it—surely, the cops must have considered this, even if no one ever discussed it with me—or if it's just a coincidence.

Tears threaten, and I backhand them away. It's funny how I miss my mother, when she always drove me crazy before.

Oil and water, we were.

My mother—tiny, feminine. Me—a carpenter on one of my father's framing crews. Always a little lost, even after I was found.

I make a difference. I build homes, change landscapes. "I like what I do!" I scream into the ravine, as if she's still down there, as if she's still fighting with me about my every life decision.

Blip, blip, blip.

The sounds of those machines at the ICU ring in my ears, even when I haven't been to the hospital in days.

Blip blipblipblipblip . . .

I cover my ears as if I can block out the sound, and the world fades to black in the periphery, like I'm running through a narrow tunnel. A dizzying effect overtakes me, and I crouch, keeping myself low to the ground to keep from tumbling into the ravine.

Images flash in my mind:

The lock of blonde hair at the bottom of a box.

A little girl, staring at me across a dim expanse—a house under construction, with a stretch of open floor joists between us.

Ghostly blue eyes practically glow at me, but instantly, the image goes black.

Blipblipblip . . .

In an instant, the ravine starts to blend back into focus.

My hands are splayed against the earth, the creepy humanlike doll between them.

My fingers close around a stone.

The scents of soil and newly sprouting grass enter my lungs with a deep breath. For a few seconds, I'm still caught in that half-baked image of the blue-eyed girl and the half-finished house.

But like a fleeting thought that escapes you just as you're about to put words to it, it's suddenly gone.

I squeeze the rock I'm holding, and I feel in it an odd sense of lingering energy, as if my mother is still here, part of the landscape, like this rock. The sensation makes me want to stay.

But the world around me won't be ignored, even for the sake of half a dreamlike memory.

Get up.

Finally, I get to my feet and prop the doll against a tree.

It's probably expensive. Whoever left it there will probably be looking for it before long.

I return to my truck, where I set the stone on the dashboard and stare at it for a second, trying to conjure the image of that little girl again. Something specific: the shape of her nose, her approximate age, whether there were any gaps due to lost teeth. To see if I'm picturing myself. Because if I am, it might say something about the time I was gone.

But I can't do it. She's nothing more than a ghost now. With shaking hands, I put the car in gear.

I take one last look at the doll, and then I roll away.

Cecily

For weeks after the kidnapping, our house was filled with endless casseroles, police, and neighbors, specifically, the Hersheys.

I'd been hiding in Holly's room, a pretty usual occurrence those days, when Matt knocked on the door. "Ceci?"

When the door opened and he came in, I found myself looking at a man where a boy used to stand. Matt was nearly seventeen, a good-looking kid with his father's brawn, golden hair, and chiseled, dimpled chin and his mother's narrow nose and blue eyes.

The trauma of the kidnapping had caused him to make the leap from child to adult within weeks. Other boys his age were playing basketball, talking about which colleges to apply to, trying to get laid. He was taking care of his little sister, helping Trevor at TrevCon Homes, our then newly established construction company, and stapling pictures of my missing child's face to telephone poles.

"You should eat." He placed a tray at the edge of Holly's bed. "It's a Mexican casserole from Mrs. Garrity at All Saints. A little bland at first, but Mom doctored it up, and it's actually edible now."

I waited for Matt to leave, but something out of the ordinary happened then. He pulled Holly's chair out from under her built-in desk, took a seat, and faced me. "She's going to come back, you know. I feel it."

I sat up a little straighter.

"Do you ever just *know* something?" he asked. "And you can't explain how you know it? Well, it's like that. I just feel this connection with her, like she's still out there. Like she's close."

I'd been trying like hell to find some sort of cosmic connection to my daughter. Something that would give me reason to carry on. But, true to form, as much as I reached for her, I never felt her reach back.

Although I didn't want to admit it, I, like the police, expected the search dogs to find her body on the side of a country road one day after the snow melted away.

"She's close," Matt said again.

I managed to keep my tears at bay, and while all I really wanted was to be alone, I didn't ask him to leave.

"There's someone here to see you. I'll send him away if you want."

"Who?"

"Alan Kohlbrook, from church."

The way he said it—*from church*—as if *his* church were also *my* church, when I hadn't been to a service since the one in which I became Mrs. Trevor Gebhardt, made me feel as if I were part of a bigger whole. Something warm sparked in me for the first time since before Holly was taken.

"I'll come down."

When I finally found my way downstairs, it was only to interrupt an embrace. I'd taken the rear staircase, so maybe they thought they'd be hidden from public view, but Trevor had his arms around Susan, who was crying on his shoulder.

Isn't that rich? I was suffering alone in a shrine to our daughter's existence, and he was comforting the woman more suited to be her mother. It's more complicated than that, and I understood as much even back then, but it stabbed at my heart.

Susan saw me and backed out of my husband's arms. "It's Kitten," she said.

I wasn't interested in the explanation, which was probably valid. Kitten had witnessed the kidnapping, after all, and hadn't slept much since. I walked past the two of them to the front room, where Matt had asked Kohlbrook to wait. "Cecily." He stood the moment he saw me enter. He'd become something of a friend to me in the weeks leading up to the abduction. I'm sure he must have been present at the candlelight vigils and the neighborhood canvasses. But this was the first time I remembered speaking to him since it had happened. His eyes were bloodshot, and his clothing was wrinkled, and even in my state of disarray, I knew he likely hadn't bathed in days.

I'm sure we exchanged pleasantries, meaningless hellos and how-are-you-holding-ups. But the way I remember it, he jumped right into things: "The type of person to do this . . . He thinks he's doing something kind. He sees her: she's beautiful. Maybe he thinks she's sad, and he thinks he can help. You know what that's like, don't you? When you see a little girl crying, and you just want her to be happy?"

I felt my brow furrow. "What do you mean? How do you know—"

But he was suddenly on his knees, gripping me by the waist, talking again, as if he'd shaken a fizzy drink in his mind and it was exploding out in words.

"I never want this to happen to little girls. It breaks my heart. It breaks my heart, *breaks my heart.* What can I do? Tell me what to do, and I'll do it."

Trevor appeared in the doorway.

Instantly, with one eye on my husband, I pried at Kohlbrook's hands, but his fingers only tightened against mine. "He thinks he's caring for her. He's in love. He loves her."

My husband and Susan inched closer. Watching, judging.

I didn't know then about Kohlbrook's previous conviction, about the three months he'd served the year prior for luring two girls into the back of his minivan, where he photographed them. He took pictures of my daughter, too, but from a distance. The police found the candid snapshots hidden in a shoebox under his bed after Holly's return, along with half a dozen letters he'd written to her.

"Did you know he was writing to her?" a detective asked not long after she came home.

"What? No. I mean, she can't read more than a few words. Why would he—"

"Maybe it's best you have a look."

I didn't want to touch the letter, encased in one of those plastic sleeves and tagged with a case number (1224, Holly's birthday), but I took it from the cop reluctantly. Trevor didn't even wait to read it; he instantly exploded in anger, a primal, guttural caveman roar, followed by his hurling a side chair against the wall.

"Cecily, tell me—"

His words were a cacophony in my ears as I read:

> Dearest Holly,
> I want you to be happy today. You're special, the prettiest almost-five-year-old I've ever seen. Are we friends? I'd like to be your friend very much.
> I love you.
> Alan

My fingers trembled to the point that I dropped the letter.

"Did you know about this?" My husband shook me by the shoulders.

"Trevor! I—"

"*You're* the one who brought him into this house. *You're* the one who made him a friend. Did you know what he was planning to do? Did you help him do it?"

No! If I'd known about Kohlbrook's problem, his . . . deviance, I wouldn't have let him anywhere near Holly. But even now, it seems surreal, almost unlikely that Kohlbrook could have been the one who took her. He wasn't the man I thought I knew.

"It's all my fault." It came out in a whisper. Suddenly, everything was foggy and numb. I felt as if I were tumbling through a kaleidoscope. I wanted to explain to Trevor that I hadn't known, that I'd never left Kohlbrook alone with Holly. But the funny thing about inebriation: it silences you as soon as it steals your ability to think and walk in straight lines.

Weeks upon weeks of the same questions followed. It felt like a witch hunt, a ducking. Toss me, bound, into deep, riotous water. If I drown, I'm innocent. If I survive, I'm a witch.

Before I knew it, even I started to consider that maybe I knew more than I was telling. If the cops thought I knew something, I must have known something. If only I could remember what I refused to reveal.

"Ma'am?"

I focused on the cop talking to me.

"This is very important. Did Kohlbrook say anything to you that might've hinted at his condition?"

No. But I couldn't form the word.

Trevor paced, shoved his hands through his hair, screamed at me: "You retreated into her room! You never helped us look! Did you *know* Kohlbrook had her? Did you stash her with your friend?"

There are few things you never forget. Your husband accusing you of allowing a kidnapper access to your daughter is one of them. His words slammed into my chest, and for a few seconds, I couldn't draw breath.

"Did you let him take her? To hurt me in the process?"

I dropped my head into my hands. If he would say such a thing *in front of the police*, I must have given him reason to question my loyalty, my sense of responsibility for our daughter, and my commitment to her return.

But for the life of me, I couldn't remember what I knew, or even what I didn't. I just wanted it all to be over. She was home. She was safe, and her innocence was intact.

I wanted to count our blessings and be done with it, but even after the police left, Trevor kept at me, shook me, kept saying those awful words: "Did you know?"

Across the room, the ice cubes in my bourbon melted as slowly as the wheels turned in my mind. Why would he say that, unless I gave him reason?

I wouldn't do what he was suggesting. Would I?

Maybe. Hadn't I wanted him to hurt? Hadn't I bottled up years of resentment and pain and hoped it would rain down on him tenfold?

Think, Cecily. Think.

There *was* something Kohlbrook had said once.

I'd love to have a daughter.

And what was my reply? *Borrow mine for an afternoon.*

In hindsight, maybe Kohlbrook was inappropriately concerned with Holly's happiness. But had I, in some drunken haze, helped him hatch a plan? Knowingly or otherwise?

The police had profiled the abductor early on: someone we knew, according to Kitten, but she couldn't tell us who. She'd seen him before, and often enough that he was recognizable. Someone who was bigger than her but not old.

Her vague account of the man she'd seen take Holly drew one conclusion: it was someone who'd been around for a while, someone Holly knew and wasn't afraid of. Someone Kitten didn't see as a threat until it was too late.

After Holly came back, Kitten suddenly conjured the name: Al.

Now that I've had all this time in this white space to think about things, it seems rather convenient, doesn't it? Blame the resident weirdo, for lack of anyone else to suspect. Plant the seed in a five-year-old's mind, and watch it bloom.

Beep. Beep. Beep.

I try to move my little finger, still nestled in Trevor's hand.

"There's been another kidnapping," he says.

Oh no.

"They're wondering if they convicted the wrong guy for what happened to Holly. The police asked me what I thought about it. They've been poking around."

Oh no.

"Are they going to find anything, Cecily? If you know anything, now's the time to tell me."

I do know something.

It's all coming back to me.

CHAPTER 7

HOLLY

June 6

When I arrive home, a black two-door sedan is parked at the arc of the drive. A man paces in the shade of the barn, a cell phone to his ear. If that's Guidry, he's shorter than I thought he'd be, maybe five ten, and he's wearing jeans. He turns toward me; I see a badge hanging from a lanyard around his neck. A vintage White Sox logo spans the width of his T-shirt.

Maybe it's silly, but seeing the name of the baseball team puts me a notch closer to at ease with him. If he's a Sox fan, he can't be too bad.

He wraps his call when my truck comes to a stop, and shoves his phone into the front pocket of his jeans.

Even though I spritz myself with an apple-scented spray before I hop out of the truck, I'm practically drenched with sweat and probably reek of it, too. I wish I'd thought to give myself a cushion of time between work and this meeting. I more than *need* a shower; I'm *craving* one right about now.

The cop leans through the open driver-side window of his sedan and emerges with a thick accordion file, which he tucks under his arm. "Miss Gebhardt?"

"Yeah." I walk toward him with an only slightly dirty hand extended. "You can call me Holly."

"Detective Jason Guidry."

"I assumed." My fingers tremble as he shakes my hand. The shakes. Side effect of too much alcohol at night and too much Red Bull the next day.

"I was just trying your cell phone."

"Oh. I turned off the ringer. Text messages. It was distracting, and . . . Sorry I'm late."

"I understand."

"You'll uh . . . have to excuse the mess. Me, *and* my place." I toss my head toward the stairs we're about to climb. "I had a late night and an early morning."

"Not a problem."

As we ascend, I ramble about the bridal shower and my role in the wedding, as if he cares, but once I start, it seems awkward to try to shut up. It's a problem, I know. I sometimes fill silence with meaningless chatter. My last therapist said it's a way to avoid intimacy, as small talk is actually a barrier to deeper interaction. "And I'm . . . oh." I stop at the top of the steps, just as I'm about to put my key in the lock.

The door is not only unlocked but standing slightly ajar.

"Well, I guess I did leave in a hurry," I mutter under my breath. I push open the door and lead Guidry into the wide, open space with vaulted ceilings, which follow the roofline of the barn. When Dad and I designed the apartment, we incorporated the existing rough-hewn beams and built only enough walls to provide privacy for a bedroom and a bathroom. I have to admit, I love coming home to this place, even if it's nearly impossible to hide my clutter.

"Nice digs," Guidry says.

"Thanks. Built it myself." But I know almost instantly that something isn't right. I can't put my finger on it. It feels as if someone else was in here, or moved my things around, while I was gone. A moment later, the intruder comes barreling out of the bedroom at me: a cream-colored chusky—husky and chowchow crossbreed. "Dog! Down!"

"Clever name."

"I refuse to say her name." I look to the detective. "I don't like it."

"Here's an idea: give her a new one."

"Wish I could, but she's not mine. She belongs to a friend."

Sterling. I'm already texting to ask him when he plans to retrieve the she-devil with the happily wagging tail. It's not that I minded dog sitting while we were dating, and I probably wouldn't mind even now, had he asked if I had plans.

Besides, didn't we just discuss a clean break last night?

With the thought of male-female relationships, Matt flits into my mind. Again, I wonder about the extent of what happened between us—if anything at all happened—last night.

"May I?" The cop indicates my kitchen island.

"Huh?" I look up from my phone and quickly pocket it when I consider it must seem rude, especially since I was so late. "Oh, absolutely. I'm sorry, I'm just . . ." I dart to the island. "I'm dealing with some personal drama." I gather yesterday's mail into a pile, making room for his file. "Now." I turn to fill a dish with water and place it on the floor for Dog, who happily collapses and starts slurping with her purplish-black tongue as if she just emerged from the Sahara. "What can I do for you, Detective?"

"First, thanks for meeting me."

"My pleasure." I pull two bottles of water from my refrigerator and slide one toward him. He thanks me.

Out of the corner of my eye, I catch sight of the time on my oven: 1:42.

It has to be wrong. I knew I was running late, but *forty-two minutes* late? I glance at my phone. Yep. 1:42. How long was I sitting at the side of the road contemplating my mother's accident?

The detective's talking: "And I understand that this must seem out of the blue, my calling yesterday."

"Was it that obvious?"

"To be honest, this meeting is overdue."

I take a sip of water. "What happened to me happened twenty years ago. But you said I might be able to help you draw parallels to another case?"

"It's a long shot." He squints, as if assessing me. "But maybe. Mind if I record our conversation?"

"Not at all."

He produces a digital recorder from the file and presses a button. "This is Detective First Grade Jason Guidry. Lake County PD. At the residence of, and speaking with, Holly Gebhardt. For the record, state your name—first, middle, last."

"Holly Adryenne Gebhardt."

We go through the rigmarole. I state my address, my age, my date of birth.

"Do you have any questions? Before we begin?"

"I looked online," I tell him. "I couldn't find any recent cases involving missing girls around here."

"Right."

"But there's one from Indianapolis." I raise a brow, but he replies with a deadpan stare.

I try again. "I suppose a detective from Lake County, Illinois, wouldn't be working a case in Indiana."

"Miss Gebhardt, you might help with any number of cases."

"How so?"

"You were recovered alive three months after you were taken. In most cases of children missing that long, we expect to recover only bodies. Your case isn't unusual. Plenty of abducted children come home, even after extended periods of time. But it's not the norm. This puts you in a unique position to be able to help us profile abductors, to offer an interesting perspective as to how they plan, how they think."

I nod. "I'm sure you read my file. I don't remember the time I was gone. Have you tried speaking with the man who took me? Alan Kohlbrook?"

"I have." Guidry continues: "He isn't interested in helping. His lawyer approached me with a theory—that whoever is responsible for your abduction is still out there, and still at work."

"But who's gone missing in the area since me?"

"That's what's tricky: the geography. My team and I were focused on nine unsolved cases of interest, all taking place after your recovery, all within a five-hundred-mile radius of Chicago, until—"

"Nine?"

"Until a tenth girl was taken. Skyler Jane Kipniss, from the Indianapolis area. I'm working across state lines with a number of detectives in Indiana, Tennessee, Wisconsin, Iowa, Minnesota . . ." He pulls another object from the accordion file—a banner folded twice, so as to fit it into the file. When he opens it, I see it's a time line.

The first incident of note is the day of my abduction twenty years ago, followed by any number of events, including the kidnapping of other girls and the release of known pedophiles from prison. The last notch on the line is the day Skyler Jane disappeared, March 18 of this year.

Guidry points to the second-to-last notch, which denotes the recovery of Gretchen Klemm's body. "Aged five. Dubbed, until her identification, the Alleyway Angel, as she was recovered wrapped in a white blanket in the middle of an alley. She'd been dressed all in white—"

So was I, when I was recovered.

"And posed with her hands in prayer, tucked under her left cheek." He slaps a picture down on the countertop. "She was posed and swaddled *after* she was killed."

In death, the girl, Gretchen, is as white as her nightgown. Her golden hair appears to have been brushed prior to her placement in the alley, and the pajamas are riding up her right leg so her ruffled panties are visible.

"Was she . . ." I swallow over the thought of what I'm about to say. "Assaulted? Sexually?"

"Unfortunately, it's the number-one motive in taking a little girl," Guidry says. "But no."

It was one thing that had lent credence to their zeroing in on Kohlbrook in my case; he'd admitted pedophiliac tendencies, and even preferences, but had never acted on them—or so he said. And the shrinks who testified confirmed that people with his tendencies often *don't* act on them.

"Where was she from?" I ask.

"Gretchen represents the southernmost girl on the list. Her family lives on the outskirts of Memphis, Tennessee, but she was recovered near Evansville, Indiana. The site of her kidnapping is just out of range, but the recovery is well within our radius."

"That's a lot of ground to cover."

"Over seventy-eight thousand square miles."

I glance at the time line. Gretchen was found a year ago, come fall, on Halloween. "And a lot of time to consider."

The incidents marked in red represent kidnappings, and it's easy to see they occur every eighteen to twenty-four months, with a few longer gaps stretching up to three years in between.

"We have a long list of child abusers who covered a lot of ground like this. Back in the late eighties, there was a piece of shit who snatched girls up and down the West Coast and even went as far east as Arizona. It happens, when you consider the length of time we're talking about."

"Why do you think the cases are related? To each other *or* mine?"

"I mentioned the lawyer earlier."

"Yeah."

"He received a manifesto recently." Guidry opens another compartment in the accordion file and produces a stapled report. "Twenty-seven pages about why Kohlbrook couldn't possibly be the guy. The theory presented was that Kohlbrook couldn't have done it because whoever *did* is still at work. This manifesto includes the names of all the victims on our time line, up to and including Gretchen Klemm. The last words in these twenty-seven pages indicate that it's about to happen again. And a few weeks after the lawyer received this, a little girl went missing. Just as this guy's manifesto predicted."

"Skyler Jane Kipniss."

"That's right." Guidry now points to the event at the end of the time line: *disappearance of Skyler Jane Kipniss.*

"You think this is the guy who took me," I say.

"That's one of the things we're trying to determine," Guidry says. "Prove the same guy who kidnapped any of these girls was the one who kidnapped you, and Kohlbrook goes free because he was incarcerated during the time of the other abductions. It's a tough row to hoe, as most of the victims, all but you and Gretchen, have yet to be recovered. We presume they're dead, but we don't know for certain."

I imagine how that must feel: a child stolen and decades passing with no resolution in sight. No closure, no moving on.

"However, Gretchen *was* found, which means we have evidence. Not the kind of evidence I'd like, mind you, no DNA, but if Kohlbrook's attorney manages to prove parallels between your case and Gretchen's, or God willing, if we happen to recover Skyler Jane in time, Kohlbrook could be walking the streets by Christmas."

"But you *do* have DNA evidence against Kohlbrook, right?"

"We do."

"There were skin cells scraped from under my fingernails, and a hair fiber was found on my clothing, isn't that right?"

"It is. But," Guidry says, "it appears there's some trouble with its interpretation. Kohlbrook's lawyer hired an analyst who makes a pretty strong case that the forensics were flubbed. Added to the fact that Kohlbrook had been in your parents' house, your parents and the

Hersheys held you *before* the evidence techs took your nightgown for analysis. The hair could've been a secondary transfer, meaning we've got DNA worth squat."

"But it doesn't matter: He'd been stalking me. He planned to stalk other little girls. You said he had a list."

"Making a list isn't illegal."

"Still. He shouldn't be out there—"

"It's an imperfect system sometimes." He looks back to the time line. "Earlier this year, a letter was sent to newspapers in three major cities: Los Angeles, Chicago, New York. It was probably a quest for attention. The letter called out Deanna Renee Rhine." He points to the name of the fourth missing girl on the time line.

I remember hearing something about a letter, but I can't place any details.

"The letter didn't get much press," he says. "We tried to quash the story after we pulled a partial print from one of the letters."

"Why?"

"It's an ongoing investigation. We can't leak too much information."

"Oh."

"In theory, because the letter didn't get much press, the guy turned around and wrote the manifesto to garner more attention. I personally think that after the press leaked the partial fingerprint and still no one brought the guy in, he got a little cocky. So we're working on ways to keep drawing this guy out. But in the letter . . ." He pulls a copy of it from his file and points to one line:

you're not looking in the Right Place(s).

"Some investigators take this to mean the remains are divided. Others think it's a blatant reference to other victims, especially considering this." His finger lands on another line:

the truth of what happened to the Hag.

"*Hag* isn't usually how we refer to little girls," he says.

"Unless they're her initials," I say. And they're mine. "So this letter may have referenced me, and *this* is the first I'm hearing about it?"

"To be honest, it's a weak reference. You'd be surprised how many false alarms we ring in cases like these." The detective slides the manifesto toward me. "But this is a little harder to deny."

I flip from page to page. The third page begins with a name, in bold caps, centered at the top of the page: HOLLY ADRYENNE GEBHARDT. *Sweet girl. If you love something, you set it free. If it comes back, it's yours. Until then . . . and since then . . .*

I skim from page to page, each offering a possible explanation as to what happened to Enna Scotsman, Selena Truesdale, Jenny Bock, Alyssa Carter-Friese, Deanna Renee Rhine, Bethany Sparrow, Sophie Cousins, Lauren Bunting, and Gretchen Klemm. As much detail as the author of this manifesto included, however, there's no real information that might help solve the cases.

I read the last line: *It's the way of the world. Who will be next?*

"You think he did it again." I can barely get the words out. "You think this was a warning, and he made good on it by abducting Skyler Jane Kipniss."

I meet Guidry's gaze.

He sighs. "I'd say we can count on it."

CHAPTER 8

Holly

June 6

The afternoon sun beats through the windows behind me and bakes my sweat-drenched T-shirt to my body.

My skin feels grimy, greasy, dirty. I look toward my shower the way my mother used to eye her bourbon from across the room. Like it's part of me that has been taken away.

But Guidry has more to discuss. He slaps an eight-by-ten photograph onto my kitchen island. "Do you know what this is?"

"Um . . ." At first glance, it appears to be a picture of a small, angular rock, but the shape is too distinct, too symmetrical. "God, is that a tooth?"

"It is. From a small child."

Instantly, the taste of the bloody nub in my gums returns to me.

"Holly, you lost a tooth while you were gone."

"It was over twenty years ago." I wonder how long a tooth remains in good shape after it falls out of a little kid's mouth. Surely mine, wherever it ended up, has long since disintegrated.

"Has anyone asked you about losing your tooth before?" Guidry asks.

"I'm sure they have."

"What did they ask?" He leafs through his file and holds another page between his thumb and index finger, as if he's about to yank it out.

"It's been a long time. I don't remember *exactly*—"

He pulls the page free. "May I?"

It's a rhetorical question; he proceeds to read from what is apparently an old report:

Question: Do you know what happened to your tooth?

Answer: It falled out.

Question: Did the tooth fairy bring you a prize?

Answer: I didn't know I lost it.

Question: Where is your tooth now?

Answer: It's too dark there. We can't find it.

When it's clear he's finished, I look up at him through teary eyes. I remember the interview. I don't remember being upset back then, as much as I was matter-of-fact about things. I was, however, irked that I didn't get a chance to wiggle my tooth and wait up for the tooth fairy like Kitten had the summer before I was taken, when she lost her first tooth.

"I'm sorry to raise difficult subjects," Guidry says.

I shake my head because talking about the tooth isn't difficult. "I didn't know what happened to me back *then*. I don't know why I'm affected *now*."

But I *do* know. I'm bothered by the memories of what happened shortly after I returned. But it's not because of the memories themselves. It's because of my mother, because of what life was like then. Once I came home, my mother didn't let me out of her sight for months. She slept on the floor of my room, forced me to hold her hand at the grocery store, and never let me walk through the field to Kitten's on my own anymore.

It annoyed me because it was out of the norm. My aloof mother was gone, replaced by an overbearing basket case. I wasn't used to her standing over my shoulder all the time. Dad was the one I relied on when I was sick, the one who tended to me 90 percent of the time. He took me to work often, although my mother was a homemaker and easily could have taken care of me. But suddenly, after I came back, I couldn't shake her.

And I retorted with sass that a teenager would aspire to spit out.

I didn't want *her*.

I wanted Daddy.

I pushed her away. I'm sure I hurt her feelings.

Eventually, because she couldn't calm down when she was around me, and she couldn't find peace when we were separated (for school, sleepovers, you name it), the doctors prescribed her antianxiety pills—some version of the medication I took earlier today.

And then, she was lost to all of us.

She'd medicate with the pills, or alcohol, or both, and retreat into her world of old trinkets and antique furniture.

Dad and I carried on as if she were on the fringes of our lives, instead of an integral part of it.

This division coincided with the separation and subsequent divorce of Kitten's parents. They say there's nothing like trauma to test the strength of love. In enduring the trauma of my disappearance, the Hersheys' marriage crumbled, and our family dynamic forever changed.

Paul Hershey disappeared. Dad and I paired up with Susan and Matt and Kitten for vacations, while Mom stayed close to home. It was a pattern established when I was little, and it continued until the day she ran off the road and into the ravine.

I guess I never knew how much I'd miss her until she was just out of reach.

"Can we continue?" Guidry asks.

I clear my throat. "I'm fine."

"Mm-hmm." He looks at me for a moment, as if making sure I'm really okay before he resumes the conversation. "There's some indication in the dialogue I just read that you might have attempted to look for the lost tooth in a dark place. I know it's been a long time, but do you have any recollection of doing so? And if so, with whom?"

I shake my head. "Maybe, after I came back, my parents made a show of pretending to look with me or something. I don't really know."

"Do you know the process of obtaining DNA from a tooth?"

"No, I—" I clamp my mouth shut as realization dawns. "You can't possibly mean you think this is *my* tooth."

"Our dental expert says it's a central incisor, which are usually the teeth kids lose first—the first tooth *you* lost, as a matter of fact. Central incisor, lower right."

I press my tongue against the spot, remembering the odd feeling of the tooth's absence.

"We can extract DNA if we grind the tooth down to powder."

"Okay."

"And we did. DNA testing was a rather new tool in forensics the year you were returned to your family, but we used it to confirm your identity when you turned up all those years ago. This was before my time on the force, you understand. In any case, we compared your DNA on file to that of this tooth."

"And?"

"It takes a while at the lab, but now we know. It's not your tooth."

"Then why do you want to talk to *me* about it?"

"Care to know where we found it? Or when?" He pulls another sheet from his file. This one is a picture of skid marks on pavement. He raises a brow.

Now I'm thoroughly confused. "What's this?"

"We found the tooth at the scene of your mother's accident. Fifty-two days ago."

Numbness slides through me, but this time I know it's not a result of my hangover or the energy drinks. "So you're saying the day she slid off the road . . . ?"

"What if I told you I'm not sure it was an accident, what happened to your mother?"

"You think she did it on purpose?"

"No, I don't mean to imply *that.* Do *you* think that's what happened?"

Forgive me, Mom, but it isn't the first time the thought crosses my mind. I take a breath to explain, but Guidry's already elaborating.

"The marks on the road"—he stabs at the photograph of the skids with his index finger—"suggest another vehicle came up behind her and came to a screeching halt at the bend in the road. There were dark-blue streaks on the rear fender and the rear driver's side panel of your SUV. As if the vehicle had been nudged. It was your vehicle, isn't that right?"

"Yes. She borrowed it that day."

"Unless you were in an accident you didn't report previously?" He looks up.

"No." I feel for a counter stool and pull it under me.

"My evidence techs matched the tread marks to an all-season tire we often see on work trucks. Do you know anyone who drives a dark-blue truck?"

"I'm sure half a dozen guys in TrevCon's employ." I think for a second. "Craig Vellerman, one of our foremen."

He writes down the name. "Anyone else?"

"I'm sure there are others, but right offhand, no one specific. We have five crews out for rough framing right now. And then come the subs—plumbers, electricians, HVAC."

"Mm-hmm."

"Does my father know this?"

"I've spoken to him, yes." Guidry presses his lips together and pauses for a second before moving on. "There were a lot of scratches and marks on the vehicle by the time it came to a stop at the bottom of the ravine. Right now, this is only a theory of mine. My colleagues . . . well, given your mother's blood-alcohol content, most of my colleagues think the blue scratches must have been preexisting—maybe from someone scraping you in a parking lot, that sort of thing. And the tire tracks a coincidence."

"I don't remember seeing any blue marks on my car."

Guidry nods. "Are you aware 9-1-1 operators registered a call from your mother's cell phone around the time the accident occurred?"

"Yeah, they told us." Dad and I assumed Mom had managed to place a call via Bluetooth.

"Did they tell you we've determined the call was dialed by hand? Her device wasn't paired with the Bluetooth system in the car, and the phone was found out of her reach on the passenger-side floor. She made that call *before* she went over the edge."

So she was afraid of something. Someone was probably following her. My eyes burn with tears I'm trying like hell to ward off.

"If someone was following your mother a bit too close, maybe she was scared and didn't let up on the gas when she rounded the bend."

"You think someone was following her?"

He watches me a few seconds too long for comfort. Finally, he pulls a small spiral-bound notebook from his pocket and flips to a free page. He clicks open a ballpoint pen. "I've also considered someone may have thought they were following *you*."

Jesus.

Mom borrowed the car because she was shopping for a large piece of furniture at the Antiques Warehouse. She was supposed to be back within a few hours, but as often happened, she'd obviously stopped for a drink and lost track of time.

My head spins with the thought of her ending up in a coma because someone had a beef with *me*.

"She'd stopped drinking, you know," I tell him. "Twenty-two, twenty-three days, I think."

"That's what your father said. But relapse is part of recovery."

"I've always thought that if my mother had been drinking that much, she would've taken the long way home. At the very least, she would have crawled around that bend. She wouldn't have been going fast. Not with that awful rain."

"Funny thing about being impaired. It affects your judgment."

I stare down his sarcasm. He shrugs. "She was willing to drive, my colleagues say, and she was willing to take the shortcut past the ravine. If her judgment lapsed to that extent, we don't know that she would have been careful about it."

"Here's the thing about my mother," I offer. "Point-oh-seven blood alcohol might have been impaired from a scientific standpoint, and it's one one-hundredth from the legal limit, but she probably didn't feel it. After the accident, I looked it up. For a woman her size, that's about the equivalent of two drinks in two and a half hours. That's *nothing* to my mother."

"Your father agrees."

"So I thought it was just one of those things. It would have happened even if she'd been stone sober. But now . . . if you think it wasn't an accident . . . or maybe that I was the target . . . I don't know."

"Do you have any enemies?"

"Not that I know of."

"Do you know anyone your mother may have had a disagreement with?"

"She was quiet, but could be, shall we say, *contentious* at times. When she was drinking, especially."

"Mm-hmm. What was her relationship with Paul Hershey like?"

"Kitten's father?" My brows rise. "I didn't know they *had* a relationship."

"He and your mother spoke in the week before the accident. And on the day of."

He lets the information hang there.

I wonder aloud: "Did she call him, or . . . ?"

"Yes, she initiated contact. He reciprocated the day of."

I nod. "Susan Hershey seemed upset that he didn't make the drive for Kitten's engagement party the weekend before, so maybe my mother reached out—"

"So your mother and Paul remained friends after he moved away?"

I shake my head. "He was a good friend of my father's, but I don't think they saw each other after the Hersheys divorced. Paul's the one who introduced Alan Kohlbrook to my parents and recommended him for odd jobs. Paul met him at church, and as I understand it, he never got over the guilt of introducing him to us."

"Mm-hmm. Well, a few hours before your mother had the accident, they spoke for eight minutes. And her call log registered several missed calls from his mobile just before her car went off the road."

"What does this have to do with the tooth?" I ask.

"Do you know how it ended up in the glove box?"

"It was *where*?"

He clarifies: "The glove box of your Ford Explorer jarred open in the wreck. The EMTs noticed the loaded firearm, and that led the officers to search the vehicle. We uncovered the tooth from there."

I take another sip of water, but it doesn't help steady me. My hands are all out shaking now. "I don't know why Mom would've put it there. Or even where she would've gotten it."

"The tooth was enclosed in a small glass bottle. We dusted it for fingerprints. We didn't even pull a partial match to her. Your mother never touched that bottle. You know who did?"

He pulls another picture from the file. This one is of the bottle in question. It looks like a miniature mason jar, about an inch and a half tall, the diameter of a penny, pale-green milk glass, but instead of a screw-on lid, it's sealed with a tiny cork.

My heart drops.

Might come in handy for a collection of atoms, Kitten had said when we'd seen the tiny bottles sitting on a windowsill at the Moonbeam.

Or, according to my mother, I could keep my ambitions in there, I'd joked.

I remember seeing them, for sure.

I don't remember taking one.

I must have, but I just don't remember doing it. I think hard. I cast my mind into the past as I remember the night: Karaoke (Blondie's "Heart of Glass"), whiskey, a game of darts.

Sterling showed up late. We argued. He left. The beginning of the end for us.

Kitten and Eliot disappeared on the dance floor, I went home, and she texted me the next morning:

I fucking LOVE this guy.

I'm a total slut.

But

Oh.

My.

God.

We're getting MARRIED!

I called her instantly. "You're *marrying* this guy?"

"Holly, I know you're going to love him instantly. He's so *posh*, you know? You should see his apartment. It's right across from the Lincoln Park Zoo. You're gonna die!"

"Okay. But Kitten . . ." A thousand concerns rushed through my mind at once. At the top of the list: she'd known him only a couple of months. There was the fact that he was, as Kitten said, *posh*, and she'd always been an outdoorsy girl. What did they have in common? And the age difference . . . But I bit my tongue. "Are you sure?"

"When you know, you know."

That was the end of it. I didn't ask if she really wanted to be part of this guy's midlife crisis. I let her be happy. She was doing the logical, grown-up thing to do. She'd found someone to spend forever with.

And I was still kicking around a disaster of a relationship with legs barely long enough for middle school.

"You recognize the bottle," the detective says.

I pull myself back to the present.

He continues: "Your prints are all over it."

"I . . . I remember seeing it, but I didn't think I . . ."

"You remember seeing it."

"Yes."

"In the glove box."

"What?"

"The vial was in the glove box. That's where you saw it?"

"No. It was at Moonbeam. It's this little pub we go to."

The detective nods. "Do you remember the date?"

"Um . . . around the time Kitten and Eliot got engaged."

"And when was that?"

"I don't know the *exact* day. Early to mid-March, I think."

I should tell him about my tendency to take things. I should make him understand the twitch in my fingers, the discombobulating feeling that cloaks me until I grasp whatever it is that pulls me in. I don't remember feeling that way about the little green bottle, but . . .

"It comes from the time I was gone," I begin. My stomach churns. I might get sick. I take a deep breath and slowly exhale.

"Holly."

"Yeah." I meet his gaze.

He tilts his head to one side; his brows come together.

"I didn't know there was a tooth inside it."

He nods, a curt movement—a quick jut of his chin in a downward motion. "There were no prints on the tooth itself. Whoever put it there didn't leave prints."

"I just don't know how . . . I don't remember taking it—"

"Let's talk about the firearm."

"It's registered to my father." The police returned it to him about a week or so after the accident, after determining it hadn't been fired.

"You have a concealed-carry card."

"I don't always work in the nicest neighborhoods," I explain.

"Your father is licensed for concealed carry as well."

"Yes."

"Your mother is not."

"She doesn't like guns. She didn't like the fact that my father taught me to shoot when I was a kid, but when you survive something like being abducted . . . He sent me to martial arts classes, too. She didn't like that, either."

"The GLOCK had your prints on it, your father's, and your mother's. Any chance you borrowed your father's firearm and left it in the glove box?"

"No." It's a .45, for one thing. That's a hefty caliber for self-defense for someone of my size. I've never carried my father's piece, but even if I happened to . . . "I never leave my firearm in the vehicle."

"So your mother must have brought it with her."

"I guess."

"Any idea why she would have brought a firearm with her?"

I shake my head.

"Do you know where she was going that day?"

"She said she might stop at the Antiques Warehouse off Route 41. She was always lugging home these run-down pieces and refinishing them, and we'll have a concept house to furnish, come September. It looked like rain. She couldn't haul in the pickup in the rain, and her Camry's too small."

"Did she happen to mention anything about seeing someone that scared her, or—"

"To be honest, I'm not sure she would have. We don't have that kind of relationship. We don't share a lot. You might ask my father."

"I have. Holly, your father tells me your mother took a vacation in March of this year."

I nod.

"Tell me," he says. "Do you remember where she said she went?"

"Door County, I think? A retreat of some sort."

"Your father tells me your mother wasn't much for the outdoors. Didn't ski—"

"Not on water. Not on snow."

"Snowmobile?"

"Not a chance."

"Then winter is an unusual time to go to Door County, don't you think?"

My eyes start to go cloudy. *It is.* Most tourists who aren't the snow bunny type venture up to the thumb of Wisconsin only in May through October. Maybe visits stretch into November with the leaves changing, but March?

"Maybe it was an AA retreat. All you need for that is a fireplace and a circle of chairs."

"True." The cop continues: "But I called the resort where she told your father she was staying. They were closed for renovations in March."

I feel faint.

"Holly, do you know . . . is it possible your mother was having an affair?"

I remember something now that seemed unimportant at the time. I dropped in at my parents' place a few weeks before the accident. Mom was at the kitchen table with a laptop in front of her. Her email account was up on the screen, and she closed the laptop the moment I entered. Was she hiding something? Correspondence from a man? "I don't know." I drop my head in my hands. "Maybe. My parents aren't like other couples. They exist in the same space, but they don't seem to *share* it, you know?"

"If she broke it off, whoever it was with might be angry enough to nudge her over a ravine."

"No." It comes out in a whisper. I try to cough over the lump in my throat, but it's all too much to process. Maybe my mother was cheating on my father. Maybe that affair resulted in an accident. And it's somehow all tied up with a tiny tooth.

I draw in a slow breath. Before the detective has a chance to ask if I'm okay, I blurt, "You'll have to excuse me. I worked in the sun this morning. Haven't had much to eat. I'm feeling off today."

"I've thrown a lot at you all at once. Maybe we'll continue some other time." He gathers his papers and shoves all of them back into his file with the exception of one: the time line. "I'll leave this with you. We've got more copies. See if anything jumps out at you, if you will. Dates that coincide with anything that might have happened to you. Anniversaries. That sort of thing."

"Sure."

"Can you come down to the station? Tomorrow? Monday, the latest?"

"I can come tomorrow for sure, but if . . ." I press my palm to my cheek. It's warm to the touch, and I feel an ache where the enormous sliver was embedded in my hand. I need to clean the gash. "If this is about a missing child"—or ten—"I want to help."

Guidry slides a business card across the island toward me. "You can call, too, if you remember anything before tomorrow—about the bottle, about your tooth, or the time you were gone. Anything."

He's halfway to the door when he turns around. "You were gone for ninety-four days. Skyler's been gone for eighty now. She might not have much time." He chews his lip for a split second. "The tooth? It's hers."

Cecily

Holly had been gone nearly three weeks or so when the package arrived, postmarked from Champaign, Illinois. It was addressed not to Trevor and me, but to me alone, using a standard computer-printed label. There was no return address.

"I brought your mail." Paul Hershey dropped a bundle of it on the table in front of me. "How are you feeling?"

I glanced at him. "How do you think?" Although I bit my tongue, I only wanted him to leave. *Take your wife and your kids back across the field*, I wanted to say. That would have mortified Trevor. I kept my mouth shut.

The envelope itself was thick and padded, about four by six inches. I tore it open, and the contents fell into my hand:

A key.

A typewritten note:

Holly won't come home.

And a blonde ringlet of hair, tied with a pale-pink bow.

"Ceci?"

"Oh, God." My hands shook, and tears came in a burst.

"Police, please." Paul already had the phone at his ear.

The moment my fingers touched the lock of hair, I knew it was Holly's. I'd fought with her to brush out the tangles every morning of her life. I'd struggled with my wiggling child to pull her hair into ponytails before playdates. And the color, a light golden blonde, was unmistakable.

I held the curl against my cheek. "Where are you, Holly?"

Paul paced the room, detailing what the package contained. "Come quickly."

I startled at his words.

The police would come. They would take her hair away.

With shaking hands, I loosened the ribbon and pulled out a few strands. I needed to keep her with me. I needed to keep her close.

Later that night, in the midst of yet another interview that aired on the ten o'clock news, an annoyed detective confirmed: "Yes, we have reason to believe the package came from the kidnapper, but I'm afraid it won't be much help. The missing child's mother tampered with the evidence."

Maybe I'd destroyed the one clue the police had been waiting for.

"Would you say Cecily Gebhardt has cooperated with the investigation?" a reporter asked.

One word came in response: "No."

Articles in newspapers followed, and Holly's case reached cities far and wide. Finally, her case garnered the national attention it deserved, but at my expense.

If people were talking about my negligence, however, they were talking about Holly. It was a sacrifice I willingly made.

Mail arrived by the boatload, convicting me on the spot of abetting my daughter's kidnapper. *Why won't you help the police? If my child was missing, I'd do anything . . .*

I looked to Trevor for help.

He only looked away.

The mail came even after Holly was returned to us. I stopped reading the letters after a while, but I never threw any of it away. Instead, I filed the correspondence in boxes, which I stored on a shelf in my basement studio, where I do most of my refinishing work.

I'm not sure why I didn't simply throw the letters away, but now, as I lie here, serenaded by the sound of my own heartbeat, I wonder if it's because I hoped the police would someday pay attention.

That's probably why I saved all the emails, too, even after the police deemed them hoaxes or attempts at harassing a hated semipublic figure.

I kept my social media pages private, but the senders of the emails always knew how to find me. The pictures were emailed from different accounts every year or so. If the police had cared to take the emails seriously, they might have been able to trace them.

"The twenty-year anniversary is coming up. Just someone trying to rattle you," the cop said when I reported receiving one of them last year: a picture of a blonde curl tied with a pink bow. The accompanying message said simply: Are you going to do anything about this?

Trevor?

In the absence of speech, I try to think my way into his head. It worked once before. The moment I tipped over the edge of the ravine, I called out to him, and he called back.

Trevor, tell the police. They'll listen to you. Find the emails.

"Cecily." His calloused hand lifts my chin. "Tell me what you know."

CHAPTER 9

HOLLY

June 6

The water beats down on my head, washing away all the ugliness of last night's whiskey, the question of what happened with Matt, the animosity and the fall at the job site, the conversation I just shared with the detective . . .

And the fuzzy memory of the half-finished house. The girl. Could it be power of suggestion? I've spent most of my life at unfinished houses, and I'd just seen the report about Skyler Jane. But maybe I should have told the detective about the glimpses (memories?) of the girl—just in case.

I try to focus on her again. I pinch my eyes closed and remember her stare.

Don't want to fall.

I gasp when the words come to me, and in the process, I inhale shower water.

I cough it out.

Don't cross.

Again, an image flickers into my mind: a signpost, peeling, white paint. The letter *P.* An *H.* It's like the woman at the 7-Eleven was saying: echoes of the past.

Kitten's texting again, but whatever she wants is going to have to wait.

A girl is *dead*, and nine others are missing. That takes precedence over wedding to-do lists and a discussion about the box I took from the mantel.

When the water turns cold, I emerge, shivering. I pull on an old robe and wrap my hair in a towel. Dog follows me to my bedroom and jumps up to the mattress when I collapse atop it. As if she can sense I'm crumbling inside and in need of an ally, she curls at my side.

She's a good dog. I'm going to miss her.

I reach for my phone and glance at Kitten's messages:

Hey, bridesmaids!

I dried all the roses Eliot's given me over the past six months.

It's time to put them to use!

Join me for a Rose Petal Peeling Party.

Let's make satchels of love and spread the love around.

Wine and cheese on me!

See you at five!

Sorry, Kitten. Not tonight.

I conduct an internet search for Gretchen Klemm, the girl abducted from a neighborhood skirting Memphis. Five years old. Missing for six weeks. Recovered, deceased, last October outside Evansville, Indiana, hours after her death in an alleyway, dressed entirely in white.

Cause of death: suffocation.

Next, I type *Skyler Jane Kipniss* into my search window. Instantly, images of the girl flood my screen.

"What happened to you?" I ask her. "It's okay. You can tell me."

I know her fate will follow one of two paths: she'll be found like Gretchen, or she'll find her way home, like I did.

"Go home," I plead with her picture. "Put it all behind you and go home."

Dad calls, but I decline.

As expected, when I don't answer, he texts: Vellerman said you fell this morning.

I swipe away the message and queue up an article about Skyler Jane.

With every word, an atom of serenity blinks out.

The child was snatched from a playground outside her parish hall.

She was wearing a mint-green beret, black leggings, a T-shirt with the word LOVE written in the same mint green, and a gray spring jacket.

Throughout the service, parishioners witnessed her wiggling a loose tooth—the tooth that found its way into the glove box of my car.

Accompanying the article is a picture of the little girl with her baby brothers, twins. Her father had taken the picture just before the family left for church.

It is, perhaps, the last picture to be taken of Skyler Jane.

This world is an evil place sometimes.

Dad texts again: You okay?

I reply, not because I want to talk about things, but because it's not fair to make him worry. Fine.

Dad: Meeting tonight. You should come.

Al-Anon.

I haven't been to a meeting in a while, since before Mom's accident. I wish he'd invited me on another night. I'm so tired. If I'm going anywhere tonight, it's not going to be until I sleep for at least half an hour.

However, maybe it's because I'm feeling vulnerable, but I could handle seeing my dad right now. A wave of nostalgia hits me, and for a moment or two, it feels like it used to feel: Dad and me, teaming up to survive the challenges of living with someone like Mom, someone who *just can't stop*. Since the accident, however, it's like Dad doesn't remember any of the bad stuff. It's like he's canonized her because she tipped over a cliff after drinking and driving.

Unless she was nudged.

I want to talk to Dad about the detective's theory, too.

Me: I'll be there. Talk then.

Dad: Grab a bite after?

Me: Sure.

Dad: By the way, Matt's staying at the house.

Don't be alarmed if you see lights going on and off.

He needs some time to decompress. Let him come to you.

Oh, I already did. But in what capacity? Is this what losing your grip on reality feels like?

I wonder how that tooth ended up in a bottle I didn't know I took—

And that's another thing. This kleptomania habit of mine is really getting troublesome. The bottle. The box.

Wait.

Something Psychic Yanneth said yesterday . . .

A rose in your garden . . .

Suppose she meant the rose petal in the pewter box.

How could she have known that?

Unless . . .

In a flash, her entire commentary floods me. She also said I was losing balance.

And I did that today, too.

I rush to the wastebasket and fish out her card.

Could she be the real deal?

CHAPTER 10

HOLLY

June 6

It feels like my eyes barely close when the image comes to me, like a clip of a movie I saw a long time ago.

A tooth in a pool of bloody drool in the palm of a hand. *Lucky girl.*

I startle awake.

My heart is beating like mad, and unlike glimpses of the past, the image of the tooth doesn't start to fade. It keeps flashing there. I can't get it out of my aching head.

Is it my tooth? The day I lost it? Whose hand did I spit it out into?

I've been lax in recording these things in a journal—probably because I've been lax with therapy, but also because these glimpses have been so incredibly vivid it's hard to imagine I'd ever forget them. Still, I rummage in the drawer of my bedside table and scribble notes about it, about the girl across the rafters.

—

I'm late.

Dad's vehicle is parked at the back of the lot, as usual. Easy exit, he always says. I pull in next to him, then sprint to the church, where the Al-Anon meeting has already started in the basement.

I pause outside the door of the community meeting room to catch my breath, to steel myself. The truth is that I absolutely hate these meetings. I get used to them if I go on a consistent basis, like Dad, who goes religiously. But I don't subscribe to the process the way he does.

I can't small talk my way out of the things we talk about here. Beyond these doors, shit gets real. And despite the fact that it was Mom who brought the turmoil of chronic drinking into our lives, the people at this meeting want me to look at me. They want me to examine my part in the tragedy.

Dad's good at letting Mom off the hook for these things and taking partial responsibility.

I understand it in theory, but I'm not there yet, not willing to do it. Or maybe I'm feeling a little guilty because lately, I'm the one with blank spaces where hours of nighttime memories ought to be.

Hello, Kettle. You're black.

My phone buzzes with a text from Kitten: You coming?

I reply: Can't. Meeting with Dad.

Kitten: Come after.

Please.

I want you to be part of this.

You're my maid of honor, and you're the only one who isn't here.

Me: Can I bring the dog?

Kitten: No!

Vera's allergic.

And so is Eliot.

Fucking Sterling.

Why is the dog your responsibility?

Drop her off at his place on your way in.

Me: Can't. I gave him back his key when we broke up.
Kitten: So he wins again.

I'm pulling rank here.

I'm the one in the big white dress.

I NEED YOU.

Me: I'll come for a bit.

Just can't stay too late.

Kitten: Yay!

She's already texting more, but I silence the ringer and enter the room in the midst of the serenity prayer.

I take the closest available seat. All the chairs surrounding the long banquet-style tables, which are pushed together end to end and span the length of the meeting room, are filled, and the stragglers, like me, have pulled chairs up, too, packing us in like sardines. A quick count tells me there are more than forty people here tonight.

Dad's hard to miss. He's six five with a shock of white hair and eyes as blue as mine. His reading glasses, black wire with rectangular frames, sit low on his nose. *Hope for Today* and *Courage to Change* are the two constant texts in his life. The miniature books, void of the brown paper covers so many of these folks fashion to hide their titles, look even smaller than usual in his hands. He acknowledges my late arrival with a nod, which I return, then returns his focus to the woman to his left, who's reading a bylaw of the group.

Her voice is familiar. Dad's large frame blocks my view of her; I see only the top of her head (a full, black bun) and plump hands adorned with at least ten rings. Costume jewelry.

When she lowers her copy of the book and leans forward into view, my fingers practically seize in a fist.

Psychic Yanneth.

Her grin is wide when she catches sight of me.

I glance away. I understand that I haven't been here in a while. Maybe she's a regular. But what are the odds that we'd frequent the same meetings?

Perhaps she's here for her own good. But the coincidence is too great to ignore: Is she here for me?

Chances are, she's here fishing. A meeting like this might be the perfect place for a predator to loiter. Some of the people in this room are searching for guidance—any type, at any cost. It's a good pool in which to cast a line to snare people willing to pay twenty bucks for a peek into the future, however fabricated. And then, once they're hooked on her prophecies, she might take them for a whole lot more than a twenty.

Or maybe she really came here looking for me. Looking to help me or to rip me off.

I think hard. Did I mention Al-Anon last night? Was I wearing anything or holding something that might have tipped her off to look for me here?

I do my best to pay attention to the group readings, the testimonials.

But every time I look up, the psychic is smiling in my direction, as if she's in my head and knows I fished her card out of the wastebasket, as if she knows I'm willing to believe in a phenomenon that doesn't make a lick of sense, as long as it might help me fill some gaps.

My fingers are closing around an object I feel on the table beneath my hand.

Flat. Spherical.

A coin.

I can't take it.

It's a hard-earned badge of commitment. I imagine the woman to my right standing, announcing her anniversary—thirty days, sixty days, a hundred twenty, whatever it is—and the room erupting in applause. The chairperson du jour awarded her this gold-toned token, but I can't let it go.

It feels like the pewter box: Cold, hard, unchanging. Permanent.

We count off to separate in groups.

Psychic Yanneth is a two.

I count ahead to determine if we'll be in the same group. I want to ask her about the cryptic message she voiced last night. The losing-balance comment, the rose-in-the-garden mumbo jumbo.

I'm a three. I stand up when everyone else does, my fist closed around the coin.

Even when the woman frantically searches the table for it, I don't give it up.

I can't help it. It feels as if I'll lose focus if I lose touch with it, as if I won't really have been here if I don't take the proof.

I slip it into my pocket and head toward the stairs, where the threes will meet in the sanctuary.

"You see I'm right, don't you?" Psychic Yanneth comes up behind me, climbing the stairs, although her group is going to be meeting elsewhere.

"What are you doing here?"

"It's an open meeting. All are welcome."

"We're a far cry from the 7-Eleven where we first met. Do you see what I'm saying? This can't be coincidence."

"There's a fine line between coincidence and logic," she says.

We're stopped in the stairwell, and people are streaming around us. The two of us, along with her enormous handbag (there's the face of a cat rudimentarily embroidered on it) are creating quite an obstacle.

She nods and, with a smile, adds: "I can help you."

For not more than a few seconds, I challenge her with a stare. She gives it right back. This is ridiculous. Rationally, I know she can't possibly know the things she claims to know.

But when she beckons toward the door at the top of the stairs, I inexplicably follow her to the church grounds. Stones crunch beneath my feet as we make our way to the garden at the rear of the building.

She sits on a bench marked with a plaque. "You want to know why I'm here," she says. "It's a fair enough question. You think I followed you. You think I somehow know where you're going to be. There's no logical explanation for it. I was called here, felt an urging to come. And here you are. I'm in the right place at the right time."

"I don't believe in what you do." I should leave it at that. But I keep talking: "But you said I'd lose balance, and I did. You said something about a rose in a garden, and—"

"And you wonder how I knew you're cultivating something that isn't your responsibility. It's like I said. I feel energy. I see echoes when I look at you. You've been through something. It keeps haunting you. You feel responsible. Sometimes, you feel as if you're floating without direction, don't you?"

"Doesn't everyone, from time to time?" I lean against a tree trunk.

"I see the number eleven. It's so clear when I look at you."

"I assume next you'll tell me what color my aura is."

"Dark blue."

Her lack of hesitation shuts me up.

"Cloudy blue. But definite. The last time something came to me so unobstructed, I saw a little boy. He was in the water. His underwear was on inside out. It was too late to save him, but his mother deserved to know where he was. So I went to Guatemala to tell her."

"You went all that way to—"

"I wouldn't have gone if I didn't know for sure."

"But how did you . . . How?"

"Now you ask me how I knew such a thing. I say it doesn't matter how I explain it. You ask that boy's mother: Would she rather know where her boy is? Or would she rather I explain a process she can't possibly understand?"

"Didn't she want to know both?"

"Hmmm." Yanneth opens her bag and pulls out a skein of yarn. She instantly goes to work, knitting.

"That's it?" I ask.

"I know what I know and see what I see."

A few seconds of silence pass before she adds, "Do you ever see someone—remember someone, maybe—who looks like you? She crosses your path, or maybe she comes to you when you're sleeping."

I'm just about to tell her I have visions of a little girl.

"If that happens, pay attention. She's a message."

I chew on my lip for a second, debating whether or not I should ask: "What message do you think she's sending?"

"Truth, maybe. I don't know yet. But I look at you, and I see . . ." She shakes her head. "You're not the only one, is what I'm seeing. And you'll see it, too. Lovely, lovely energy about you. You feel the echoes. I know you do."

"Do you know anything about a little girl? Lost tooth?"

She squints at me, as if picking through the apparently cloudy blue energy surrounding me. "I see a sign. Old. Peeling paint. You think about that sign a lot, don't you?"

Had I mentioned it at the 7-Eleven? "How do you know these things?"

"I don't have to spend my energy trying to make a believer out of you. Some things are more than black and white. You come to me when you're ready to see shades of gray. Or maybe you never will. It's none of my business, either way." She shoves her knitting back into her bag. "But if you're not ready now, I'll go back to the meeting."

"Okay." I push off the trunk of the tree and plan to walk away. "It's been stimulating."

"That scar on your arm." She glances up at me just as I cover it with my hand. "That's what I'm seeing. You're not the only one who has one like it."

The declaration stops me cold.

"Ask your mother," she says. "She knows."

Instantly, my heart pounds. "What?"

"Have a nice day."

"No, I mean . . . you said something about my mother?"

"I said, *Have a nice day*."

CHAPTER 11

Holly

June 6

I don't go back to the meeting; rather, I climb into the cab of my truck and sit and try to catch my breath.

I google: *arrow-shaped scar.*

Hordes of images pop up.

I scroll through them, but none is quite like mine. I trace it with my fingers, a thin, white scar, a small ridge in my flesh. A small arc on the shaft, and two opposing tangents, it looks as if it were cut into me with precision. There's nothing accidental about it, and of course, it's puzzled me (and the authorities) from time to time. How did it come to be a permanent fixture on my skin? But after a while, day in, day out, you just get used to seeing it. It's part of me, like a tattoo.

But Yanneth insists my mother knows something about it.

This is, perhaps, more disturbing than its existence.

The good daughter would honor her dinner plans with her father.

The good bridesmaid would go straight to Kitten's to peel petals off dried roses after.

And I will do both. I just need to take a beat. Just need to breathe a little.

Need to be by myself.

If Mom knew something about the scar on my arm, especially if she knew I wasn't the only one to bear it, I am positive this wouldn't be the first I've heard of it—let alone from a strange little lady ditching an Al-Anon meeting to knit under a tree.

Then again, it's possible Mom and Dad know something they haven't shared with me. They used to shelter me from the horror of it all.

Things that happened when I was a kid are hardly mainstream news these days; it's not like the newspapers would be printing stories about my plight all these years later, but I suppose if she did some digging, Yanneth could have read something about what Mom did or didn't know back then.

I open the browser on my phone and do a search on my name.

The last mention of me in the public arena was in celebration of the twentieth anniversary of my return—a few months ago. The *Daily Herald* mentioned my case, noted that unlike other survivors of nonfamily abduction, I have remained out of the limelight, have kept out of awareness campaigns, and have yet to write a memoir about my experience. I read the last line of the one-paragraph article: Holly Adryenne Gebhardt is doing well, working as a journeyman for TrevCon Homes. She still has no recollection of the ninety-four days she was missing. The perpetrator, Alan Kohlbrook, was convicted in her kidnapping and remains behind bars.

Still, until the detective called in the middle of Kitten's bridal shower, I was unsure even the police remembered the case, and I never spent much energy thinking about it because it never felt like it happened to me. It was like hearing stories of something you did when you were a little kid. Everyone else remembers and tells you about it. So it becomes real to you. Not because you remember it. But because everyone else does.

Too much time has passed.

And to the outside eye, I'm okay. I've never acted like a victim, and I've never let what happened to me define me. No victim, no crime.

Maybe I used to believe that, too. But . . .

I feel the outline of the coin in my pocket.

There are things the rest of the world doesn't know about me.

I glance at the mark on my arm.

It stares up at me, full of secrets.

And according to a self-proclaimed, ice cream–loving prophet, my mother shares in its mystery. I wonder if the detective knows anything about that.

I scroll through my recent calls and land on the number from which Guidry phoned last night. After a few rings, my call dumps into voice mail.

I consider the detective's theory about Mom's accident.

Chill bumps rise on my arms.

My brain is jumping from one conclusion to the next, and before I have time to organize my thoughts, the tone is sounding, and I'm leaving a message: "Hi, Detective. I wonder if you can call me. We can also talk tomorrow when I come in, but . . . you said something about Mom's accident. Maybe she was run off the road. Maybe it's because of me. Or because she knows something about me. About the time I was gone. Is that what you meant? I don't know. I'm sure this isn't making sense, but I met someone who said something strange about my scar. And . . . call me. If you can." I rattle off my phone number. "This is Holly, by the way. Gebhardt."

I hang up.

God. If this guy didn't think I was a flake before, I haven't left much room for doubt now.

I put the car in gear. I don't plan to go anywhere in particular, but I have time to kill before the meeting is over and I have to meet Dad back here for dinner. So I drive.

"Is the psychic right, Mom? Do you know something about the scar I came home with?"

Miles pass.

"You need to wake up, okay? Because if you know something the police don't know . . . or maybe you didn't know until the night you had the accident." I roll this one around in my brain for a minute. "Is that what happened, Mom? Did you learn something someone didn't want you to know?"

Maybe that's what happened. Maybe Guidry's right. Could she have been forced off the road as a means to shut her up? For good?

The thought makes me sick.

She would've been scared. She would've mentioned it to Dad, in that case.

"I talked to you before you left that day," I say to her. "You seemed fine. Nothing out of the ordinary. We bickered about the concept house . . ."

I think about it now, our last conversation before the accident. She didn't want me to start with the crew on the new concept house for Dad's next development. *Promise me*, she'd said. *You'll at least try to make strides in what you went to school to do.*

I have a bachelor's degree in social work. But like I told her: *I don't know if I can do it.* "What I meant was . . . how can I help other people when my whole life feels like fragments? I don't have *shit* together. How can I feel as if I'd be a help to someone else?"

After driving for some time and having a one-sided conversation with my mother, I'm nearly to Loyola Medical Center. I guess talking to her made seeing her all the more urgent. Dad's meeting is close to being over, and there's no way I can get back in time to meet him for dinner.

I pull into the parking garage and shoot him a quick text: Rain check on dinner?

"I know," I say to my imaginary mother. "But he'll have to understand. And so will Kitten." I pause for a second, as if Mom might reply. "Because no, I can't handle peeling rose petals tonight, either. I don't know, it seems so trivial with everything else going on. Making potpourri satchels. I mean, really."

I add another text to Dad: Decided to visit Mom.

Then I copy it and send it to Kitten, too. She can't possibly be pissed at me for choosing Loyola over dead roses, but she instantly replies: You're still coming after, though, right?

Just as I'm about to silence my ringer and get out of the car, my phone rings. I take the call. "Hi, Dad."

"Holly. You didn't stay for the meeting."

"No. My mind was racing, and I couldn't concentrate. Dad, was Mom okay before the accident?"

"Okay? She'd been drinking. You know that."

"I mean generally speaking. I mean . . . I keep going over my last conversation with her. She was all over me about calling it quits with Sterling, which I did—"

"Yet you keep seeing him."

I ignore the dig. "And about the concept house. She adamantly did not want me on that crew."

Dad sighs. "This Sterling . . . you became distant when you started dating him. More distant than usual. You're our only child. We want to be part of your relationships. We want to know the man taking you on boat trips. Is that too much to ask?"

"It was *one* boat trip, Dad. And I'm not shutting you out. It wasn't—it's not—a serious relationship."

"Just what every dad wants to hear: his daughter is involved in a casual arrangement."

"Stop, Dad. I'm twenty-five years old. You and Mom were married by the time you were my age. You already had me. Not everyone's as lucky as you . . . to find the one you're supposed to be with so early in life."

Dad takes a breath, like he's going to say something else, but I don't give him the chance.

"Look, I know you have a harder time with this sort of thing considering what happened when I was little. But you have to let go a little."

"I'll let go the day I die."

I roll my eyes.

"And as for the concept house . . . She always wanted better for you than manual labor, and considering what happened today, considering the fall, we have to have the conversation, Holly."

"I'm *fine*."

"You *fell*."

A few moments of silence later, I change the subject: "Was Mom afraid of anything in the days before the accident?"

"What's this about?"

"A detective came to see me today. He has a new theory."

"Yes, I know."

I run down the specifics about the possibility of a second car at the bend, just in case he's heard something else, but Dad's *mm-hmm*-ing in confirmation. He heard the same spiel.

"If that's what happened, if there was another car involved, it was an accident," Dad insists. "It's that cop's job to consider every possibility, and I understand that. But your mom didn't have any enemies."

"Do I? She was driving my car. Could someone have thought it was me—"

"Let's not try to make sense of a half-cooked theory."

Speaking of half-cooked theories . . .

"The scar on my arm . . . do you know anything about it? About other people having the same one?"

"*No*, Holly." He sighs. "When we found you . . ." His voice cracks, but he clears his throat and continues. "Someone called with a sighting. A little girl sitting at the top of the slide in the same park where you were snatched. We didn't want to get our hopes up, but we rushed out there—we and the Hersheys. There you were, wrapped in a police blanket."

I've heard the story a hundred times before.

"You were bleeding. You said your arm hurt. We don't know how it happened."

"Did *she*?"

"You were *gone*, Holly. No one knows better than me how the not knowing tore her up."

"You say that *now*. But at the time, didn't you think she knew something?"

"You were *gone*. I was *distraught. Everyone who'd ever come in contact with you* was a suspect."

"Okay, but . . . even if she didn't know anything then, maybe she learned something later." I proceed to give him a quick overview of Yanneth's cryptic messages. "So I'm thinking about that last conversation I had with her. I'm searching for signs that all wasn't what it seemed."

"You're basing all of this on a conversation you had with someone who claims to be psychic?"

"Dad, you know me. I don't believe in this crap usually, but—"

"These people are good at what they do. She *wants* to keep you thinking about what she said. She wants your money."

"She didn't ask for money."

"It's good you're spending time with your mother. Talk to her, you know. The doctors say she can hear you and understand what you're saying. But do me a favor. Don't talk to her about *this*."

"You think the cop is grasping at straws."

"I do. And that psychic is a crackpot."

"Maybe."

When we hang up, however, I google *psychic finds missing boy Guatemala.*

Sure enough, although Yanneth is not mentioned by name, there is an obscure report about a psychic flying to Guatemala and locating a little boy wearing his underwear inside out.

I think about this for a few minutes and what it might mean for my situation. Perhaps, if Psychic Yanneth can find a little boy halfway to the equator, she might be dead right about what she's said about me, about Mom. In my mother's current state, there's little I can do to confirm or disprove it.

I enter the hospital. "I'm here for Cecily Gebhardt in ICU four sixteen." I offer up my driver's license in exchange for a visitor's badge that allows access to the intensive care unit.

The guard nudges the sign-in registry toward me, and I fill in my name.

A few lines up, I see my mother's room number. She had another visitor today. But before I can decipher the name, written in a rushed cursive, the guard reclaims the clipboard.

I clip the badge to my shirt and walk.

It's been a couple of weeks since I've been here, but the path to Mom's room is worn into my muscle memory: past the cafeteria to the south elevators. Up to the fourth floor.

When the elevator doors open on four, I look up into the gaze of a woman about my height and weight. Her eyes, blue, like mine, arrest me. They're the blue of the eyes I imagined earlier—the little girl in the house under construction.

Her gasp is simultaneous with mine but gradually melts into a smile. "Excuse me."

"Pardon me," I say at the same time. I walk out as she walks in.

There are certain similarities in our appearance. If I think it's a sign, I have to think that Psychic Yanneth is onto something.

I glance at her arm to see if she, too, has an arrow-shaped scar. Of course, she doesn't.

But I wonder if that's what I'll do now. Every time I meet someone, will I search for proof that Psychic Yanneth knows and speaks the truth?

I feel, step-by-step, as if I'm becoming more and more unraveled. I've never felt as off-balance.

I continue down the hallway, toward my mother's room. My fingers twitch. A numbness descends over me, a feeling of desensitization, as if a buffer is shrouding me from the outside world. I usually feel this way just before I snag something that doesn't belong to me.

But there's nothing to take in this antiseptic hallway. I need something concrete to hold on to. I dig in my pocket for the anniversary coin.

I look over my shoulder for a final glimpse of the woman in the elevator.

She's well put together—blonde hair pulled high into a neat ponytail, heeled sandals on her feet, painted fingernails and toenails, and a full-skirt sundress, red with white polka dots. It's as if she's heading to a dinner date after a quick visit to the ICU.

If my mother were here and awake, she'd point out that with a little effort, I could look as couture as this stranger with the familiar eyes. If I stopped subjecting myself to slivers, my hands might be soft and smooth. If I stopped dipping my hair in dye, it might not be so split at the ends. And if I owned a dress suitable for events outside of funerals, I wouldn't perpetually be clad in denim.

The elevator girl narrows her gaze at me. I see only her blue eyes and hear an echo in my head: *Don't try. You'll fall. You'll die.*

I flinch and everything goes from fuzzy to sharp and succinct again.

The elevator doors close. I'm suddenly embarrassed I was staring, but I couldn't help it, given Yanneth's warning.

I continue down the hall to where my mother lies, draped in tubes.

She's gray at the roots, and I can't help but think she'd hate that her hair has grown out. But it's doubtful the doc would let me do a touch-up in this place even if I did ask.

I take the chair, already pulled up to her bedside, and fold my hand around hers, effectively depositing the sobriety medal into her hand. *Appropriate*, I think. I didn't take it to give it to her, but I can't think of a better place to put it. "I know you're not yet to two months," I tell her. "But you're close enough. Two months sober."

I rest my head atop our joined hands.

"I'm proud of you. I wish you were proud of me."

Her heart rate monitor answers me: *Blip blip blip.*

"What aren't you telling me, Mom? Were you having an affair? You have secrets. Tell me."

Blip blip blip.

Cecily

I was lonely, I suppose.

And so was Paul.

But that alone wouldn't have led us to do what we did.

In hindsight, it was reactionary. We did it because of what we learned.

Paul told me what he'd discovered: a black nightie in a box tied with a red satin bow. It was under a pile of sweaters in the closet. Obviously concealed.

A note in the trash, which Paul had fished out of the can on the street:

Can't wait. —T.

The more places we looked, the more evidence we found.

He'd call me and say, "Susan went shopping for shoes."

I'd say, "That's interesting. Trev just left to deal with a burst pipe."

They'd leave and return within minutes of each other. It started with short absences. An hour here, two hours there. But eventually their coincidental, mutual absences grew to days at a time.

"She had a conference last month in Baltimore. Came up out of nowhere."

"Wait. When?"

"The third through the fifth."

"That's when Trev went fishing with his brother."

We traced the affair back years.

Years.

We became allies, constantly comparing notes, often putting our spouses in situations to test them.

But they had incredible control.

A dark night. A bonfire on the bluffs.

Trevor would pull me into his arms.

Susan would snuggle up to Paul.

So at ease, so confident they were pulling it off before our very eyes.

I suppose if you've been getting away with something for years, hiding it becomes a way of life.

But not even a wink? Not even a kiss on the cheek that lingered a bit too long?

"Maybe we're imagining it," I said.

"Do you have to see it to believe it?"

Maybe I did.

So we had them followed.

I wish we hadn't.

Most people think my life changed the day Holly went missing, but the paradigm shift came a month or so earlier, when Paul and I met at a bar. He had a thick envelope tucked under his arm.

"Is that what I think it is?" I asked.

He nodded.

"You've seen the pictures?"

"Yes." He slid the envelope closer to me.

I couldn't touch it, couldn't bear to see my husband with another woman.

"It's what we thought?" I asked.

"I'm sorry, Cecily, but . . ." He sighed. "It's worse than I imagined. Seeing it . . . I threw up, truth be told."

I stared at the envelope and decided I wouldn't put myself through the anguish. I already knew, even before the pictures came, what was happening between my husband and best friend. What good would come of my leafing through the proof?

That's when alcohol began to overtake me . . . a little at a time. Progressively, I became someone I never used to be.

I started plotting: ways out, ways to hurt Trevor, ways to shred Susan.

And Paul was just as willing to exact revenge once my ideas started flowing.

The first vengeful act was strapping them with the kids while we restarted the parts of our lives that parenthood had stymied. For Paul, it was poker tournaments. He'd been on a professional tour or two but retired after Kitten was born. Susan owned an event-planning business, which she ran out of their home. As the party business grew, Paul spent more time with the kids and less time playing cards. When he went back to tournaments, Susan had to juggle her business and the house and kids.

As for me, I went out in the evenings, but not because I had a burning desire to get drunk alone. Rather, I went because I didn't have anything else to do, and I wanted Trevor to wonder: Who is she with? What's she doing? He never asked.

I was a furniture artisan in my life before Holly. I'd worked for a dealer downtown, restoring period pieces. Our clients were celebrities and socialites, and I was *good.* If someone was searching for a particularly difficult piece to procure, or if a finish had been damaged beyond repair, they'd say, "Retain Cecily. She'll take care of it."

But five years out of the business and I may as well have been a rookie. The market had shifted, for one thing. No one wanted old and traditional anymore. Everything was sleek, clean, flat, and new. There was little work to be had, and what was there, no one was awarding to someone who'd been virtually absent for years on end.

I was a failure. No career. Marriage in pieces. Couldn't connect to my kid. And my only friend was fucking my husband.

I spent my evenings at those parties where you paint methodically under the tutelage of an instructor while emptying a bottle of wine. I'd hoped to find friends, but I didn't. I'd hoped Trevor might find me interesting again, but that didn't happen, either.

Wine became brandy became bourbon. They don't care what you drink at those places, as long as you sign their waiver and promise not to hold them responsible if you drive.

I have an entire closetful of those paint-filled canvases and years of resentment stored in my heart.

Raising kids was *hard.* I thought if Trevor could understand the burden of child-rearing, he might be more forgiving when I wasn't always impeccably dressed, when sometimes the demands of caring for Holly superseded even brushing my teeth.

But wouldn't you know it? Trevor was *good* at parenting. He'd take our daughter to job sites and get on the floor and play games with her, and Holly relished the time she spent with her father while I was gone.

Paul and I only gave Trevor and Susan more reason to spend time together.

Often, I'd stumble home to find my husband and my best friend conversing in front of a fire, wineglasses perched in their hands, while Holly and Kitten slept in a blanket tent in the next room.

My efforts to prove a point fell flat and left me feeling only more inadequate. I sank further into isolation. Nothing was working the way it was supposed to. My frustration only led me to drink more.

I suppose Paul's bout with poker had the same effect, only at a greater cost. He couldn't concentrate on cards when he knew his best friend was probably sticking it to his wife, so debts were beginning to pile up.

And one night, when I'd ventured down to the bluffs to cry my eyes out, I heard his sniffle on the other side of the property line.

There we were, two lonely people fighting the same battle. We found each other that night.

He wrapped his arms around me, and I nestled into the safety of his embrace. He kissed the top of my head, and I clung more tightly to him.

And then, he brushed the underside of my chin with a finger.

I looked up at him, and the look in his eyes . . . What was he *thinking*? Something unfamiliar stared down at me, something full of longing, lust. Before I could pull out of his arms, his lips landed on mine.

I wriggled against him—"What are you doing?"—then yanked free of his hold. "You think that'll make things better?"

"Fuck 'em, Ceci. They deserve it."

Maybe they did. But I didn't want it.

It occurred to me then for the first time: what we could do. If only we could get the girls away from them, take from our lying, cheating spouses the brightest spots in their lives . . .

I wish I'd simply filed for divorce.

If I'd taken Holly back home to my parents' place in Michigan, where they'd retired, we wouldn't have been in that park that day.

And I wouldn't have done what I eventually did, and it wouldn't have destroyed my family.

CHAPTER 12

HOLLY

June 6

"Holly."

I feel Dad's hand on my shoulder, smell his classic, musky aftershave, and I sit up.

"Dad." I must have drifted off to sleep, because it feels like a blink later, but it's dark outside Mom's hospital room windows. "What time is it?"

"Nine."

"Oh." I push the chair back and stand up. "Sorry. When did you get here?"

"Just now. Did you talk to her?" There's hope in his eyes. "Squeeze her hand?" He wants to hear that she squeezed mine in return.

"Yeah, I held her hand."

"No change?" he asks.

"No change."

He nods with his lips pressed into a thin line, an expression of pure defeat.

I look out the window at the lights of the city in the distance. "It's *nine*?"

"You've been here a long time. Kitten's looking for you."

"She texted you?"

"And called. But you weren't returning my calls, either, so—"

"Oh." I check my phone. My ringer is still turned off. I have several missed calls from Kitten and Dad and a voice mail from Vellerman. I roll my eyes when I see the name on the screen and roll them again when I see the transcribed message: Hey. Let's meet for a drink sometime.

I hit the "Delete" button on the message.

"I was going to come, anyway," Dad says. "Didn't expect you to still be here. You okay?"

"Exhausted." And I must be, considering I fell asleep. My back is sore where I hit the joists that broke my fall earlier. I could use a soak in my claw-foot tub a hell of a lot more than I can use a night sipping chardonnay with Kitten and her bridesmaids. "But I'm supposed to . . . Kitten has a wine and cheese thing. Making satchels for the wedding, or something."

"Don't stay out too late." Dad kisses my cheek.

For a moment or two, I want nothing more than to curl up in his lap like I did when I was little. That was my safe, happy place—Dad's lap. It was what I thought about every time some shrink asked me to imagine safety.

"And sooner or later," Dad says, "we're going to have to talk about what happened up there today."

"Vellerman's a creep. He asked me out for a drink today."

"Before or after you fell?"

"I lost concentration for a second. Just a second, but I caught myself. I'm *fine*, Dad."

"We're still going to talk about it."

"Does that mean you're ready to keep me on the ground? With this many houses in a development, you could use another foreman."

"Are you sure this is what you want to do with your life? Your mother—"

"Yeah, yeah. She wanted more for me."

"She did. So did I. You did, too, once upon a time. You wanted to pursue social work. You'll be good at it. You can help kids like Dr. Parrish helped you."

I don't put a voice to my thoughts: Dr. Parrish helped me to continue to pretend to be okay. It's not her fault I can't remember, and I do believe in the practice, despite the fact that I failed to recall anything specific in session. But I can't possibly expect to help other people when I feel as if I'm floating in a sea of questions. It's like they say: in times of trauma, you have to save yourself before you can tend to others.

"We're going to talk about it, okay?" Dad says. "But we're also going to talk about your degree. Why you've yet to apply to grad school so you can sit for the LCSW exam."

I know what this means. He's not going to promote me. He's going to try to talk me into pursuing a career in my chosen major. I head toward the door. "Dad . . . that detective . . . Do you think he might be onto something? About Mom?"

"He's blaming the victim if he thinks she was having an affair."

"If she was or if she wasn't . . . I mean . . . Do you think he's right about her being afraid of something? Why else would she have taken your GLOCK when she left that day?"

"We'll know soon enough. When she wakes up. She'll tell us all about it when she wakes up." He resumes the seat I just abandoned and takes her hand.

My breath catches in my throat when I remember I put the sobriety coin in her hand. If the person I took it from mentioned at the Al-Anon meeting that it was missing, Dad is going to know I stole it.

I glance at Mom's hand, but the medal is gone. It must have fallen into the folds of her bedding.

I allow myself to exhale. "Did we ever look for the tooth I lost? You know, when I was . . . gone?"

Dad sighs again. "If I knew what happened to you when you were gone, we wouldn't be having this conversation."

I know this is true. And it's where Dad wants the conversation to end. He's tired, too. But I have more questions.

"Dad?"

He looks at me over his shoulder.

"Did Mom ever have a pewter box?"

"I don't think so." He thinks for a minute. "I don't know, but it's possible. So many things came through our house. Little finds she'd clean up and resell . . ."

"Maybe it had a curl of my hair inside it. And a key."

Dad frowns and allows Mom's hand to slip out of his.

"From my first haircut, maybe."

"You remember seeing these things?"

"I'm not sure if I remember it, or even if I saw it in a movie, or something, but it came to me . . . sort of like déjà vu."

Dad's fingers are tented under his chin, and he's quiet for some time.

"Dad?"

He glances at me for a split second. "We got a package in the mail when you were gone," he says. "A key to our house was inside, along with a curl of hair. There was some question about the hair as evidence, but the key was irrefutable. Mom had pinned it in your pocket the day you were taken. We knew it came from whoever had you."

A tingly sensation dances on the back of my neck. So it's real. It's a real memory.

I chew on thoughts of the box, try to remember if there was anything else in the periphery that might help determine where I was, who I was with when I dared to touch it. Because I'm pretty convinced: whoever took me had a pewter box not unlike the one I swiped from Kitten's bridesmaid's place.

A few beats pass. "Holly, are you still going to therapy?"

In my mind, I feel the cold, hard metal box in my hands, followed quickly by the sting of a whack on my backside.

"I think you should consider talking to your therapist—"

"Yeah, I have to go back." Maybe I'm placating my father by saying so, or maybe I really will go back. But I can't think about it now. Not when I've remembered something, while Detective Guidry is in the throes of another investigation.

And Dad sees right through my white lie.

"Alan Kohlbrook is in jail," my father says. "The case was open-and-shut. He wanted to be locked up. He knew he would hurt someone else if he wasn't sent away."

"But there have been other girls—"

"There are other Alan Kohlbrooks in this world, too. I don't buy that they got the wrong guy. The case was airtight. It's rather convenient, don't you think, that the police want to throw all of these unsolved cases together and call them the work of the same guy?"

"On the contrary, I think the easier thing to do would be to keep my case buttoned up."

My phone buzzes with another text. I sigh when I see the name on my screen. "Kitten."

Where the fuck are you?

"Do me a favor," Dad says. "Go to the city. Meet Kitten. She needs you."

"But if there's a chance—"

"Let. This. Go." Dad stands and looms over me. His size belies his demeanor—the gentle giant. He stands with his feet a bit wider than shoulder width apart and crosses his arms over his chest. He appears shorter than his six-foot-five frame this way. "Haven't you been through enough? If you keep at this, he wins. Do you understand that? Kohlbrook took three months of your life, and the rest of your mother's. Don't give him any more."

I open my mouth to reply, but nothing of brilliance filters out.

"You survived," Dad says. "You owe it to yourself, to others who weren't as fortunate, not to dwell on the past. Please. Concentrate on what's ahead of you, not what's behind you. What's in the past will always be there. But if you're not careful . . ." He looks down at my mother. "She never got past it, you know. That day changed her forever. You don't think that now that she's lying here, she'd rather have those years back? Those years she spent frantic and afraid even after you came back to us? He *wins* if we stay back in that time, in that place."

For some time (it feels like ten minutes but likely isn't more than thirty seconds), neither of us speaks. I understand Dad's point. I get that I'm his only child and that he almost lost me. I get that he wants me to live in the here and now instead of trudging through the ugly truth of what happened in the past.

But if he doesn't believe that this isn't solely about me, that maybe it's about other little girls, too, we're going to be in a deadlock.

I see, by the set of his jaw and his burrowing stare, that he's determined to win this one.

"You'll go to Kitten's," he says, as if I'm still fourteen, as if he still holds sway over my evening activities.

I don't know if I can do what he asks.

He must sense it, because he tacks on: "Plenty of time to pick through these theories tomorrow if you insist."

"Valid."

"We have a deal?"

"Deal."

He comes in for a hug. There's nothing like one of Dad's hugs to make me feel warm and protected. He kisses me on the top of my head, like usual.

I walk out of the ICU, take the elevator down, and check out with security, exchanging my visitor's badge for my driver's license.

Once in the cab of the truck, I place a call to Detective Guidry, and again I'm sent to voice mail.

"Detective, Holly Gebhardt here." I pause. "I'm not sure it matters, but I'm remembering a silver metal box. Maybe there was a lock of hair inside, and a key. Like I said, it could be nothing, especially because I can't quite remember where I was when I saw it, but I was little. It might have been while I was gone. In case it helps, I thought I should tell you, but . . . I guess we'll talk about it tomorrow."

CHAPTER 13

HOLLY

June 6

"Well, well. Look who finally graced us with her presence." Although Eliot flashes a grin when he opens the door, I catch the underlying judgment in his words.

He's wearing a stiffly starched french cuff button-down, tucked into black front-pleat trousers that break across polished black leather loafers. His hair, graying at the temples and parted on the side, is slicked back with some sort of gel that I'm certain would crunch if I patted him on the head—which I won't. And perhaps most cliché of all . . . his paisley gray-and-black tie is still knotted under his collar.

You're at home. Loosen up.

As if he can hear my thoughts, he practically looks down his nose at me. His round-framed, amber-lensed glasses slip, and with his index finger and thumb, he rights them. I wonder again how old he actually is. Kitten wouldn't say when I asked, so I've always assumed he's already seen forty come and go. Fine lines around his eyes deepen when he smiles. "Good to see you."

"You too." It's safe to say I think he's an all right guy. He'll give Kitten a good, comfortable life, and he seems to spoil her rotten. That's what's important.

So Eliot and I tolerate each other. But would we choose to hang out if Kitten weren't part of the equation? Ummm . . . no.

It wasn't supposed to be like this. When Kitten and I were kids and talked about getting married, it was always with the parameters that we'd each marry a guy the other loved like a brother—hence, my crush on Matt—and we'd live at the end of a cul-de-sac in a quaint little town.

The city was never part of the fantasy.

Neither was a guy like Eliot. He's *established* in some boring corporate career and a touch snooty about it, as if he's the only one in the world to have a window in his office. I don't know how to talk to someone so very obviously above our station and hell-bent on proving he's better (to and for Kitten) than I am.

But here we are.

"No boyfriend tonight?"

"Trying to quit bad habits," I say. "Where is she?"

"She'll be happy you're *finally* here."

I hand over a bottle of wine, which I carefully selected from the liquor store because it wasn't too cheap and had a fun label—half a fish skeleton melded with a vine of roses. "I told her I'd be late. You can't just text me in the morning and expect me to rearrange my day—"

"The wine and roses were impromptu," Eliot says. "But the shoot tonight . . . this was on the original itinerary."

"Shoot?"

"The photo shoot." He thumbs over his shoulder. "It's important to her. Photographers are here to commemorate our engagement with our closest friends and family. We're waiting on you to begin, and—"

"Thank God you're here." Kitten bursts into the foyer and, linking an arm with mine, pulls me into the apartment. "You missed rose peeling, and you missed gourmet cheese boards, but there's plenty to drink."

Four bridesmaids, all wearing tiny black dresses and strappy sandals and accessorized to the hilt (apparently, I didn't get the dress code memo) clink glasses over another something I've missed.

But they're not the only ones here. The place is swarming with the usual suspects, a repeat of last night's guest list, all clad in black and white. Five groomsmen in crisp, white button-downs and pleated black pants mill about the space with pretty little lady-ornaments hanging on their arms.

Susan Hershey, Kitten's mother, catches sight of me. She smiles and begins to cross the crowded room toward us. She's warm and inviting and always looks like she just stepped off the pages of a fashion magazine. But Kitten and I know that she's never been haute couture, as much as she's a thrift store upcycling genius.

What my mother can do with furniture, Susan does with clothing and accessories. They're both vintage specialists. It's probably why they've been friends for as long as I can remember.

When she reaches us, she leans in and pecks each of us on the cheek.

"Hi, Mom," I say.

"How's Cecily?" Susan's brows slant in concern.

"No change."

"Oh, honey. You'll let me know if you need anything?"

"Time for *happiness*." Kitten yanks on my arm and pulls me away. "So much to do."

"Like what?" I ask.

"God, you don't read *any* of the e-vites I send, do you? What are you wearing?"

"I call this jeans and a tank top."

"I see that. The preferred attire was black and white."

"What do you know?" I tug on the strap of my tank top. "Black."

She ignores my joke. "You didn't see the request in the itinerary to come dressed to the nines?"

No, I didn't, but that explains Eliot's looking down his nose at me.

She leads me through the crowded space.

I overhear from the cluster of bridesmaids as we pass: "Well, here's to hoping it shows up." They raise their glasses again. "Strange that it would just disappear like that. I mean, who'd take a box with nothing in it?"

"You know what's creepy?" another says. "Whoever took it is probably *in this room* right now."

I quicken my pace, and not only because Kitten is yanking on my arm as she leads me toward her bedroom. It feels like they're all looking at me, as if they know I'm the guilty party. One woman raises her brow at me. I wonder if she saw me take the box, if the lot of them remember something I don't, or if she's simply standing in judgment of a maid of honor in jeans when everyone else is in garb fit for the Oscars.

Kitten closes the door behind us. "What's with you lately?"

"I should probably just go. I'm not prepared for a *photo shoot*." I'm positively starving, and the last thing I need is alcohol on an empty stomach. I have to be more composed tomorrow when I go to the Lake County PD to continue my conversation with Detective Guidry, and if I start drinking tonight . . .

"You'll borrow something of mine." Kitten shoves her glass of wine at me and disappears into a walk-in closet she and Eliot share.

This room is dim, museum-like. Proof that Kitten's dwelling here didn't happen gradually but with a burst; it still looks like a bachelor lives here alone. Furniture of black leather and brass and glass. No sign of the girl who used to wear gingham bikini tops and cutoff denim. Two poster-size images of my best friend in black and white grace the walls—one on each side of an enormous art deco mirror.

The prints are Eliot's work. He shot the images at Navy Pier early in their relationship, the day he put a ring on her finger, when one could still see a glimpse of the girl she used to be. But it was Susan who decided the prints should be enormous and framed—*the perfect engagement gift for a man who has it all now that he has my baby*, she'd said.

I pause for a second to study the pictures, sip the wine, process how this whole thing happened.

At the bar that night, Eliot talked to me first:

I love a girl who drinks whiskey.

I rolled my eyes—*No girl loves a guy who says shit like that*—and turned my back on him. I don't know why, exactly. Maybe it was because even with a shot of bourbon in his hand, he seemed rather stiff and uppity, as if he were lowering himself to speak to me. It's been the same since: the guy never seems to relax. He's always on. Always trying to prove he's the most successful guy in the room.

But I wonder . . .

If I'd accepted the drink, would Kitten have turned her sights on someone else that night? Would Eliot be a guy we simply laughed about months later—the stick-up-his-ass know-it-all who lingered too long next to us at the bar one night?

Or maybe everything about this life really is predestined. Maybe, regardless of anything that's happened, Kitten was supposed to wind up here, rubbing elbows with the elitist crowd gathered.

But the night we met Eliot, Kitten's life changed, and she's changing along with it, leaving me behind as if I'm still wiggling a tooth in the dark by myself.

I'm glad she isn't stuck here with me, don't get me wrong. But I miss being able to hang out with her in T-shirts and flip-flops, drinking beer from the bottle on the bluffs.

"Try this on." Kitten tosses a little black dress at me. "Once we're done with pictures, we're all heading out to the Midway, or one of those chic basement jazz clubs, or something. So—"

"I didn't know we were doing all this tonight. I've had an insane day—"

"No." She plants her hands on her hips. "No, no, no. You absolutely *cannot* bail on me now."

"You said peeling roses. You said come by for a while."

"You *owe* me after last night. You were hardly even there."

"Kitten, listen." I step out of my jeans and into the dress. Thank God for Lycra, or I probably wouldn't fit into it. I reach for the zipper, but it's sticking. "I don't feel like clubbing. I had a meeting today with Detec—"

"Everyone has lives outside of my wedding," she says. "They make time to *include* wedding festivities in those lives. Never would I have assumed my best friend, my *maid of honor*, would be snubbing me this way."

"It's not that I'm not happy for you and Eliot or that I don't want to be part of this entourage—"

"You know what?" She stands, comes up behind me, and zips the dress. "I don't want to hear it. This means a lot to me. And if I mean anything to you, you'll come tonight. Matt's meeting us at the club. Straight from O'Hare."

That's a lie, but I clam up.

"If he can come directly from the base," Kitten says, "surely you can find the energy."

I bite my tongue but can't stop the smile I feel brewing. Matt managed to pull one over on his sister and mother if they think he's just now landing. Quite a feat, seeing as Matt's been one wildflower field away from Susan for at least a day now.

"If you had known an hour ago he was coming," Kitten asks, "would you have gotten here sooner?"

"Shut up. I was twelve. It was a crazy crush. Get over it, already."

"Just saying."

"I'm here, aren't I? I'm stuffing my ass into this scrap of fabric—"

"Help yourself to my makeup . . . you *do* remember what makeup is, don't you? And my hair stuff, whatever you need. But *hurry*." She takes a few steps toward the door but peeks back around the corner and blows me a kiss. "Love you."

—

The clan of bridesmaids keeps whispering behind their hands cupped over one another's ears. Glancing at me. Raising brows. Smirking.

Maybe it's my imagination.

Maybe it's the second whiskey I'm presently sipping on.

Maybe it's the tenor sax creeping into my bones, making me feel all melancholy.

But I feel like the target surrounded by a group of archers with arrows set and aimed. I suppose I deserve it. I did take the box from the mantel, and maybe Kitten ratted me out. *You have to understand*, I imagine she might have said. *She was abducted when we were kids. She's been swiping stuff ever since she was recovered.*

Next, I imagine they might google me, read my ordeal, discover Kitten's role in it, and laud her for sticking by me all these years.

I'm going to return the box, but until I do, I suppose I deserve the raised brows and judgment.

I find myself inching farther into the fringes and raising my glass less frequently. I can't help it. I'm so preoccupied with everything but this ridiculous excuse to get drunk and fawn over the happy couple for the second time this weekend that I'm almost irritated with myself for agreeing to come to this jazz club. I force a smile when someone makes a joke I don't hear—and I hope the joke wasn't at my expense.

Eventually, I'm halfway to the ladies' room, anyway, so I decide to take a breather.

The floor in the hallway is a black-and-white mosaic, which practically dances with the beat in this place, and it's dizzying to the point that the colors overlap and buzz and shift.

"Whoa. Holly."

Suddenly, there's an arm around my waist.

"You doing okay, kid?"

I look up. "Matt."

Now that I have my footing again, I remember that I woke up wearing his shirt. I remember that I don't really know what happened between us last night.

I step back and try to read his expression.

Is he looking at me like a guy who *knows* me might look at me?

"What a friggin' riot," he says. "My sister actually got you in heels two days in a row."

"I would've been more comfortable if I had tagged along in my torn-up jeans," I say. "I stick out more in this black-and-white getup than I would've severely underdressed."

"I got a pass on the preferred attire, seeing as I just now landed." He winks, as if I need a reminder of the lies he's trying to sell. I wonder how many other times he's tried to pull one over on us. All the times he had to leave to "catch his lift back" just when it was time to do the dishes . . . all the times he showed up just in time for the celebration without having to help prep for it.

If Kitten were paying any kind of attention, though, she'd realize he's come straight off the shores of Lake Michigan, where I assume he spent some time kayaking. He's tan, sporting a five-o'clock shadow, and smells faintly of coconut-scented suntan oil, which he tried to scrub off with a crisp soap.

He glances back at the table, where Kitten and her friends are congregating. He takes the drink from my hand and sips from it. "What's the world coming to when you have to treat your circle of friends like a professionally designed living room?"

I chuckle. But it's more of a nervous reaction because, looking at him, I can't tell if he's seen me naked.

He frowns into my glass. "This is terrible. What is this?"

"House whiskey."

"God, how many of these have you had?"

"It's my second."

"That's two too many if you ask me."

"Matt?"

"Hmm?"

"I don't know what to say about last night."

"What about it?"

"What happened?"

He looks back into my glass. "What do you think happened?"

"I didn't think I was that drunk." I lick my lips, which suddenly feel dry.

The sax fills the space between us.

He throws back a healthy sip of my drink and winces as it goes down. "That's the only way to drink that shit. So fast you can't taste it."

I laugh a little, but I don't know what else to say.

Finally, he breaks the awkward silence: "You don't remember anything about last night?"

"It's just that . . ." I glance again at Kitten's friends, raising glasses and toasting to a world I don't belong in. "I didn't think I was that drunk." Did I say that already?

"But . . ." A slow smile spreads onto his face. "You don't remember?"

The heat of embarrassment crawls into my cheeks.

He covers his hand with his heart. "It was an absolute pleasure, m'lady—"

"Oh no." I hide my face in my hands. "Don't say it."

"—to watch you pass out."

"Oh." I relax. "Thank God."

"Don't sound so relieved."

"It's not *that* . . . it's just that it's . . . *you*."

"Call me old-fashioned, but I prefer taking women to bed who are awake and active participants. The extent of it was me pulling my shirt over your head after you got naked."

"I . . . *what*? God, that had to be pretty."

"Well, if I'm being honest . . ." He shrugs.

"No, I didn't mean . . . oh, you know what I mean."

"You kept saying you were uncomfortable, and pulled off that *kickin'* dress—"

"It's my mother's."

"Looks good on *you*." He indicates with his palm up toward my chest but doesn't break eye contact. "Like this one."

"*This one* is your sister's."

"Okay." He shrugs again. "It looks good."

"So nothing happened," I confirm.

"Stop, already."

"Kitten would be absolutely *insane* if something did."

"She's sort of lost her mind on all this wedding crap, anyway, hasn't she?"

"I plead the Fifth."

"So I don't think Kitten saw me walk in." He sways a little on his feet and smiles. "You want to get me out of here?" He raises a brow. "So nothing can happen between us again?"

"Shut up. We should stay for at least one more round."

"Oh, I really can't bear it." He puts an arm around me, and we turn back toward the party. "But if you insist . . ."

It's then I see him through the crowd, a face that doesn't belong in this scene: Vellerman. "On second thought . . ." I pull my phone out and tap on the Uber app. I spend enough time on the job with my foreman. I have no desire to hang in such proximity to him tonight.

What's he doing here?

I suppose he has every right, but it's a big city. And maybe I'm wrong, but I assume jazz isn't usually his bag. I'm guessing he's more Metallica or even Toby Keith.

Oh no. Eye contact.

He narrows his gaze and begins moving toward me.

"Let's go."

Matt puts a little more weight on me. "You all right?"

"I should be asking you," I say when I realize he's using me to stay upright.

"Strong whiskey."

I laugh. "Yeah. You want a Red Bull?"

Cecily

About a month before the abduction, as I was about to leave for my painting class, I lingered at the kitchen doorway while Trevor and Susan spun through the space, together creating a fabulous dish.

"Holly? Give Mommy a hug?"

"Busy." She and Kitten sat at a child-size table and created shapes with the cucumber and carrot slices Susan had served them.

Oblivious to Holly's rejecting me, Susan measured a tablespoon of olive oil. "God, I'd love a kitchen like this!"

"Say the word, and I'll build one for you," Trevor replied. "Now, what do I do with the garlic?"

"Holly?" I tried again.

"I'm *busy*," she sassed.

This time, Susan took notice. "Holly!"

Trevor looked up then, went to Holly, and scooped her up. "Give your mommy a hug."

Reluctantly, my daughter patted my shoulder when I embraced her.

The moment her feet hit the floor, she scampered over to Susan, clung to her leg, and said, "Chocolate milk, please."

"One second, honey."

Tears threatened, but I turned away.

"Cecily, wait." Trevor followed me into the foyer. "You'll call if you need a ride?"

I eyed my daughter in the distance and watched as she thanked her pseudomother for the milk. All smiles. Polite. "I'll take a cab. I wouldn't want to interrupt your night."

"Ceci—"

"I'm fine."

I rushed out the door and stopped at the liquor store for a bottle on the way.

I sipped a bourbon neat and dragged green paint over canvas. I looked around at all the others in the painting class, laughing, sharing the experience, toasting with one another.

People usually came to these classes in groups. People with *friends* did, anyway.

If things were different, Susan and I might have planned a girls' night out. Maybe we would've sat side by side, sharing a bottle of pinot. She would have laughed at her attempt to make a tree look like a tree, and . . .

I couldn't stop the tears, which rolled silently down my cheeks.

"Are you all right, ma'am?"

I looked up at the man who'd asked. *Ma'am.* That's who and what I was to everyone in the room, everyone with whom I'd spent the past four or five Friday evenings. A nondescript, nameless *ma'am.*

I drank faster and cried harder, conscious of the fact that I was beginning to draw stares. People raised their eyebrows, whispered about me.

Around four in the morning, I awoke in a hotel room across the street, alone. I couldn't find my keys. I couldn't remember how I'd ended up there. Had I come alone? Had I come straight from the painting class?

I called Paul, who came to my rescue.

"What happened?" he asked.

My head was on fire. "I don't know."

But I was sure that when I hadn't shown up as expected around ten the night before, I'd given Trevor an excuse to bitch about me. Susan would have listened willingly. She would've put an arm around him. *Poor thing,* she might have said. *You work so hard, and all she does is drink.*

Paul elbowed me and laughed. "Did you wake up alone?"

"Of course."

Paul grinned. "Is there any better revenge? Maybe you should let him know what it feels like." He put his hand on my knee.

With the bitter taste of my rejecting Paul not long ago still on the tip of my tongue, I stared at his fingers, naturally molding around my flesh. And the heat of his touch . . . it felt *good.*

As if he knew what I was thinking, he said, "It's going to happen eventually. You need to feel like a woman. You need to feel needed, don't you? Wanted? The way your husband wants my wife? Wouldn't it be better with someone you know? Someone who loves you? Someone like me?"

Years of respect and partnership and blurred lines between the four of us rushed at me at the speed of light. All the late nights playing board games and sipping wine, all the neighborhood dinners. Smiles across the table.

And recently, catching tender moments between our spouses while we grieved alone and waited for the opportune time to tell them we knew about their affair. "Turn around." I pulled the room key card out of my purse.

And we went at each other with reckless abandon.

The sex was incredible. All the anger, resentment, and hard feelings bottled up with fizzing emotions, and when we shook it, it exploded.

When it was over, life was a fallout shelter.

Quickly, I realized what a mistake it had been. Maybe Paul didn't love Susan anymore, but my husband was the love of my life. I still loved Trevor, despite everything he'd done.

That's how it happened between Paul and me: we wanted them to know what it felt like to hurt, but in the end, we hurt only ourselves.

We weren't careful.

In fact, it's accurate to say we were downright stupid.

I cried all the way home.

Paul was distant after that, almost as if he blamed me. I would've blamed me, too. Not one but two women had chosen my husband over him.

I was even more alone after that because Paul was lost to me, too. I couldn't look at him without reflecting on what we'd done; I couldn't pretend nothing had happened between my best friend's husband and me any more than I could pretend she and Trev hadn't been shagging for years.

The week after, our families congregated on the bluffs for a bonfire, and I decided I no longer fit into the dynamic.

I feigned a headache and went home early.

I opened a bottle of bourbon.

I drank.

Every sip shut out more of the world.

The periphery of the room started to go fuzzy. The room started to spin. My gut churned. Every part of my body warned me to stop: the ache in my head, the loss of control in my fingers, my inability to speak.

If I thought I could still stand, I'd throw back another shot.

I was so tired of trying to be a good mother and wife. What was the use? No matter what I did, I couldn't hold a candle to Susan. I suppose I figured I ought to jump right into failing for a change. Or maybe I thought Trevor might take notice and wonder what had changed between us to send me spiraling into self-destruction.

I wish I'd known what the long-term effects would be, particularly in regard to my relationship with Holly. If I hadn't been constantly obliterated the whole month before she was taken, maybe I wouldn't fear that she subconsciously blamed me for the whole ordeal.

If I had been sitting on that pavement next to her, focused on my child, no one could have snatched her to begin with.

But the effects reached far into the future. Even now, I know my behavior embarrasses her. Even now, I fear she wishes I were more like Susan.

A colossal disruption was about to shake both of our families to the core.

The nail was set.

All it took now was the tap of a hammer, and soon, all our lives would be upended.

They asked me who swung the hammer.

I told them I didn't know.

But I never told them what I suspected: that Paul wanted revenge, that he was scorned and hollowed out and he wanted me to hurt. More than that, he wanted Trevor to suffer.

CHAPTER 14

HOLLY

June 7

You can't cross.

I see only the outline of her body at the far end of the space, across the open floor joists.

There's no floor.

I can do it, I say.

Don't try it. You'll fall. You'll die.

I sit up, surrounded by darkness.

The moment feels real, somewhere between a dream and a fuzzy reality. Real enough that it's a distinct possibility the blonde-haired, blue-eyed girl is in this room with me.

I look for her, stare into the miles of pitch-black nothingness before me, reach out to touch something tangible, anything to confirm I'm not floating in make believe but grounded in reality.

But there's nothing there. Just space. And darkness. And more space.

I reach down, down, down, trying to touch something concrete, but it's like trying to touch the bed of a deep, murky lake. I can't touch the bottom.

Eventually, it's as if the darkness is swallowing me whole, filling my lungs. I can't breathe, and everything is black, and the ringing in my ears just won't stop.

Blip, blip, blip. I hear, in the distance, my mother's heart rate. I try to get mine to sync up. But I'm not sure my heart is beating at all.

Someone pounds on my chest, trying to get it all going again.

Compression, compression.

C'mon, breathe!

Dog hurtles onto my chest, effectively zapping me out of a deep sleep. "Jesus! Dog!"

Before I even open my eyes, I fold an arm around her warm, fluffy body. "Shh. Calm down." I try to concentrate on the voice I heard in a dream, try to grasp it.

You can't cross.

The voice of a little girl.

Think.

Who is she?

Is she real? A memory?

A figment of my imagination?

Or . . . is she a premonition? A vision to deliver the echoes of the past?

I focus. Think about the girl with blue eyes.

Just as I'm about to grasp the image of her again, Dog gets restless and whacks her tail against my face. "All right, all right. Give me a second."

I pull myself out of bed. My new roommate circles me as I brush through my hair, then brush my teeth.

A text comes in from my foreman: You okay? And another: Grab a drink later?

I delete the texts. He's getting too creepy.

Dog runs laps around the apartment as I head toward the closet near the front door to grab a leash.

I wish I had half her energy this morning.

If I'm being honest, I wish her owner were the one dealing with it.

I dial Sterling, who actually answers this time.

"Well, hello." So casual, as if he's surprised to hear from me.

"You have to come get the dog. I have a long day tomorrow, and I can't leave her here."

"Might be tough by tomorrow. I'm in South Bend."

"You're visiting your brother in Indiana." I roll my eyes. "I've been a good sport about taking the dog while you're working, but is there a reason you couldn't bring the dog with you this time?"

"If you want to get technical, I'm stopping by on my way from an assignment. I'm working with a team of investigative journalists on an interesting story, and if we're the first to break it . . ."

"What's it about?"

He ignores my question and continues as if I haven't inquired. "Besides, it's my niece's birthday. And come to think of it . . . I'm texting you some options. If you were a seven-year-old girl, tell me which of these presents you would want."

"Sterling."

"Look, I know you're busy. I appreciate you taking the dog. She's stir-crazy in the car."

"She's stir-crazy *in my apartment*."

"You know I only really got her because I thought we were going somewhere. I never would have—"

I stab at the "End" button and swear under my breath when the text message of birthday gift options comes through a second later. "He is *not* going to put the decision to get a dog on me!" I like dogs. I'd like to have one *someday*. Maybe I even told him as much. But I didn't decide he should adopt Dog.

I think Mom would agree.

"But you're cute." I crouch and rub the dog's ears. "Aren't you? You're adorable."

Knock, knock. "Holly?"

I startle but quickly relax when I hear: "It's Matt."

I open the door.

He's holding a coffee in each hand. "If your head's aching like mine, I thought you might need a boost." His gaze then trails downward. "Oh. You're going for a walk."

"Just a quick loop around the property."

"I'll join you." He exchanges a coffee for the leash, which he clips to the dog's collar. He fingers the tag. "Wait a minute. Is her name—"

"Don't say it." I follow him down the steps.

"Since when does a die-hard Sox fan name her dog—"

"*Don't* say it."

He chuckles and sips his coffee. "You're the one who named her."

"Actually, she isn't mine. She's Sterling's."

"Gotta love a girl who refers to the man she's sleeping with by his last name."

"Past tense. *Was* sleeping with. We broke up."

"That's not what Kitten says."

"Well, it sort of depends on the day, I guess."

We walk toward the path that leads to a creek at the rear of my parents' acreage, sipping, until he breaks the monotony: "It's beautiful, isn't it?"

I glance around at the prairie grass and trees I see every day and raise a brow. "Uh-huh."

"Seriously. You don't know how beautiful Lake Bluff can be until you're gone for months on end."

I know what he means, but I can't help drawing a parallel between his absence in the call of duty and mine, as a survivor of Alan Kohlbrook.

"There's something about coming home when you're not sure you ever will."

After a few silent moments, I pipe up: "We don't have to talk about it, but . . . do you still feel the effects of being there?"

He shrugs, as if donning a uniform and marching into heavy artillery fire is no big deal. "Just doing my job. And I survived."

"So did I. But at what cost? Sometimes I think it's a blessing I don't remember. But you do. It must haunt you some nights."

"I'm sure it haunts you, too, when you think about it. And like you said, you survived. You're still here to tell another tale."

"Hardly. What happened to me is still a blank space in my mind. *You* remember."

"Residually, I think you do, too."

I think about it for the space of a few steps. "I remember being really happy to be with my dad." He was warm; I was cold. He smelled like a crisp, snowy day. "But I don't know what it was like to be gone. I don't remember missing anyone, although I'm sure I must have, and I don't remember being afraid, even when they told me what happened. But Kitten says she was scared the whole time I was gone."

"Even after," he confirms.

"She says that's why it was harder for her."

Matt sighs and gives his head a shake. "Leave it to my sister—"

"I'm sure it was."

He rolls his eyes and takes a sip of his coffee. "You're always giving Kitten a break. She can be a spoiled brat sometimes. It's okay to admit it."

"Listen," I explain. "I equate it to dealing with my mother when she's wasted and says or does something stupid, usually at my father's expense. She's over it instantly the next morning because she doesn't remember what happened, but for the rest of us, the pain lingers. Because we were there. We were present. It's the same thing with me and the time I was gone. I don't remember, so I don't feel the effects. See?"

He shrugs. "I suppose."

"And then . . . the way your dad left so quickly after I was taken—"

"He came back. They tried to make it work."

"Do you think the added stress of my abduction made it impossible for them to work things out?"

"It's not your fault my parents split." Laughter laces his words. "Did Kitten blame *that* on you, too? It was about money. My father was a compulsive gambler. He lost tens of thousands of dollars in the matter of a month."

"Oh."

"You didn't know that? Kitten never told you?"

"No." I contemplate this for a moment, consider whether my best friend would want me to feel guilty for the abrupt ending of her parents' marriage. "But it doesn't matter," I decide. "Think about it from Kitten's point of view. All at once, her world changed. You were older, but Kitten . . . she was only *five*."

"She went through her own ordeal," Matt agrees. "I'm not saying she didn't."

"So the day I was taken, life changed for the rest of you, but nothing changed for me until they told me what happened to me. And what changed wasn't that I was scared. I thought everyone had lost their minds, that they were playing a weird joke on me, or maybe even that I was suddenly invisible. They sat me down and said, *Holly, you were kidnapped.* I remember being sort of . . . *No I wasn't. I'm right here.*"

"They didn't want to scare you."

"Fine, when I was five. But even now . . . no one ever talks about it around me," I say. "The thing is that they still talk about it. It's like this big thing they just can't get over. And it's all about me, but they don't want me involved."

He doesn't say anything for a stretch of time. "It was touch-and-go for a while, Holly. You have to understand that. At first, we were optimistic. The cops were saying we'd have you back by sundown. And then, hours became days, days became weeks and turned into months. We stopped expecting to find you alive and started looking for your body."

My fingertips tingle.

It feels surreal to hear someone speak of it now.

"My dad and I spent a lot of time with your dad when you were gone," Matt says. "We tried to occupy him, you know. We went hunting, fishing, to the shooting range . . . And we dressed this enormous deer at the camp, and . . ." He sips his coffee. "I don't know what we were thinking. We weren't thinking at all, probably, that maybe a slaughter table and spilled blood wasn't what your dad needed at that time, but we were just trying to keep him busy. And on the way back from the hunt, we drove past this wide-open field. There was a ring of turkey vultures circling overhead, and to most people, that wouldn't mean anything. But Trev knew those birds wouldn't be there without catching the scent of decaying meat. He thought it might be you in that field."

The thought chills me to the bone. I imagine what Dad might have said, how he might have crumbled at the sight of the circling carrion feeders.

Matt was almost seventeen at the time. Although Kitten and I certainly considered him more adult than peer back then, he was a *kid*. Too young to be dealing with that sort of thing.

"Dad and I didn't want him wondering," Matt says. "We decided the best thing to do would be to have a look. And truth? That field stank. Even I knew there was something dead nearby. I kept thinking . . . *God, how are we going to tell Trevor if she happens to be lying here dead?* And up until we came across that dead opossum, I really thought you would be."

I don't want it to sink in, the horror Dad must have been feeling while they searched the field and came up under the circle of birds.

"Can I ask you something?" I don't wait for his reply before continuing: "Kitten saw it happen."

He nods, a curt bob of his head.

"Kitten's testimony helped put Alan Kohlbrook behind bars—or so I'm told. She ID'd the guy—someone your parents knew from church? Someone my father hired on your dad's recommendation?"

"That's right."

Kitten and I don't talk about it now. I'm not sure we ever did. But I know because I've been told: "He had her by the arm. He tried to grab her, too."

"Mm-hmm."

"So I'm wondering . . . Do you think they have the right guy?"

He thinks for a few seconds. "Why do you ask?"

"Because there are other girls." I give him a quick synopsis of my conversation with Guidry. "And it just doesn't jibe. The original team of detectives assumed it was someone we knew, and then, once I'm back, Kitten remembers something? She says it was Kohlbrook? And everyone agrees?"

"Yeah, that's about the size of it."

"And furthermore, the guy first wanted her but took me because I didn't fight as hard? Tell me this makes sense to you, because it doesn't add up if you ask me. If they profiled someone focused on *me*, someone we knew, that would mean that I was the specific target, but that's not the way Kitten says it happened."

He sighs. "The thing about my sister . . ." He studies me for a second—a long, hard look that lingers just long enough for me to wonder if I have something stuck in my teeth.

"What?"

"Have you ever noticed that she craves drama?"

Oh. *That.*

"Consider that maybe the guy didn't try to grab her, too. Consider she, as she often does, inserted herself into the action. When you grow up thinking the world revolves around you, and something major happens that doesn't have anything to do with you . . . Maybe she didn't see it. Maybe he *didn't* try to grab her. Maybe she looked away for a second, and then you were gone when she turned back. It doesn't mean we don't have the right guy."

"The cops believed her version of events when she said she saw it."

"They had DNA evidence to back it up. And one of his hairs was on your nightgown the day we got you back. *Of course* they believed her."

Things are silent, except for the sounds of the rushing creek below. When I was a little girl, I used to think the creek was talking to me. *Holly. Holly. Holly.*

If I concentrate now, I can still hear my name disguised in the gurgling water, so distinct, as if someone's hiding in the trees, beckoning to me.

A sense of déjà vu washes over me, and I think, not for the first time, that that's how it must have happened: Alan Kohlbrook must have called to us. I must have gotten there first, before Kitten, because I was the one whisked away.

Matt nudges me with his elbow, a subtle invitation to cop a squat on the rocks on the edge of the bluffs.

Dog sits, so I sit.

From this vantage point, I can see clear to the other side of the ravine. I imagine how the place used to feel before my mother's accident—serene, private.

But now, this place feels like a panic attack waiting to happen. My chest tightens, and until I force a deep breath, it feels as if my lungs won't inflate.

My eyes travel over treetops to the bend in the road, where the accident happened in April. And then I see it . . . the doll I saw there yesterday.

It happens without warning. The world tilts to the right and feels as if it's spinning before my eyes.

I close my hand around whatever is beneath it. Have to hold it. Have to *have* it. And I squeeze until the horizon once again levels.

"Hey." Matt's thumb travels over my knuckles.

I refocus, zero in on what I was holding: a few of Matt's fingers. I pull my hand out of his. I seem to be hell-bent on making an ass of myself in his company the past couple of days.

"You okay?" he asks.

"Honestly . . ." I look back to the curve, to the doll. "I'm not sure."

He follows my gaze.

"There's something about a doll . . . ," I say. "There was one in the park before I was taken."

"There were hundreds there *after* you were taken, too." He drags a few fingers over my hand.

His touch evokes a tiny gasp, and I can't help the flush of embarrassment in my cheeks.

God help me, it feels damn good to be with him.

But I don't want him to know I'm affected.

I straighten. "I recently remembered seeing a doll posed on its side, and there was one yesterday . . ." I point toward the ravine.

"What's going on?"

"I was *fine*. It was just something that happened to me a long time ago, and then that detective called . . . and suddenly, I feel like my grip on reality is slipping. I don't know if I can handle this."

"I know you can handle *anything*, Holly. It's one of the things I love about you. But if you need anything . . ."

I can't find words. He *loves* things about me?

He drapes a stray strand of my hair behind my ear, and for a second or two, his stare is intense. He leans a little closer. My breath catches.

Abruptly, he turns back toward the ravine. "Sorry," he says. "I don't mean to make you uncomfortable."

"You didn't." But I'm unmoored, for sure. For a second there, I thought he was going to kiss me.

Would that be so bad, Mom?

Would you approve?

I don't want to start relying on him. He's here now, but he could be gone tomorrow.

"Are you, uh . . ." Matt sips his coffee. "You interested in hitting the shooting range later?"

It's not exactly a date, but a rush of adrenaline darts from my heart to the pit of my belly. "Yeah."

"Yeah?"

"I always welcome a chance to outshoot a US soldier."

He laughs. "It's on."

Movement on the other side of the ravine catches my eye: a blue pickup truck rolls to a stop at the site of my mother's accident. It's too far away for me to register the plate number, and it's not there long enough for me to do more than nudge Matt and point.

"What?" he says.

A blue truck. Like the vehicle Guidry thinks hit my mother.

CHAPTER 15

Holly

June 7

Each round fires into the target in front of me.

Most at dead center.

It took a while for me to be comfortable with firearms, but I've honed my skills and taken enough drill-oriented classes, most of them right here on this outdoor range, that I'm adept at the practice. My father encouraged my mother to learn, too. But she never was able to find comfort in the practice. I wonder . . .

If she had, and if Guidry's right that she was afraid of something, would she have been able to defend herself against whatever happened on April 16? Would she have had the courage to draw to protect herself, instead of driving away from whoever had scared her? Would she be in the ICU right now?

Earlier, the blue pickup lingering at the ravine rolled away before I could register a plate number or snap a picture. Was that truck there the night my mother tipped over the edge?

I place my firearm on the table and pull in my target.

Fifty rounds, and not one of them outside the second circle. If someone dangerous were to be staring me down, the only way I wouldn't walk away is if he were a faster draw. Which is also unlikely.

Matt's in the lane next to me.

As I ensure my mag is empty, as well as the chamber, and begin to stow my firearm, I hear the pop of his .45, muted thanks to my ear protection.

One of his casings ricochets over the divider and pings off the bill of my Sox cap. I stare where it lodges in the sand at my feet.

I can't help it. I have to have it.

I crouch and retrieve it, shove it into the pocket of my cutoffs.

I pack up and head off the range toward the pro shop, where Matt and I will meet once he's emptied his rounds. Like I said, it's not exactly a date as much as it's a mutual, solitary practice. And it's hotter than hell in the sun today. I'm a sweaty mess.

We rode together, we'll compare targets for accuracy, and the loser will buy drinks tonight after my visit to the Lake County Police Department. But that's about it.

Once I'm farther down the gravel road, far enough away from the firing range, I pull the protection from my ears.

It's then I see the blue truck parked in the lot at the pro shop.

I recognize the truck, the rust spot at the bottom edge of the driver-side door, the permit hanging from the rearview mirror allowing the driver access to the gated development we're building in.

Vellerman.

What's he doing here?

Was this the truck at the ravine earlier?

I haven't mentioned coming here recently, or even since I've been on Craig Vellerman's crew. But it's no secret Dad and I frequent this place. Any number of guys on-site might have clued him in.

Then again, I don't own the place. And if he wants to hang out at the Second Amendment Sports complex, it's his right to do so.

He's not on the range right now, so that means he must be inside the pro shop, where I'm supposed to meet Matt. I consider I could avoid seeing Vellerman if I text Matt to meet me in the parking lot, but I'm not going to let any guy intimidate me or stop me from going where I want to go.

I enter the pro shop and give the place a quick once-over.

Vellerman's back is to me, and I know (because I've been coming to this pro shop with Dad since I was issued my first Firearm Owners' ID card at age sixteen) that he's mulling over the knife display.

Great. He's going to buy a knife. That's all the world needs. Vellerman with a knife.

As if he's turned on his Holly radar, he looks over his shoulder at me and pins me with a stare.

I offer a hand up in a sort of wave—what else can I do? And quickly, I glide to the counter to check in my piece. "Is it all right if I leave my target here for a second?" I ask. "I want to wash up."

"No prob."

I glance back toward the knives just in time to see Vellerman look my way again, then I beeline into the ladies' room.

Once in front of the mirror, I take a deep breath. My heart is beating double time, but I don't know why.

Sure, the guy invited me out for a drink, and he's an asshole onsite, but who cares? Why am I borderline freezing up whenever I see him like a kindergartener who sees her teacher outside of school? It's probably Guidry's suggestion that a blue truck nudged my mother off the road, and its connection to the Skyler Jane Kipniss case. There's the manifesto, and the fact that a little girl is still missing and that her case might be tied to mine, and that I can't remember a damn thing to help save her . . . No wonder I'm a mess.

I wash the firearm residue off my face and hands and even scrub up past my elbows to my shoulders. I thoroughly rinse and let the cool water run over my hands for a bit longer than necessary. I have to calm down.

I wonder if such a thing is possible with Vellerman just outside these doors.

Vellerman expressed interest in my scar—the same scar Psychic Yanneth insists others bear. I wonder if he knows something about it, or if he suspects I might remember something, and he's following me—the way he followed my mother around the ravine?—to ensure I can't tell Guidry whatever it is he's afraid I'll remember.

Or maybe it's just that he makes me uncomfortable. Asking me if I want to get a drink . . . it's over the line, isn't it? And he's my foreman . . .

Again, I splash my face with water.

When I look into the mirror, I meet my own blue eyes, but the periphery darkens, and again, a flash of open floor joists appears before me. A little girl is at the end of the run. *Don't cross.*

I gasp, and suddenly, the vision is gone.

I turn off the water and towel off.

My head is pounding.

When I hear Matt's laugh beyond the door, I exit back into the pro shop to see him chatting with a clerk at the counter. When I hear the usual key words, *tour*, *over there*, I know they're trading stories.

A quick look around confirms Vellerman is no longer here. I breathe a bit easier.

"There she is," Matt says when he sees me. "Bought you something."

A balled-up T-shirt flies at me, and I catch it.

The front of it boasts Rosie the Riveter, captioned ARMED AND DANGEROUS.

"Truth in labeling and all," he says.

"Thanks, smart-ass."

"Saw your target. Damn, girl."

"Don't cross me."

The second the words escape me, I hear it in my head again: *Don't cross.*

I don't know what happened to me. And I don't know if it might be happening to another girl right now.

I have to go. I have to talk to Guidry.

CHAPTER 16

Holly

June 7

A uniformed officer puts me in a positively frigid room labeled CONFERENCE and asks me to wait here because Detective Guidry will be along soon. He doesn't close the door.

The room is sparse, save a laptop on the lone table and several folding chairs, but the walls still feel as if they're closing in on me, attempting to envelop me in nothingness.

I imagine that's what it felt like for my parents when I was gone—as if I'd simply been swallowed up by the universe.

Considering Alan Kohlbrook is riding out a twenty-five-year sentence at Stateville, you'd think there wouldn't be such a gap in my memory. You'd think Kohlbrook would have answered all my questions by now, let alone the questions of the cop assigned to the case.

But with Yanneth's comment about the scar on my arm, Matt's theory that maybe Kitten didn't see what she said she saw, Guidry's theory about my mother's accident . . . and the *tooth*, God, the tooth . . .

My brain feels as if it's twisting and wringing in my head.

I took an aspirin once we left the firing range, but it isn't doing much good. And that's another thing. I'm hungover way too often these days. The blackout moments I had after the party in Edgewater, the thinking I had a couple of drinks, only to wake up with no memory of the second half of the night, how the pewter box came to be in my possession, or whether Matt and I . . .

"Coffee?" Guidry appears with his accordion file tucked under his arm. "It's not exactly *good* coffee, you understand, but—"

"Sure. Thanks."

He leans back out of the room, asks someone to bring me a cup, and sits across from me. "First. We're in a conference room. We're being recorded."

"Okay."

"Standard procedure."

"Sure."

"Now, down to business. You left me a message yesterday."

I nod. "I thought of some things that might not matter, but I thought I should let you be the judge."

The blue-eyed girl flashes in my mind again. I try to hold on to her, but in an instant, she's gone again.

The same officer who greeted me leans in with my coffee.

I thank him, then gather the right combination of words for the detective: "Do you think there's a chance he took two of us at the same time?"

Guidry slides the cup of coffee toward me across a delaminating table. "Why do you ask?"

"Lots of reasons." I sip my coffee—*not good* is an accurate description—and glance up at him. "First off, I should tell you that I've recently had something I call a glimpse. It's a flash of a memory—or maybe it's not a *memory*, but . . . it's something *like* a memory. It bubbles up. Just an image, and then it's gone before I can grasp it, but here's what I know: It's a little girl. She has blonde hair and blue eyes, and she's looking at me across an unfinished second floor of a house."

"Hmm."

"And I know it sounds crazy, but I'm wondering if she was there with me." I pause, but he isn't looking at me like I'm crazy, so I continue. "Kitten said Kohlbrook grabbed her before he took me."

Guidry nods.

"So, what if he wanted two of us and had to settle for one? What if he eventually grabbed another girl? Is there anyone, case presumably solved or otherwise, who went missing shortly after me?"

"I'll look into it." He pulls his little spiral-bound notebook from his shirt pocket and jots notes. "Why else?"

"Huh?"

"You said there were lots of reasons."

"Oh. Yeah, there are. For starters, I stopped at a 7-Eleven the other night." I tell him about the self-proclaimed psychic I met there. About my dark-blue aura at the Al-Anon meeting. About what Yanneth said about my scar and me not being the only one who has it. "Doesn't it seem possible? That maybe he got another girl."

He raises his brows when I suggest it. "Interesting."

"I also have a vague memory of a wooden sign with white, peeling paint. There's a letter *P* on it. And maybe an *H*."

"Mm-hmm." He writes that down, too.

"I don't know if it's real," I explain. "It could be just a dream, but I thought . . . I don't know. Maybe it's nothing."

"Everything and anything might help."

"And Matt said something today—"

"Matt?"

"Hershey, Kitten's brother. He seems to think his sister embellished details about what may or may not have happened back then." I reiterate Matt's theory about Kitten fabricating part of what she said, so as to remain at the center of my kidnapping.

The detective sits back in his chair, and for a moment, he doesn't verbally respond. He clicks the end of his pen several times, and judging by the knit of his brow, he's mulling things over. Finally, he speaks:

"The truth is it's a tough call. Her story wavered. It grew from the first time she told it. The state brought in child psychologists to explain that as children become more comfortable with the adults they're relaying information to, they begin to impart more of it." He straightens and pulls a clipped-together report from his file. It looks like a portion of the court transcripts. "The defense brought in their own experts to debunk her testimony and prove she was lying, or at least stretching the truth." He finds a page riddled with notes in red ink and turns it toward me. I glance at it:

Witness: I'm not lying.

Defense: Come on, now, Kathy.

Witness: My name is Kitten.

Defense: This is a place for the truth. When you lie in a place like this, it's called perjury. Grown-ups can go to jail for perjury. Do you want to go to jail?

Prosecution: Objection! Badgering.

"The trouble was," Guidry says, "it made the jurors distrust the defense. Not good business, calling a five-year-old girl whose best friend just survived a horrific ordeal a liar."

I digest this for a minute. "Can I ask, then . . . surely the case wasn't balanced on Kitten's testimony alone. I know there was Kohlbrook's prior conviction for the two girls he photographed."

"Mm-hmm. Served three months the year before he snatched you."

"And I know there were pictures of me . . ."

The detective nods. "It seemed he had been following you for a long time. He had several pictures of you, all taken from a distance: in your pajamas at the breakfast table, with your father at work. One of the pictures showed you in a swimsuit at a water park the summer before. He'd tracked your movements for months, which is exactly what we tend to see in these types of cases. And there's the fact that we recovered evidence suggesting he was about to strike again—a list of possible targets by name and age."

"He didn't testify on his own behalf."

Guidry narrows his gaze, which tells me he's trying to figure me out, as if to ask why I'm mentioning all this now when for so many years I've been removed from any discussion of it.

"I don't remember what happened to me," I remind him. "A few years ago, my therapist suggested I revisit the documented evidence in the interest of closure, but I have to be honest: it was like reading about something that happened to someone else. I want to help. I just don't know *how*. Maybe, if he offered an explanation for having pictures of me—"

"It was more than that. He recorded your every move in a journal he kept."

"Okay. But there's nothing in court documents about his explanation," I say. "Surely, he must have told the team of detectives why he would've done such a thing if he expected them to believe he was innocent."

"I don't know if he did expect people to think he was innocent. I don't know if he wanted to be found not guilty. There's old interview footage. You're welcome to watch it. He doesn't make a good impression. He all but begs to be put away."

"Maybe I'll take you up on that. Someday."

After a few seconds of silence, he leans forward. "Holly, do *you* think the right man is serving time for what happened to you?"

I used to think so, or maybe it's safe to say I assumed so. Until the tooth, central incisor, lower right, of a missing girl happened to turn up in my possession. "I don't think I know enough to answer that question. But as I understand it, there was DNA evidence—"

"Mm-hmm."

"And a strand of Kohlbrook's hair."

"Mm-hmm."

"Correct me if I'm wrong, but . . . if that's not airtight, what is?"

"A DNA profile that *doesn't* cause problems, for starters." Guidry fires up the laptop, and something that looks like a series of dots appears on the screen. "Here's the profile of Kohlbrook's saliva." He clicks an arrow, and another picture shows up. "Here's the profile of Kohlbrook's blood. They don't match up. According to this profile, these specimens didn't come from the same guy, but we know they did. These profiles are far less complex, however, than the one that convicted him. This one"—another picture appears on the screen—"profiles the DNA gathered from beneath your fingernails. If our profiler screwed up simple profiles, known to be of the same man, how can he be expected to decipher your DNA from the perpetrator's?"

"Wow."

"So, there are certain elements that show inconsistency in our profiler's analysis. We've come a long way in the realm of DNA profiling in the twenty years since you've been back. Kohlbrook's lawyer knows that."

"Okay, then. So it's a wonder he was convicted."

"Maybe. You know about the white nightgown Gretchen was wearing when she was found."

"Yes."

"That parallels your case, but there's more. The man who abducted you mailed a package containing two objects to your parents about three days after you were gone. Authorities never released the details of what was inside that package, but you mentioned them in the message you left for me."

"My dad actually just told me about it. A lock of my hair and the key my mother had pinned to the inside of my pocket that day." I think about this for a second. "Is that weird? That she pinned a key in the pocket of my romper?"

The romper. It was one of my favorites—light green with white polka dots and eyelet lace trimming the shorts.

I never saw it again. And despite the fact that I probably would have outgrown it by the time the weather turned warm again, I always longed to wear it that next summer. As a child with a three-month-long blank space in my memory, I couldn't comprehend where it had gone.

"Is it weird? Maybe not." Guidry raises a finger and leafs through his file.

"I was four," I continue. "I mean, Matt usually walked me back and forth, but if he was out with friends, I was trusted to walk across the field to Kitten's, with her mom watching from one window and mine from the other. I wasn't roaming around town on my own. I certainly didn't let myself into my house. Why would my mother pin a key to my pocket?"

The detective finds whatever he's looking for. "The police asked your mother that very question a few days after you disappeared." He slides another packet of transcripts toward me.

I read:

Question: Why did you pin the key to Holly's pocket?

Cecily Gebhardt: I didn't bring a purse that day. We walked to the park. I wore a dress . . . I didn't have pockets.

Question: Did you do this sort of thing often?

Cecily Gebhardt: No.

Cecily Gebhardt: It was the first time.

Question: Did you anticipate being separated from your daughter?

Cecily Gebhardt: What?

Question: Is that why you pinned the key—

Cecily Gebhardt: No! Why would I . . . ? She's four.

Cecily Gebhardt: I may not be supermom, but I don't let my kid wander the county on her own.

I hear my mother's voice in my head as I read her responses. If I remember correctly the neurotic mess she was after I came back, I can imagine the desperation she must have felt when I was taken, the guilt laced in that desperation—after all, I'd disappeared on her watch, and when she'd been drinking. Her pinning the key inside my pocket, and the police presuming it meant more than it likely did, probably made things worse.

I rarely think of things from her point of view, but now that I've considered it, I feel terrible for what she must have gone through. "They made her look like a bad mother." My voice is hushed.

Guidry doesn't split hairs: "Yes. Cops, media, neighbors . . . everyone wanted to know how it happened right under her nose. And then there was the matter of the cash."

I don't know about any cash, and it must be obvious, because the detective inhales deeply and nods once. "About ten grand over the course of the time you were gone. She opened a new account."

"Where did it come from?"

"She wouldn't say. But about six weeks after your disappearance, your father found a letter in her belongings and brought it in."

I don't have time to process the fact that my father was nosing through my mother's things and that he turned in evidence that certainly didn't help his wife appear innocent. A copy of it lands atop the pile of evidence Guidry's already stacked before me. The letter is handwritten in a rushed half-print, half-cursive.

"Presumed male author, according to our graphoanalysts," Guidry says.

I read:

> Cecily,
> It's clear you don't want me to have anything to do with this situation. Be that as it may, we got into this mess together, and I don't feel right walking away now, not when so much is about to happen.
>
> Perhaps this small gesture will help you to carry out some of our plans, and the plans you have yet to make.

> There is more to come, as things progress.
>
> I hope all we've put into place serves as a small way to get back at Trevor. He doesn't know what's about to hit him, but then again, he never knew what he had in you.

"It isn't signed. Who wrote it?"

"We don't know. Your father didn't know, and your mother wasn't saying."

"And the money?"

"Your father didn't know anything about the money, either," Guidry says. "Suffice it to say, we assume the author of this letter is referencing the money with 'small gesture.' It put her further under fire for sure."

"You don't mean that she was somehow in on the kidnapping."

"It was a theory. Before you were recovered, and before it had been determined that you hadn't been sexually abused, some cops figured she was renting you out. Selling you. Especially when the detectives determined she'd tampered with the lock of your hair."

The detective flips a page and begins to read:

Question: Do you realize that by dividing this hair, you've potentially destroyed it as evidence?

Cecily Gebhardt: It's my baby's hair. The hair I brushed every morning and every night. The hair I wrestled into ponytails. I don't know if she's coming back. That hair could be the only tangible thing I have left of her, and I'll be damned if it's going to sit in a plastic bag buried in a box somewhere. You people have already stopped looking for her. You're going to forget about her hair, too, when the next big case comes along.

Question: So you untied the ribbon—

Cecily Gebhardt: Hell yes, I did! It's part of her! Part of my baby!

I don't believe for a second that my mother could have known what was about to happen to me and stepped aside to allow the events to transpire, but I see how the police, in absence of any real leads, might have considered the possibility.

But my poor mother! I feel an urge to throw my arms around her and tell her I understand, and furthermore that I appreciate her wanting to feel close to me when I was gone. The aching she must have felt when she couldn't simply walk down the hallway to catch a glimpse of me . . . And now we're in the middle of a role reversal. I want to feel close to her right now, too. As soon as she wakes up, I want to tell her how much she means to me.

Such a contrast from the distance that's loomed between us for most of my life. A distance stretched out over years and years of slurred speech, overconsumption, and hangovers.

I clear my throat. Back to the matter at hand: "I think the hair and the key were kept in a pewter box. I saw a box like it the other day at Kitten's bridal shower . . ." I don't tell him that I took the damn thing. "And I had a feeling that I'd seen it before. When I touched it, I remembered something: I'd reached up to grab it and opened it and seen a lock of hair and a key."

"Before or after your father told you about the package sent by the kidnapper?"

"Um, before. I asked about the box, whether it was Mom's, and that's when he told me about the package they received in the mail with the hair and key. That confirmed, to my mind, that it was a valid memory."

He writes this down.

"So my abductor mailed a lock of my hair home, and I'm guessing Gretchen's did, too?"

"No, but Skyler's parents received a similar package."

"Maybe Gretchen isn't a victim of the same guy."

"Well . . . we have this."

He leans to the laptop and clicks on an icon, and an old photograph appears on the screen: it's my five-year-old arm, a close-up of the strange arrow-shaped mark that I came home with. "Recognize this?"

"It's my arm."

He clicks another key on his laptop, and then another image appears on the screen, alongside the picture of my scar: a nearly identical image.

"Holly, this is Gretchen Klemm's arm."

I cover my gasp with a hand, and a chill chases up my spine. "Psychic Yanneth was right." I'm not the only one who has an arrow embossed on her forearm. And if she was right about that, maybe she was right about Mom knowing something about it. Couple this with news of the money Mom stashed away, Guidry's theory that my mother was afraid of someone or something the night she plummeted into the ravine, and . . . *fuck*. Maybe she learned something about my kidnapping just before she went into the ravine.

"Did you say *Yanneth*?" Guidry sits back in his chair again and chews on his lip, as if in deep contemplation. "Could it be *Jan-neth*? Pronounced with a *J*?"

"Maybe. She never said her name . . . she gave me her card. I assumed it was a phonetic pronunciation. Why?"

"I assume you can contact her, this psychic?"

"I *can*, but—"

"Would you be willing to talk with her?"

"I guess. But I thought you cops didn't take stock in that sort of thing."

"Depends. I don't usually, but occasionally, when I'm contacted, I'm willing to listen. Any lead's a good one, and considering what I just showed you . . . I have to ask you to keep it to yourself, you understand. The authorities haven't released the information about the scar to the press."

I'm not sure I'm willing to bear such a burden, but as Guidry already let me in on the information, I have little choice.

I offer the closest to affirmation I can under the circumstances—an almost nod.

"I'm going to do some digging on this Yanneth, and I'll let you know if we need to reach out to her. In the meantime, can you get me her contact information?"

"Sure."

"We can't ignore the possibility, Holly, that Gretchen might be the handiwork of whoever snatched you."

"But Kohlbrook's in jail, which means he couldn't have—"

"Exactly. And we have the tooth of the latest victim, found in your vehicle, in a bottle covered in your prints."

An unsettling feeling wells in my gut and rises through my rib cage, through my heart, as realization dawns. It's as if a sense of fear is expanding in my chest and threatening to burst. "You think whoever did this is still watching me."

Guidry's studying me carefully. "That's one possibility."

"Do you think he planted that bottle where he knew I'd see it?"

The rest of my explanation plays out only in my head; I don't speak the words aloud: *Look, I have this problem. If I'm feeling off-balance, I hold on to something concrete, and sometimes I happen to take whatever item helps me feel grounded.*

He holds up a hand. "Either the wrong man's in prison or there's someone out there copying his crime," Guidry says. "But either way, it begs the question: If we were to find the other victims, would they, too, have odd arrow-shaped marks on their arms? Will Skyler Jane, when we find her?"

He leafs through his file and presents two reports, side by side. One is my medical examination, the one that determined what had happened to me while I was gone, and a likely reason I didn't remember it: high levels of flunitrazepam in my system, more commonly known as Rohypnol, or roofies.

The other report is Gretchen Klemm's autopsy, which reveals her similar plight: a meticulously cleaned body so as to remove DNA evidence, and again, flunitrazepam in abundance.

Twenty years ago, the case of my kidnapping was tied up neatly with a bow. Open and shut. Now, to think they got it wrong . . .

"Do you know, Holly, what most serial abusers and offenders have in common?"

I go to shake my head, but he's talking again.

"A severe, traumatic, childhood incident. Not unlike one you survived."

This makes sense.

"Do you know how many victims of child crimes turn into offenders later in life?" he asks. "We have a partial print on a letter that may or may not reference you. A bottle with your prints all over it, containing the tooth of a missing girl."

The reason for his careful look at me is obvious now. "I don't know how the tooth came to be in my glove box. I told you I saw the jar at the Moonbeam, but—"

"And flunitrazepam . . . you've had access to drugs that act like flunitrazepam. Your mother's been prescribed Xanax, Klonopin, Halcion, isn't that right?"

"Yes. You aren't saying that *I*—"

"And your father says your mother rarely *takes* the medication."

"That's right, but—"

"The tooth was in your possession. How do I know you didn't clean it before putting it in that vial?"

"You've been to my place. Do I strike you as a particularly neat person? You know what?" When I stand, the chair skids on the linoleum and screeches something awful. If this guy's going to accuse me of something, I'm leaving. "If you don't believe me about the tooth, ask Kitten. She was there when we saw the little bottle for the first time."

"Holly—"

"I'm here. I'm helping. And you already know, because you've probably cross-checked my FOID and concealed-carry records, that my fingerprints don't match the partial print you picked up on that letter."

"You're right."

"I didn't write it. I don't know who did. And I don't even know how the vial ended up in my car to begin with."

He extends a hand, palm up, in offering. "Have a seat."

"I don't know what happened to that girl."

"Okay."

"Why are you acting like I might?"

"Holly, if the real culprit is still out there, he's probably keeping an eye on you. Maybe even trying to frame you. You survived what he put you through. That could be motivation for revenge."

I shake my head in disbelief.

"As I said to you yesterday: you're in a unique position to help us profile this guy."

I look him in the eye. "I don't remember what happened."

"That doesn't mean you never will."

"What else can I do to help?"

"If you can't help me figure things out before we're looking at victim number eleven, I don't know if anyone can. And we're running out of time."

I swallow over the tears culminating in my throat.

"People who do this don't stop but for two reasons," the detective says. "One: we make them stop. Or two: they die."

If only I could remember. I cradle my aching head and massage my temples. A déjà vu sensation teases at me, but before I can center on it, it's gone again. "What do the experts say? About his psychological profiling?"

"For your case, we centered on a young man, aged roughly eighteen to thirty. White. Inferiority complex countered with delusions of grandeur, that sort of thing. Now, in later cases—Gretchen's, Skyler's—we're focused on someone older. Maybe someone seeking approval."

"So pretty much every guy on the dating circuit."

He cracks a smile. "Funny. But if we're right and the same guy who took you is out there with Skyler Jane right now . . . it means he could be anywhere from late thirties to early fifties. Kohlbrook was a young man when he was incarcerated," Guidry says. "He spent over half his life behind bars, and if he didn't commit this crime . . ."

"Maybe *he* can help," I say. "He needs a way out of prison, we need help deciphering all this. You said he was watching me. Maybe he noticed someone else was watching me, too. Win-win, right?"

"If he saw things that way, he might be willing to help. But so far, he's extremely uncooperative. I don't think he wants to get out, to be honest."

This doesn't make sense to me, but I suppose it might be difficult to reenter society after all that time. Or maybe, if he has a conscience, he knows he'd be a danger to little girls if he were let out.

"You have a degree in social work," Guidry says. "You have clinical experience talking with incarcerated subjects."

"Some." Which means *enough to earn an undergraduate degree.*

"It's another reason I think you might be useful here."

"But I don't have a master's degree, so I never sat for the exam."

"You went to class, though, right? You learned stuff? You graduated?"

"Yeah."

"Okay, then."

"Do you . . ." I can't believe I'm about to suggest such a thing, but here I go. "You don't mean you think he'll talk to *me*?"

"There are only two names, aside from his lawyer and deceased mother, on Kohlbrook's approved visitors list: your mother's, and yours. Will you talk to him?"

Cecily

People often commented that the girls looked more like sisters than friends.

Kitten was less than a year older than Holly, and when they dressed in the same outfits, which they loved to do, some people even assumed they were twins.

I used to find it charming.

How lucky I'd been to have found an extended family in our best friends, and how serendipitous it had been that we happened to purchase the acreage right next door to their farmette.

But I began to look at Susan Hershey and her children as a curse instead of a blessing.

I was so on edge, pretending not to know about Trevor and Susan's affair, that I'm sure I occasionally snapped at Matt when he'd arrive at our doorstep with my daughter in tow just after dark. *Hi, Mrs. Gebhardt. Look who I found hanging around my house again. Mom fed her dinner. You're off the hook.*

He was a kid; he didn't mean to make me self-conscious about my less than stellar maternal instincts, but it felt as if everyone was judging me, even before Holly was taken.

One evening, I balanced a second glass of bourbon on my knee and stared out the window at the house across the field, determined to catch sight of my husband's silhouette in Susan's bedroom window.

Holly was in the tub, calling to me: "Mommy! Mommmmmy!"

But I figured, if she was talking, she was keeping her head above water. I couldn't afford to miss what I was certain I'd see. And when he came home, I'd pull him in for a hug, I'd inhale the scent of Susan's perfume, and we'd finally confront the issue, head-on.

I couldn't take it anymore. So many times I'd thought to blurt it out, but Paul had the pictures. I had nothing to back up the claims, and Trevor was good at arguments. I imagined if I accused him without proof, he'd make me feel crazier than I already felt. I relied on his carelessness, his willingness to return to me with her scent smeared all over him.

But I didn't see them together, didn't even catch a glimpse. I peeked in on Holly, who was crying in the tub. "One more minute, sweetie."

"I'm cold," she said.

I looked into my glass, which was nearly empty. "One more minute."

I managed to make my way down the dark staircase to refill my glass while she wailed. "Mommmmmmy!"

"Cecily."

I turned when I heard Trevor's voice.

"What are you doing? Where's Holly?"

Her scream came again: "Mommy!"

"Sheesh fine."

"Mommy!"

He bolted up the stairs.

Our daughter's cries echoed down the hallway, down the stairwell.

"Holly-Dolly. It's okay, Daddy's here. I'm here now. Oh, you're so cold! Let's get you in a warm, fluffy towel."

I stumbled to a chair and knotted my fingers in my hair and pulled and let out a roar. *Daddy's here now. I'm here to take care of you. Everything's better.* He may as well have said, *Your mother is a fucking loser.*

Images of Trevor and Susan entwined, naked, flashed in my mind. They probably laughed about my inadequacies behind my back: Can't catch us in the act, no balls to even look at the pictures she paid a PI to take. Can't make a decent dinner. Can't even give the kid a bath.

I cried alone.

Drank some more.

The numbers on the clock blurred.

"Cecily."

I looked up from my bourbon, and through the blur of alcohol and tears, I saw my husband.

"How long was she in that tub? The water was ice cold."

"Not long."

"Her lips were blue, her fingers were like prunes. She was shivering. What the hell were you thinking?"

"I just needed to see it," I say.

"You needed to see *what*?"

"I needed to see you for what you are."

"I don't even recognize you anymore," he said. "When she was born, I understood. Postpartum. It happens. But she's our *daughter*, and it's like you can't be close to her. Do you know what some people go through to have families? We're *blessed*, and—"

"Blessed? That's what you call this life? *Blessed?*"

"I love you."

"No you don't."

"But if you don't get it together, if you can't give our little girl the upbringing she deserves—"

"What, Trevor? What are you going to do?"

We stood eye to eye in a stare down.

Finally, he spoke: "She was freezing."

"So am I." I slammed my glass down on the table. It cracked with the pressure and cut my finger. I walked out the door, biting the blood from my finger. He didn't follow me, but that was just as well. One of us had to be there to tend to Holly should she have trouble falling asleep.

I followed the path to the rear of our property. When I looked to the right, I saw Paul, a black silhouette against the setting sun, making his way in the same direction.

We met just shy of the creek, about halfway down the bluffs.

"Ceci." He took me in his arms, but I pulled away.

"What do you want, Paul?"

"I think I interrupted something in the shed. Just before dinner."

"What else is new?"

"He stuck around after. Can you believe it? To be so smug, so sure you couldn't be caught—"

"I don't care anymore."

"You couldn't look at the pictures. I understand that. But there's more." He shoved an envelope into my hand.

The return address read: DNA ReSource.

My heart started beating like crazy. "What did you do?"

"This has been going on between Susan and Trevor for a long time."

The envelope was open.

"A long time." He nodded toward the envelope. "See for yourself."

Inside were two sheets of paper, each indicating a test result.

The first subject, Male Child, age 16 years 9 months: 99.9% match to mother; 99.9% match to father.

The second subject, Female Child, age 5 years 2 months: 99.9% match to mother; 0% match to father.

I looked up at him, silently asking for confirmation of what I already had guessed.

"Matt and Kitten," he said.

"Okay, okay, okay." I started pacing, matching my steps with the rapidity of my heartbeat. "Okay, so Kitten's not yours. That doesn't mean she's Trevor's. Or . . . or, you know what? I hear there are certain cases, with certain kids . . . the tests bring about a false negative."

"Ceci."

"I mean, these things aren't one hundred percent accurate."

"Think about it, Ceci. *Think.* We dug back three years and found coincidences in their calendars. Do we have to dig back five? Or six? The four of us are very close. All the vacations, all the late nights. Who knows when they first crossed the line?"

I shoved the envelope back into his hand. "Believe what you want to believe. I'm going to believe in my husband."

Despite it all, I realized, I still wanted to do just that.

"You're a fool, Cecily," he called after me as I walked away. "A fool."

Fool or not, I didn't want to believe Trevor was Katherine Hershey's father. I didn't want to believe that the woman I'd confided in during the pregnancy, and after, when postpartum depression hit me hard, had carried my husband's firstborn . . . and seamlessly, effortlessly mothered her children and mine.

I had to calm down. To get my thoughts in order.

If Trevor had fathered Kitten, I had more to overcome than I could probably handle, but did I have a choice? I had Holly to think about. And I wanted to be a good mother. I wanted to mend what was broken. And now, with one typewritten genetics report, it was all about to implode into pieces that couldn't be glued back together.

I continued onward, drunkenly maneuvering over the brush and ridges in the path.

"Ceci, wait."

"Go home."

I walked all the way to the road, and even down to the bend, and stared over the ravine.

So easy.

It would be easy to throw myself off the edge.

Given the rocky terrain below, I'd certainly split my skull when I landed.

I climbed over the guardrail and stared down, down, down.

I wondered, if I jumped, how long it would take before the authorities found me dead at the bottom.

A few hours?

A day or two?

Would Trevor secretly be happy to be rid of me? Would he and Susan forever raise my daughter as their own and leave the memory of me to fade away?

I wasn't like Susan. I didn't love the park, I hated mommy-and-me yoga, and arts and crafts with a four-year-old was damn near frustrating. And I couldn't handle watching a kid puke. None of this meant I didn't love my daughter, but did I love being a mother?

I swayed in my inebriation, closed my eyes to the evening breeze, and imagined my body on a cold steel table, doctors cutting at my flesh to determine my cause of death.

Maybe she was pushed, they might say.

They'd zero in on Trevor first, Paul would blab about Kitten's DNA test, and they'd run my husband through the wringer.

Good. Maybe he deserved it after all he'd done.

It would be easy.

All I had to do was lean into the wind, and eventually, I'd go.

Maybe just another step closer.

I leaned another degree of an inch.

"Cecily."

I felt the grip on my arm as soon as I heard the voice.

I turned to see who'd saved my life.

Alan Kohlbrook, a recent TrevCon hire, had come recommended by Paul Hershey. *He goes to our church. Good guy. Down on his luck.*

"You okay?"

Stones beneath my feet plummeted fifty feet downward, spurring a dizzying sensation.

"What are you doing here?" he asked.

"What are *you* doing here?"

"Your husband hired me to fix the rotted posts in the paddocks."

He was still at it? It was dusk; the sun was dipping down the horizon.

"I heard you crying," he said. "I wanted to be sure you were okay, so I followed."

"You followed me here?"

"Are you okay?"

In hindsight, I wish he had left me alone to fall.

Why had he saved me only to tear my heart out a few short weeks later?

"I want to die," I said.

"There are worse things than dying, you know."

I didn't know. But I was about to find out.

CHAPTER 17

HOLLY

June 7

Kitten texted Matt and me during my meeting with the detective: Bonfire on the bluffs. Let's kick it old school.

Ah, there's the Kitten I know and love.

I reply: I'm in.

I call Sterling, but he doesn't answer, so I follow up with a text: If Dog is still at my place . . . when will you pick her up?

Next, I call Kitten, who picks up on the first ring. "What time are you thinking? There's this thing I have to do first . . ."

Guidry said Kohlbrook might refuse a video visit, but I figure if he put my name on his list, it's worth a try.

Before I left the station, Guidry helped me register with the state, making me eligible for the video process, and I now sit at my laptop and log in to the system. He says the security team at Stateville will do their part to expedite the visit on their end, but he warned me that because video visits are monitored in real time and recorded, Kohlbrook might not show. Whatever he says to me today, if he says anything at all, could be used against him in any upcoming parole hearing. If I were in his shoes, I'm not sure I'd want to risk it, either.

After a few minutes, an empty room appears on the screen, and my visit has officially begun. A countdown ticker in the lower right of the screen tells me I have three hours, fifty-nine minutes, and fifty-three seconds remaining in my visit. A window pops up reminding me that the session will be monitored and recorded and that it may be terminated for any reason at any time. I also have to follow dress code, which means I have to toss a flannel over my tank top because even tank tops are considered too suggestive for inmates to look at. I click to confirm I understand the rules.

But Kohlbrook isn't on the other side of the screen.

A modicum of relief washes over me.

I'm nervous to see him.

Bourbon will fix that. I pour one on the rocks.

I hope he doesn't keep me waiting the entire four hours, but it's possible that I might sit here all that time for nothing, which simply isn't going to work. Dog is going to have to go out eventually.

But in the meantime . . . I open another window on my laptop, keeping the video link live, and navigate to Mom's email. I figure if she was having an affair, maybe there will be evidence of it in her emails. It's a gross violation of her privacy, but if ever there was a reason to invade her privacy, it's now, when Guidry is hypothesizing that an affair gone wrong could be the reason she went over the edge of the ravine. I type in her address, then stare blankly at the password prompt.

I click *forgot my password,* then attempt to answer her security questions. Father's middle name: Michael. Childhood street: Elmwood. First pet . . .

And I'm stumped. It'll come to me. I drum my fingertips against the tabletop. Was it a cat? A dog? A fish?

As I ponder it, I open another window and begin researching the other missing girls the detective assumes may have been victims of the same psychopathic danger to society who took me.

If, that is, Alan Kohlbrook is innocent.

I use Guidry's time line as a reference, and I write notes on it as I research. Their stories are heartbreaking. Each has a web page detailing what little is known about her abduction, and I see why Guidry and his team might be taking the manifesto seriously, as there are definite parallels between their cases and mine.

Each of the kidnappings took place in a park or on a playground.

Each child, prior to being taken, was mild mannered and introverted. Polite, if you will. Perfect targets: children taught to listen to and respect adults and fear strangers, children too afraid to fight or talk back.

Most are blonde, but some, like Deanna Renee Rhine, have darker hair.

But every girl on the list has blue eyes.

And each of their mothers holds out hope that they're alive year after year, after five, nineteen.

There's virtually nothing to go on in most of the cases. Gretchen's body was wiped clean. Her murderer even meticulously cleaned beneath her fingernails. I can't help but wonder if he did so because he neglected to do so before he released me and they were able to pull a DNA profile.

I move on to another girl.

Enna Scotsman disappeared from rural Iowa a year or so after me. She was with her cousin at the time, riding bicycles on a trail, making hers the second and last kidnapping on the list categorized as a witnessed stranger abduction. After that, he was more methodical, more careful. Even girls playing in plain sight disappeared at a moment when no one happened to be looking, as if they were simply deleted from existence at one particular second, as if God's finger hovered over the "Delete" key and punched it only at the most precise moment.

There's a composite sketch of the kidnapper on Enna's site.

I stare at him, try to burrow back through the annals of time, and concentrate. Is this the man who took me?

There's nothing familiar about him. His most distinguishing feature is the wild crop of hair on his head, but given this was nearly nineteen years ago, and hair is easy to cut, shave, or dye, there's no way this sketch is going to help anyone find the culprit or tie this case to mine. This composite looks nothing like the man Kitten described as my kidnapper, and it looks nothing like Alan Kohlbrook.

Next, I search for Deanna Renee Rhine, and the letter the abductor sent to major newspapers pops up instantly. Right Places. Why are these letters capitalized? Suppose it's a clue. The word *hag* is capitalized, and Guidry thinks that's a clue, so maybe Right Place is a street name . . .

"What do you think, Mom? Is it possible?"

I study Deanna, focus on her picture until it becomes blurry, until the periphery of the room fades to darkness and I see her face across the room, at the other end of what looks like a dark tunnel.

Don't cross.

The sound of scuffling jars me out of the trancelike memory.

I catch movement in my video visit.

I maximize the window and see a door opening and a harsh fluorescent light illuminating the tired-looking space. In walk an officer and the prisoner convicted of stealing me and hiding me away for ninety-four days.

An odd thought crosses my mind, one of gratitude. Despite what he did, *he let me go.* How do I not thank him for that? Because of a decision he made, I was able to go home to my family, attend school, fall in love—sort of, if what I shared with Sterling constitutes as such—and explore a career.

As Guidry just outlined for me, nine other girls were not afforded such opportunity—ten, if Skyler Jane doesn't make it home.

Kohlbrook, who is not shackled but clad in prison denim, is led into the room and directed to sit. He does so and folds his hands atop a table. His eyes seem to travel about the closet of a room into which he was led, as if he doesn't yet notice my image on the screen—or maybe they've yet to queue me up.

He looks much older than he appears on news broadcasts and positively ancient compared to the twenty-year-old photographs with which the newspapers depict him. He isn't an old man. He's a bit older than forty, but his eyes put him somewhere closer to death. It's as if he's aged before my eyes.

After a good fifteen seconds of silence, he says, "What the fuck's this about?"

There's an edge to his voice that's nothing short of chilling, and when coupled with his hard stare, it's a wonder I don't instantly sign off.

"You have a video visit," the correctional officer says.

Kohlbrook's gaze then lifts, and his stare is so hard, so unrelenting, that it feels as if he's boring into my soul. I'm glad I'm in the privacy of my own home. I can't imagine a traditional visit with this man, face-to-face.

The officer exits, and my nerves kick into high gear. It's silly, I know. There's nothing that can happen to me here with or without the officer chaperoning the visit, but I don't like being alone with Kohlbrook.

"Home Sweet Barn." His gaze is aimed to my left. I know, without looking, that he's reading the sign my mother hung on my wall just before I moved in.

I shift my laptop, so that there are no more discerning details of my place in his view, but I only give him reason to look at me.

"You don't look like you live in a barn."

"Mr. Kohlbrook." I swallow hard. "I'm not sure you remember me."

A moment or two later, realization dawns on his face. His features soften; the hard, vertical line between his brows melts away, and a smile appears at the side of his mouth. "Holly."

"Yes."

"Holly Adryenne Gebhardt." He nods with each name. "Goddamn, you're pretty."

"I'm here today because—"

"Would you look at you? It's like God brought me a present and tied it up with a bow."

I clam up. I don't know what I thought this was going to be like, but . . .

This guy brings a whole new meaning to the word *ogle.*

His gaze combs over me and lingers at my chest, although Guidry instructed me to button up the flannel far past my cleavage.

His tongue appears at the center of his lower lip, and he nods, as if in approval.

An *ick* courses through me.

I know what I'm here to accomplish, but already, I feel myself veering off course to the fast track. I just want this to be over.

"Mr. Kohlbrook, I need you to help me understand something."

He grins. "Never thought you'd need me for anything."

"You followed me when I was a little girl. Why?"

"According to the state, I was planning to take you."

"*Did* you take me?"

"According to the state, I did."

"According to *you.*"

"Doesn't much matter, does it? Here I sit."

"You're up for parole again soon," I say. "If you didn't take me, maybe I can help you."

"Nothing can help me now, and I'm not going to help the cops do their job, so . . . You got me to come all the way up here. Let's talk about something else."

"There's a chance you'll be released, Mr. Kohlbrook."

For a few long seconds, he doesn't respond.

"Mr. Kohlbrook—"

"Al."

"Pardon?"

"I think two people with such integral histories ought to refer to each other by the first name, don't you?"

"Al."

"That's better."

"You *have* been in jail for a long time. I'm told you might be serving time for someone else's crime."

"No, I'm here for mine."

"So, you . . . you did it? You kidnapped me twenty years ago?"

"I followed you. I photographed you. I obsessed over you—"

My gut churns. It's unsettling to consider his thinking of me that way *now*, let alone when I was in preschool. But I try my best to stay composed, not to let this creep know how his words affect me.

"I dreamed of doing more with you," he says. "*That's* why I'm here."

"You were convicted of kidnapping. Did you kidnap me?"

He holds my stare. "It doesn't much matter, now, does it?"

"If you didn't, you can help me find whoever did. You can get out of there."

"You don't want me getting out of here."

"If you're innocent—"

"I'll tell you exactly what I tell the parole board every fucking time I'm up: I have urges. I can't control them. They ask, if I'm out, will I be a danger to society? The answer is: probably. If tempted, given the chance, I might do every despicable thing running 'round in my head. That's why I sit here, year after damn year, rotting."

It occurs to me: "That's why your lawyer is trying to get you exonerated. Because you won't get paroled if you keep saying things like that."

"If I keep telling the truth, you mean?" He sits back in his folding chair a little, as if he's getting comfortable. "Yeah, I signed the papers and let the lawyer do his thing. But that lawyer's not interested in helping *me*. He didn't even know who I was until some asshole sent him twenty-seven pages of reasons I'm innocent. He's trying to make a name for himself.

Everyone wants to make a splash. But I've made peace with myself, with what I've done, with what I want to do. I'm okay to die here."

"For something you didn't do?"

"How's your mom?"

"She's . . ." I sigh. "Actually, she's not doing so well right now. She was in an accident."

"No one told me."

"She hasn't regained consciousness."

He drops his head in his hands. "Lord, watch over your child, Cecily . . ."

He's *praying*. I let him finish.

When he utters *amen*, and looks back up at me, he asks, "How long's it been?"

"Almost two months now."

"She was a good friend of mine. A good friend." He's quiet for a few moments, then pipes up. "What's your life like, Holly? Do you have a boyfriend? Job? Still pal around with that girl, Kitten?"

Guidry warned that this guy might try to pry personal information out of me. We're not old friends. He has no right to know these things about me.

"I'd rather talk about the girls, Al." I read the list of names: "Enna Scotsman, Selena Truesdale, Jenny Bock, Alyssa Carter-Friese, Deanna Renee Rhine, Bethany Sparrow, Sophie Cousins, Lauren Bunting, Gretchen Klemm."

"You're missing Skyler Jane."

"Is Skyler Jane Kipniss a victim of the same guy?"

"I won't do their job for them. I give them a tidbit, next you know, they're all over my ass."

"Then do it for me." I bring my hand to my heart. "If you loved me the way you say you did—and if you loved my mother . . . If that's true, you'll tell me."

"Yes." He leans forward in his chair again. "She's the eleventh."

Psychic Yanneth's comment returns to me: *I see the number eleven when I look at you . . .*

I glance at her purple business card, which is lying abandoned on my kitchen island.

The world tilts, and the edges seem to cloud up.

My fingers close into a fist, only there's nothing on the table but a tiny Elvis saltshaker for me to grab on to. I flinch, force myself out of it. I cough when I try to draw in a breath.

After a moment, I refocus on the screen.

Kohlbrook is just as zeroed in. But he's tight lipped. He won't talk unless I specifically ask.

"Do you know who's doing this?"

His stare is steady and unrelenting; he gives his head a slow shake.

"You have a boyfriend these days?" he asks.

"How is that relevant?"

"I have a lot of time on my hands. Give me something to think about."

So he's playing the quid pro quo card. For a second or two, I consider how to answer. I could simply say no and end it at that. But if I don't give him anything to go on, he might then ask more questions about other things. The truth is harmless enough, anyway. "It's on-again, off-again."

His lips turn up into a grin.

For an uncomfortable few seconds, he doesn't say anything.

I brace myself.

"Let me guess: he's an older guy."

I don't know why it matters, but . . . "Somewhat, yes."

"Boys your own age can't relate to you," Kohlbrook says. "They're too busy shooting tequila and getting lap dances."

"I didn't know that behavior was relegated *only* to boys of a certain age."

He smiles at my joke. "You're more complicated than other girls."

I suppose if that's not true, it's a convenient enough excuse for my being a romantic mess most of my life. But I wonder, and not for the first time, if maybe this is where my schoolgirl obsession with Matt began. He was the older boy, uninterested in and unaffected by the melodramas of boys my age.

As was Sterling, come to think of it, the trade-off being that Derrion Sterling is more complicated than even me. A week or so before the couples' shower, he crawled into bed with me upon an unannounced return from a business trip in Michigan. "Went to a winery," he whispered and kissed my cheek. "I brought you some Riesling."

Thinking about it now, my heart aches for the thoughtful man he could be. But we'd broken up before he left for that trip. *Too little, too late*, Kitten had said, and I'd agreed. Why couldn't he have done things like that more often before we called it quits?

"What's this guy do?" Kohlbrook asked.

He'd hoped to be an investigative journalist, but at thirty-eight, he's still paying dues on grunt analyses, working for a team of journalists instead of calling himself one. "He's a researcher."

"Stable. Boring."

Before I can disagree on both counts, he asks, "You in love with him?"

"I used to think so."

"Do just about anything for him, don't you?"

"Not really. We're on the off-again part of the cycle." I uphold my end of the staring contest, despite feeling as if worms of his imagination are burrowing into my brain, my body. "Tell me about guys like you, about what's going to happen next with this little girl."

Finally, he speaks again. "My guess, if it were *me*: He's eluded the cops so many times, gotten away with it so many times, that he's thinking he's untouchable. The last thing he should do is kill again, probably the last thing he *wants* to do, but he's worried she's going to remember something and blab about it, so he can't possibly let her go. He got lucky with you. He's thinking he won't get that lucky again. Your freedom haunts him. He worries. He's too tired, too paranoid"—he taps a finger to his temple in time with the words—"to think. This. Through. So, yeah. He's gonna kill her to save himself, to save his family, maybe, from finding out."

"He has a family?"

"Maybe. I feel like the risk is greater, if he does, which might explain why he didn't kill you but he killed the recent one."

"Gretchen."

"Yeah, Gretchen. Not as much at stake with you, but the others . . . maybe he got married. Suddenly, it wasn't about just him anymore. He can't risk the exposure."

"But he wants attention. He sent letters."

"He wants notoriety." Kohlbrook laughs. "He wants everyone to know he's smart. My guess is he spent his life hearing that he wasn't. He'll dangle this girl on a string, send the cops on a wild-goose chase, maybe. But it's all the same in the end. He'll kill her."

"How much time do we have before that happens?"

"He had you for ninety-four days. There's a reason for that, but I can't guess what it is. How long has this Skyler been gone?"

"Eighty-one days."

He considers this for a moment. "She's probably still breathing, but—"

"Do you think her time is running out?"

He crosses his arms over his chest. "What do you do for a living?"

"If you're reading a lot these days, you already know."

"The paper said you're a journeyman. A journeyman what? Trim carpenter? Electrician?"

"I'm a rough framer. I build the skeletons of custom homes."

"A dainty thing like you?"

"I'm not dainty."

"You'll always be that sweet five-year-old girl in my mind." He closes his eyes and takes a deep breath, as if he's breathing in the aroma of homemade pumpkin pie. "Sweet, sweet girl. That's how I think of you." His hands disappear under the table.

Sweet girl. The same words in the manifesto.

I jot down a note for Guidry: *Possible Kohlbrook had something to do with manifesto?*

It would make sense, if this whole *I-belong-in-prison* thing is by chance an act, and it might be, considering he signed an agreement with a lawyer. Why retain a lawyer if you don't want things to change?

I can't imagine Kohlbrook could send even a paragraph from prison without the authorities first reading it, so he didn't author the manifesto. However, maybe one of his associates wrote the entire twenty-seven pages to start the conversation that Kohlbrook is innocent of the crimes for which he's doing time. Maybe he's playing the whole system.

"Sweet girl," he says again. "I still see you in my mind's eye: skipping rope in that cute little romper."

I practically shiver with the possibility he's just admitted to seeing me the day I was kidnapped. But I shake it off.

"I'm twenty-five," I tell him. It's a social worker's trick, one I learned in clinical study. A small reminder of the here and now, that whatever fantasy he entertained two decades ago is past. "Not a girl. And I'm not sweet."

"Journeyman. Means you're skilled. But not in charge. Why aren't you in charge?"

I sigh. "You're asking why I'm not a foreman. Why I'm not running sites."

He nods.

"My father, out of respect for my mother, doesn't want to promote me."

"Why not? Isn't that the benefit of working for your dad? Climbing over others to get to the top?"

For a good minute, we're locked in another stare, a contest of wills.

"Fine, I'll tell you," I say. "My mother thinks I should be doing something else with my time. She wants me to pursue another career, and if Dad promotes me, I'll remain in construction, which is, from time to time, unbearable at journeyman status."

"Your foreman's an asshole."

"Accurate."

His smile is slow to spread on his face. "But you like what you do."

"Yes."

"Good." The word itself isn't all that threatening, but he says it as if it's three syllables, and he licks his lips soon after.

"How do we save this girl in Indianapolis?"

Dog stirs across the room and diverts Kohlbrook's attention.

"You have a *dog*."

"She belongs to my boyfriend."

"You have good sex with this guy?" He closes his eyes. "Tell me about it."

"You don't want anything to happen to this little girl," I say. "Help us save her."

"The time I spent with you and your mother," he says, "was the best time of my life. I would've done anything for either one of you. Well worth the twenty-five-year sentence, especially since you've come back to me."

"I'm not interested in reconnecting with you if not for Skyler," I say. "I'm focused on one thing: the safety and well-being of a little girl."

"Of all little girls."

"Right."

He shrugs. "C'est la vie."

"Al. It's been long enough. If you didn't take me, who did?"

"You think I have that kind of knowledge? You think I'd be sitting here if I could've pinned it on someone else? Truth be known, I'm here for one reason: to save your mother from incarceration."

"My mother? You think she had something to do with it?"

"If they weren't looking at her, I probably would've kept my damn mouth shut and watched them fumble the whole investigation from the sideline."

"Tell me why, then, if you don't know who it was. Tell me how the urges work."

"You want to get inside my head." He grins.

"I want to be sure no little girl goes through what I went through."

"You can't do that," he says. "No matter how hard you try, it's going to happen. He'll strike again and again. That's why he wrote the letter. He wants everyone to know what he can do . . . what he *will* do again."

"What do you make of Right Places being capitalized? Seems blatant, overt. I think it's a reference to wherever she's buried. I'm sure the authorities are already looking for a road called Right Place."

"Smart girl."

"Like I said, it's overt."

"He thinks the cops are idiots," he says. "Thinks they won't figure it out. But they will. They always do."

"Yeah, but will they figure it out in time to save Skyler?"

"That's the real trick, ain't it?"

This guy can't—or won't—help. And judging by the way he's staring me down, he's getting much more out of this conversation than the police will.

"It's been great catching up," I say. "But I have to go—"

"I suppose you aren't interested in hearing about the dolls."

Chills pass over me. My finger hovers over the "Exit" button. "What dolls?"

"Your mother could tell you, if she were feeling better."

"Well, she's not. So stop wasting time."

"You'll visit again?"

"Is that what it's going to take?"

"Your mother used to."

I wonder if that's true.

For a few seconds, he stares at me in silence.

Finally, he clears his throat. "For years after you came back, in the weeks between your birthday and the anniversary of your recovery, someone left a doll in the exact place you were taken from. Your mother reported it, but nothing ever came of it. Find out who left the dolls, and you'll find the guy responsible." He smiles. Waves. My screen goes blank.

I look out a window, toward the ravine. I wonder if the guy responsible also left a doll at the scene of my mother's accident. Maybe he thought it was me in the SUV that night. Maybe he's back for me.

Cecily

"I want her home for Christmas." Trevor always did the talking when we agreed to speak with reporters. "Her birthday is Christmas Eve. We need her home. If you have her, just bring her back. Drive her to the park, and make sure she's warm. We'll take it from there. No questions asked. We aren't interested in revenge. We only want our daughter back. And, Holly, if you come home, we'll have your favorite for Christmas dinner: macaroni and cheese."

Her fifth birthday faded to Christmas morning without a sign of her, but we visited the park, anyway, just in case.

"There's a doll." I pointed to the dense brush on the park's east end. "Call the police. They'll dust it for prints."

"Cecily," Trevor said. "People have been leaving dolls here for months." And under his breath he muttered something about how I'd know it, if I hadn't been so unabashedly wasted all the time.

No one paid any attention to the doll. Not then, and not when I'd call every other time a doll happened to turn up.

They'd believe me now, if I could get through to them. They'd take Paul aside. They'd ask him to explain.

CHAPTER 18
HOLLY

June 7

Guidry calls shortly after my video visit comes to a close. He thanks me for speaking with Kohlbrook, then jumps right into the reason for his call:

"Have you spoken with Katherine Hershey?"

"Earlier."

"I'd like to talk to her about what happened the day you were taken. See if maybe her perception has changed."

What he doesn't say: he wants to ensure our stories match up regarding the little bottle I stole from the Moonbeam.

"I can give you her mobile number."

"I have it."

Of course he does.

"Went well with Kohlbrook, I think."

"Not that I want to make a habit of it," I say, "but if you think it might help for me to talk to him again . . ."

"I'll let you know."

"Do you know what he's talking about?" I ask. "The dolls?"

"My team is pulling all reports your mother may have made," he says. "But I've already got my hands on the most recent."

"How recent?" I ask. "Five, ten years ago?"

"Last Christmas. And then a couple of months ago."

My heart sinks. To think this case has preoccupied my mother so thoroughly that even after twenty years, she still visits the park to see if someone left a doll . . .

"There was a doll at the scene of her accident yesterday, too."

"Hmm."

"Maybe it's still there. If it's relevant . . ."

"What kind of doll was it?"

"An expensive one. The kind that feels like a real baby."

"No detective thought the dolls were relevant to your case, especially with Kohlbrook in prison," Guidry says. "But now that we're looking at the cases of these other girls, it's hard not to see common threads between the day you were taken and the dolls in the park."

"For example?"

"The dolls . . . according to your mother, they're posed on their sides."

"Just like Gretchen," I say. And just like the one I remembered in the glimpse of the past yesterday morning. *Drink your juice.* I shake free from the memory before it takes hold of me again.

"And the dolls are dressed in white," Guidry adds. "Just like you were when you were recovered, and just like Gretchen."

It's more proof. More fuel to back up the claim in the manifesto that either the same sicko who took me went on to take more girls, or there's someone out there copying the crime.

"Your parents received this photograph while you were gone, too. There. Just texted it over."

My phone blips, and I open Guidry's text.

"It's me." I'm dressed in a white nightgown, posed on my side, with hands folded beneath my cheek. I'm lying on a mattress, but there are no discernible details of the room I'm in.

"And . . ." He clears his throat. "There's been a development in one of the other cases. About an hour ago, just after you left the precinct, I got a call from authorities in West Des Moines, Iowa."

"What happened?" I almost don't want to know. I'm not used to praying, but I do so now. *Let Skyler Jane be okay.*

"They recently located remains of a female child, aged approximately three to six years old. Missing a lower central incisor."

"Oh no." I have to sit down. "Is it Skyler?"

"No. The remains are skeletal, and authorities in Iowa estimate they've been there ten to fifteen years."

I scan the time line. Iowa, Iowa, Iowa . . . "Enna Scotsman?"

"That was the initial thought, but Enna's permanent lower central incisors had already begun to come in at the time of her abduction, and these bones had no sign of that. Based on clothing remnants buried with them, the remains are thought to be Deanna Renee Rhine, abducted from a park near Minneapolis."

Tears burn my eyes. I struggle to draw in a breath.

"She was posed on her side prior to interment. Hands folded under her cheek. One leg bent over the other."

Just like Gretchen.

"God." I hiccup over a sob, which I try to stifle.

"She was found outside West Des Moines in a rural field on a road locally known as Right Pass."

I think of the letter sent to news outlets in Los Angeles, Chicago, and New York, and the words *Right Place(s)*. "He was taunting authorities with the location in his letter."

"Yes," Guidry confirms. "We have reason now to take those taunts seriously."

"And the remains weren't divided, so he wasn't talking about one girl buried in several places. He was probably talking about more than one girl."

"That's right."

There's one more line in that letter that raised suspicion: *the truth of what happened to the Hag.* I'm afraid to ask if they've decided it's a reference to me or ruled it out.

"And there's one more thing. Authorities were led to the location after a motorist reported seeing a baby on the side of the road. It turned out to be a posable silicone doll. It seems he marked the grave with it."

I wonder if the doll I saw yesterday marks the ravine for the same reason. No one died there. But was that where he'd intended to end my life? Did someone leave a doll at the ravine to mark what was supposed to be my grave?

Cecily

After he stopped me from falling into the ravine, I saw Kohlbrook frequently. It was as if my near suicide brought us closer together, bonded by the secret we shared.

He came to the house often, after work and on weekends, whenever Trevor and Susan were off sharing sweat and secrets of their own.

He met us at the park one day . . . the same park from which my daughter was stolen.

And I've often wondered if what I told him during those visits made it easier for him to do what he did. I wonder if it implicates me in the process.

Was I an accessory to my daughter's abduction? Did I say something during one of those secret meetings to put a plan in motion?

One day, when we were in the park, Holly found a doll. It was one of those like a newborn baby. I allowed her to play with it during our stay, but when it came time to leave, I insisted she leave it where she found it, in case its owner returned for it. It was an expensive toy. I was sure someone would be missing it before long.

Naturally, Holly threw a tantrum, and I was powerless to stop her screaming. She drew stares, it seemed, from miles.

Later, after she'd been taken, mommies recalled the spectacle and marched into the police station to report it.

I'm not sure it matters, but last week at the park, I saw that woman and her daughter, the girl who's missing . . .

They told the police I'd shouted at her.

She said things you shouldn't say to a kid.

I don't remember what I said, but I know that before long, Holly and I both were crying. I dropped my head into my hands, fell to the grass, and sobbed. My shoulders shook, my head ached.

Alan Kohlbrook picked me up that day.

He held my hand at the picnic table while I cried.

He held Holly on his lap, and the three of us had a tea party.

I didn't know at the time about his urges.

But I let him hold her on his lap.

Those mommy-vultures told the cops about that, too, once Kitten pointed him out in a lineup.

Look. If I'd known he had a penchant for young girls, do you think I would've let him anywhere near my kid?

Alan Kohlbrook was there for me the way no one else was. He is perhaps the only person who knew the extent of my depression, of my secret desire to die.

Alan Kohlbrook is the only person I told about my sole reason for staying alive: to avoid Susan and Trevor raising Holly as their own. I was honest with him. I didn't think I was suited for the job, either, but I didn't want to give my husband and Susan the satisfaction.

Maybe Kohlbrook thought Holly would have been better off away from the drama about to unfold.

"Something this precious doesn't deserve to be caught in the middle," he said.

A few short days later, she was gone.

In her place lay the doll.

The police asked about it: "Witnesses say she was playing with it. But it isn't hers?"

"It's been here for days. Someone must have left it."

No one in our small town came forward to claim the doll.

"Witnesses say they overheard you threaten to, quote, *sell your daughter to the gypsies*, so you could have a normal life. Can you explain why you'd say such a thing?"

I tried to explain that when Holly was kicking and screaming, in public, no less, there was no consoling her. I was embarrassed and upset. And, as they'd soon learn, I'd been drinking.

If I hadn't said those words, however, I wonder if they would have considered the doll as evidence and dusted it for prints. If I was right, if the doll was meant to lure Holly away from me, maybe Kohlbrook's prints would have been on it, or maybe the cops would have found someone else's.

It hardly matters now.

I didn't say things normal moms say to their children, so I was a villain, and my daughter stayed gone for ninety-four agonizing days.

CHAPTER 19

Holly

June 7

Sterling's phone rings incessantly, but he hasn't answered a call or text since he explained his niece's birthday trumped being a responsible dog owner.

I leave another message. "I have plans tonight. When are you coming home from Indiana? Your dog misses you." I hang up.

Dog follows at my heels as I pace about my apartment.

"Do you think he's innocent, Mom?" I ask. "Is that why you reported seeing the dolls in the park after Kohlbrook was found guilty?"

I let the question simmer, as if she'll answer me from her bed thirty-nine miles away, as if I'd hear her even if she did.

"You were gone in March," I say. "We know you didn't go where you said you went. Where did you go? Were you doing what Guidry assumes? Were you cheating on Dad? So much is happening. They found another girl—"

Knock, knock.

I stop in my tracks and look toward the door.

"Holly?"

"Matt." Is it already time to meet Kitten and Eliot on the bluffs? I go to the door and open it.

He enters with caution and a twelve-pack of bottled beer dangling from his hand. "Do you have company?"

"No."

"I heard you talking to someone."

"Oh. *That.*" I take a deep breath and wipe another tear from my cheek. I can't stop the random tears. Just when I think I get them under control, another round gears up.

"Are you okay?"

"They found another girl, Matt. They think whoever killed her might be the same guy who took me. If they're right, it means he probably killed most of the others. I have to wonder: Why did he let me go? Why *me* of all people?"

"You can't think of it that way. You can't begin to understand how someone who could do something like that decides who should live and die. Maybe you were meant to survive to help figure out who's doing this."

"There's a whole lot of *diem* I've yet to *carpe*, if you know what I mean. I'm sure not the type singled out for a higher purpose."

"I'm not so sure about that." He takes a seat at my island and cracks open a couple of beers—one for me, one for him.

"My mom used to say I was destined for more. I've been talking to her a lot lately, and I'm starting to feel as critical of myself as she always was. Maybe she's rubbing off on me. And how crazy is that? I talk to her like she's here."

"I had a few conversations, myself, in the desert."

"Here's to insanity." I clink my longneck to his. "Who'd *you* talk to?"

"Honestly?" He looks at me for a second in a way that pricks the hair on the back of my neck. "You."

My beer suspends halfway to my mouth for a split second—"Me? Why?"—before I bring it all the way home.

"You'd just sent an email. Told me you met Sterling. You wrote about that boat trip to Mackinac."

I remember the note. I'd been writing to him for years, but it was the first time since I was about twelve that I treated Matt like an older brother instead of a potential boyfriend.

"It was different." He takes a pull off his beer. "I didn't like it."

I probably should leave it at that.

But if I could let sleeping dogs lie, I wouldn't be digging into the (officially solved) mystery of my abduction twenty years after it happened.

"Why?"

His forehead crinkles with the frown he wears when he's analyzing something. "I think it was because you said he remembered the day you were kidnapped."

So what? I want to say. Lots of people remembered it. It's not like that sort of thing happens all the time in the Chicago suburbs, and my case garnered national attention. Sterling, like Matt, was a teenager when it happened. It stands to reason he'd be familiar with the story.

"You said he knew a lot about the case. He followed the news when it was happening. You said it made you feel like you'd known each other a long time."

The warm and fuzzy feeling returns to me now. It had been a relief not to have to explain that yes, I'm the same Holly Adryenne Gebhardt who was taken all those years ago. And no, I don't have any recollection, but this is what they say happened . . .

"It made you feel comfortable," Matt says. "Like he cared and understood what you'd been through. But the thing about feeling comfortable . . . sometimes you feel comfortable in a bad situation because you're used to it. It's comfortable because it's familiar. Not because it's good for you."

I'm about to ask him how he presumes to know what's good for me, but he cuts me off.

"I had a bad feeling about it. Like he knew too much about it, or like he thought you were some sort of anomaly. Or that he was getting close to you for information about what you'd been through—given his job, and all."

"That's not the type of research he does," I remind Matt. "He mostly analyzes numbers and stats and things like that. For business and stock market trades."

"Still. He does that for a *news outlet.* What could stop him from writing some exposé about you? To get a leg up in his career? And you were so blind to the possibility, and I was half a world away, so I couldn't exactly warn you about it, and—"

I straighten. "*Warn* me? Like I'm too dense to realize when a guy's using me?"

"I don't mean that you couldn't take care of yourself. I just mean—"

"That's what it sounded like."

"It rubbed me the wrong way, is all."

"You weren't here. You didn't meet him."

"Exactly my point. *No one's* gotten to know him except Kitten, and she doesn't have many good things to say about him. And my sister's a terrible judge of character. She likes *everyone,* but even *she* doesn't like him. Your dad says he's met the guy a handful of times but can't get a sense of what he's like. Sterling is not invested in you the way he should be."

"News flash, Hershey: *no one* is."

"You're good enough to dog sit when he needs you, but will he be there for you when *you* need *him*?"

"I don't need you to tell me another man is falling short," I say. "You don't get to arrive here with discharge papers and tell me how it is. You've been gone half my life."

"I've been gone, yes, but I think you'll agree it was for a pretty noble cause. Where's he been the past couple of days, while you're tearing through everything that happened twenty years ago? Consumed in his own world, that's where."

As if on cue, my phone chimes with Sterling's text alert, a measure of Ozzy Osbourne's "Crazy Train":

> Researching a project I think you'll find interesting. Be in touch soon. Take care of the dog?

Matt and I both shut up at the same time, locked in a staring contest.

"Touché," I say. I stare at Sterling's text.

"See what I mean?" Matt asks. "Everything's on his terms."

Simultaneously, our phones alert.

"Kitten," we both say.

Her text to both of us: Coming?

He offers a hand. "Truce?"

"Truce." I tap my fingers against his palm, then hit the back of my hand to his on the backswing.

Without another word, we exit with Dog on a leash between us. An awkward silence hangs between us as we make our way to the bluffs.

I don't like the icy feeling. Why I was defending Sterling is beyond comprehension, for starters. And I had no right to infer that Matt, himself, has been falling short of obligations when he's been serving our country.

He finally breaks the silence: "You okay?"

"I'm sorry I said that. I just . . . with my mom and the case—"

"Hey." He catches my hand in his. "I just want you to be happy."

"What is *this*?"

I pull my hand from Matt's when I hear Kitten's voice.

She and Eliot already occupy a space on the rocky bluff, where we've been coming since childhood to welcome summer, celebrate Independence Day, and toast marshmallows at bonfires well into the autumn season. There's a fire burning, which Kitten must have built, as I can't imagine Eliot was ever a Boy Scout. His idea of a fire probably involves a light switch and a ceramic log.

I breathe in the scent of the forest beyond and the creek below in the ravine.

Home.

This place is germane to our existence in this town, practically synonymous with the sense of togetherness our families share, and I can't help but remember that Kitten is choosing to leave it for the sake of the man sitting next to her. Everything is about to change.

"Were you two *holding hands*?" Kitten asks.

"I don't know what you're talking about," Matt says.

"I *saw* it," Kitten persists.

"Just a peace offering."

"For what? Not taking her to the prom?" She plants her hands on her hips, and her red lips form a dramatic O. "Better late than never, huh, Holly?"

"And *you* . . ." Matt extends a hand toward Kitten's betrothed. "You must be the luckiest guy on the planet. Or the deafest. Can't figure which."

Eliot stands, but before he shakes Matt's hand, he slides his wire-framed glasses up his nose. Although he's wearing jeans for what might be the first time in his life, they're stiff and inky, and he's still sporting a crisp white button-down, the sleeves rolled to his forearms. On his feet are preppy leather sandals. Never has anyone seemed as out of place on the bluffs as this guy.

And while he's out of his element here, I can't help but see he's at least trying to fit in.

"Holly." He nods at me, too, and opens his arms for what can only promise to be an uncomfortable hug for the both of us.

I take half a step into it.

He squeezes my shoulder, and then it's over.

Not so bad, actually. I have to wonder if maybe I'd find him more pleasant and tolerable if I had my life together. If Sterling turned out to be someone I could spend the rest of my life with, for example, would I begrudge Kitten's decision to move in with this guy? To make a life with him? To *marry* him? I've assumed Eliot was smug and always looking down his nose at me, but what if it's really just that I'm bitter and envious that he turned out to be unafraid of commitment, ready to dive into forever, when I've been dating a guy who can't be bothered to take care of his own dog?

Kitten sidles up to Eliot and sinks against his body. He's tall and broad, and my best friend practically disappears in his tan arms.

"So . . . ," Matt says. "Are you two going to have kids?"

"Are you kidding?" Kitten says. "At least *four*. Isn't that right, babe?"

Eliot kisses the top of her head. "Whatever my girl wants."

I refrain from rolling my eyes.

"But *first*, the *wedding*." Once she raises the subject, there's no getting her off it. "Did you pick up your dress yet? We have to be at the tailor for fittings—"

"Tomorrow," I say. "I promise."

"And, Matt, you have to get measured for your tux. Trevor's gonna walk me down the aisle, but I need you there to seat the guests."

Matt helps himself to the bag of marshmallows his sister brought, pushes one onto the end of a toasting stick, and hands it to me.

But my gaze is drawn to the ravine in the distance, the bend around which my mother sped and lost control.

I wonder if the doll is still there, if Guidry was able to get to it in time to determine if it's evidence or coincidence.

Kitten and Matt rib each other, and Eliot laughs.

"Beer, anyone?" Matt's handing out bottles. "Familiar scene. It's like old times, isn't it?"

I remember back to a night like this, when our parents led us out to the bluffs at dusk to enjoy the sunset. The Hersheys and us. A pack of seven . . . or eight if Matt happened to bring along some company—a girl du jour, or even a buddy from the baseball team he played on.

We spent so much time together back then, but I can hardly picture Kitten's father now. It was as if he were lifted out of the equation the moment they found me in that park.

"The police say my mother and your dad talked the day of the accident," I blurt out. "I didn't even know they were still in touch."

"We all know *how* to reach him," Kitten says. "The point is that we wouldn't *want* to after what he's done . . . or what he hasn't, as the case may be. He's ignored every major milestone in our lives."

"Yeah," I say. "But you know, my mom's screwed up quite a bit, too. She missed graduation, remember? But still . . . I can't imagine getting married without her there."

"Do you want Dad involved, Kitten?" Matt asks. "It's not too late. I bet if I call him—"

"I don't think so," Kitten says. "He gambled away your college tuition."

"Oh, we're talking about that in public these days?"

"I tell Eliot *everything*. He already knows about our deadbeat dad. You don't get to do the things he did and call yourself a father, am I right?"

Conversation continues between the siblings, but thoughts of the doll at the ravine distract me. Deanna Renee Rhine was found in Iowa, the resident state of Enna Scotsman. I wonder if the killer was marking a location close to my home as a place to bury another of the victims. Maybe my mother saw something. Maybe that's why she started drinking again. And the fact that she spoke to Kitten's estranged father the very same day it happened . . .

I burn my marshmallow.

I shove it between grahams with a slab of chocolate and eat it, anyway.

Or maybe my mother will simply *always* drink. Maybe it's the only way to carry on after everything we've been through.

I finish my beer.

Eliot offers me another.

"My mother." I realize a moment too late that Matt was about to say something and I cut him off. "She had a knack for interrupting the most serene of nights with her cacophonic bullshit, didn't she?"

Kitten leans to Matt. "How much did she drink before you came?"

"Please," I say. "I'm *fine*, and you tell Eliot *everything*."

Kitten tries again. "Out of respect for your mother—"

"Since when do I have to censor myself *here*?"

"Not on my account." It's the first time Eliot says something that doesn't totally annoy me.

We share a glance.

Maybe he's not 100 percent stick-in-the-mud.

"I'm just wondering why no one ever called her on it," I say.

"She wasn't the same after it all happened," Kitten says. "None of us were."

It's nice of Kitten to give my mother the benefit of the doubt, but . . . "I'm talking about a night before I was taken, when Mom stood up in the middle of a verse of 'Kumbaya.'"

I glance at Matt, at Kitten. When they don't hold my gaze, I know they remember the night in question.

If you think I'm gonna sit here an' preten' nothin's wrong . . . preten' I don't see . . .

She tossed a half-drunk bottle of beer into the fire and turned toward home. *Well I do. So I won't. Not for a single second.*

Dad got quiet, but still, we stayed out on the bluffs and enjoyed the night sky. After a while, someone started singing the next verse, and the evening resumed as if my mother hadn't interrupted at all.

"Here's my point," I say. "She wasn't always like that, but she didn't start drinking because of the kidnapping. If none of that had happened, would you be saying things like *out of respect for my mother*? Or would you be talking about her the same way you talk about your dad?"

Matt's knee brushes against mine. "Holly—"

"The detective I've been talking to . . . he hinted the cops thought she had something to do with what happened. Or that she knew something about it. And all I can think about is that there were signs. She was *different.* She had secrets. Did you know she'd been visiting Alan Kohlbrook in prison?"

"Holly." Matt's hand lands on my knee. "Let's take a walk."

Maybe he thinks I wouldn't be saying these things unless I were drunk.

Really, I'm just tired of no one talking about it in front of me.

"Why would she do that?" I ask. "Why, unless he was the only one who'd listen to her? What if she knew that what they all assumed about my kidnapping was bullshit?"

"Let's take a walk," Matt says again.

And now they're embarrassed of what I might say because they think my words are influenced by how much I've had to drink.

"I just don't want you to say something you'll regret," he says.

I'm not out of line.

These things should be said.

"You stay." I pick up Dog's leash. "I'll go."

"Holly, come on," Matt says.

"I'm *fine.*"

I hear Kitten's whisper as I walk away: "She doesn't usually drink that fast."

She's making excuses for me the same way Dad used to make excuses for Mom. *She's had a rough day. It's the hormones. It's my fault; I set her off earlier.*

I sip my beer and walk farther down the bluff until I put enough distance between us that they can't see me. I cop a squat on a rock and stare out over the ravine.

Tell me what you know, Mom. Help me understand what you were going through.

The conversation from above carries down.

Matt: "She's fine, Kitten. You have no idea what she's been dealing with today."

"Yes, I do. That cop called me and asked if I knew Holly stole something from the Moonbeam. She took a box from Vera's place the other day, too."

"I'd rather not talk about this now."

I hear the words Matt doesn't say: that he'd prefer to keep *my* shortcomings out of Eliot's ears, too.

"Her mom's in a coma, and if she's not careful, she's heading for the same fate. She's drinking too much, Matt."

Maybe I am.

As if proving Kitten's point, I gulp down another healthy sip.

Dog perks up and walks to the edge of the bluff. She lets out a bark and happily wags her tail. A flash of light reflects from the ravine. Someone is parked at the curve again, but it's not a blue truck.

I recognize the black crossover idling there—Sterling's.

Before I'm on my feet, however, the world spins.

Whoa.

I sit back down.

I count my drinks. A bourbon at home during my video visit with Kohlbrook, a beer with Matt on the way to the bluff, two since we met Kitten there.

I count the hours—less than two.

Yeah, Mom. That's too much, all at once.

But still . . . I shouldn't be feeling like this.

I close my eyes.

The world turns black.

CHAPTER 20

Holly

June 8

Everything's fuzzy, from the light shining through the slivers my eyes have become to my numb fingers.

My eyes are heavy. I can't open them.

I don't know where I am.

Where's the dog?

What time is it?

I try to say the words, but it's like I'm in a deep sleep and I just can't wake up.

"Are you all right?"

The voice is familiar, but I can't quite place it.

"Holly?"

In the periphery I hear Dog's distinct, sharp bark.

I peel my eyes open, but everything is blurry.

"Are you with me?"

I focus on a hand but only for a moment before my eyes close again.

I've seen that hand before. When?

Concentration brings an image to the forefront: a tooth in a pool of bloody drool. *Lucky girl.*

Is it the same hand?

Can't tell.

I feel something soft, like flannel or some sort of cloth, beneath my hand. I close my fingers around it. I feel a button . . . I'm gripping someone's sleeve.

"Come on, Holly."

I peel my eyes open and glimpse the hand again. This time, the scar on the back of it registers.

Vellerman?

But no sooner than I see his face, the world fades to black.

Don't cross.

The whisper reverberates in my brain, along with the flash of a silhouette in the dark.

I feel the world shifting beneath my feet.

Everything is fuzzy and out of focus. But this time I don't fight for clarity. I sink into the blurriness.

Close my eyes.

A bumpy road.

Drink your juice, Holly-Dolly.

I'm in a truck of some sort.

A peeling painted sign. The letters *P* and *H.*

It feels like only a blink later that I'm squinting into the sunlight pouring into my bedroom. I bring a hand to my forehead, which pounds with the force of a thousand framing nailers.

I sit up.

Oh no. If it's this light out, I'm going to be late for work again.

When my feet hit the floor, it's like pins and needles dig into my heels and toes. What happened to me last night?

I took a walk with Dog, intending to cool off after Kitten started judging me, and the next I knew . . .

Sterling's car was at the ravine.

And Vellerman . . . was he there on the bluffs?

Or was that a dream?

How did I get from the bluffs back home?

Don't cross.

You'll fall, Holly-Dolly.

I pull myself out of bed.

Why can't I remember?

My stomach churns.

This isn't right. Even with what I drank, I shouldn't be feeling this sick, this unsure of what happened. I shouldn't be missing half the night.

All I can think about now, however, is that it happened twenty years ago, too.

I was jumping rope.

I blinked.

Drink your juice.

And suddenly it was winter, and my father was holding me, apologizing, promising everything was going to be all right.

Through the fog in my mind, a light bulb clicks on.

This has been happening lately, since my mother's accident, for certain. Maybe even a few times in the months leading up to it.

The toxicology reports told us the reason why I didn't remember back then.

Standing upright, I shiver. It's happening again. What if whoever kidnapped me knows me now? Maybe he knows me very well. Maybe he's been watching me.

Drugging me.

Waiting for me to be incapacitated before he finishes what he started twenty years ago.

But who could it be?

Vellerman has been around about as long as I've had this problem, and if I saw him last night, maybe he's involved. He's been creepy, to say the least, and I knew the second I met him he was an asshole. He has a scar, and he was interested in mine. Not to mention, he drives a blue truck, and someone in a large blue vehicle may have nudged my mother over the edge of the ravine. And Mom . . . the night before the accident, she was adamant that she didn't want me on the concept house crew. Did she know Vellerman was the foreman? I assumed she was gushing out her usual opinions about wanting more for me than physical labor. But what if she just didn't want me near Vellerman? What if she knew something about him?

It's possible.

He's been showing up lately where I least expect to see him—at Kitten's black-and-white party, for example. But he's not the only one. Sterling's been coming and going as he pleases a lot lately, too.

Sterling and I broke up around the time of the accident. I'd swear that he was poking around the ravine last night, and by strapping me with his dog, he knows I can't stray too far. Maybe he was taunting me with the message hinting at a project I might be interested in.

The horror of possibility cloaks me. What if his project was *me*? He's brilliant . . . too brilliant to be stuck at his level, researching for other writers. What if he prefers the menial position so he has time to be on the road, so he has time to kidnap and stash girls around the Midwest? I pull out Guidry's time line.

The kidnapper would have needed time on his hands to cover this kind of ground. And this radius . . . I can't remember the last time Sterling traveled outside of it. What's more, he knew everything about my ordeal before we even met. I think hard. Was there anything he knew that most people didn't?

My mind is a scramble. I can't focus, can't remember. And my head is pounding!

"Oh, God." I pace around my kitchen island, putting possible pieces of the puzzle together. Sterling kept a careful distance from my parents. Was there a reason for that? Last Christmas, for example, he came back to town a day late. I asked if he was still coming to my parents' place for dinner, and he danced around the answer, ended up not coming . . . He bailed on my family's gatherings every time. Was he afraid one of them might remember seeing him twenty years ago?

I talk it out with Mom: "And then there's Matt's point: sometimes when something feels comfortable, it's because it's familiar, not because it's good for you. And I think we can all agree that Sterling isn't exactly *good* for anyone."

I sink into a chair at my island and queue up my text thread with Sterling. Maybe he'll have a good excuse for being at the ravine last night, especially when he told me he was still working. I scroll through our messages, which have become sparse in the months since we broke up.

I pause at the link he sent. He asked me to weigh in on a gift for his seven-year-old niece, but I'd never replied. Hesitantly, I click on it.

"Oh, God!" I drop my phone, but when I retrieve it, the web page is still there: *Real Life Dolls.*

Have I been sleeping with my captor?

My hands are numb. It can't be true.

Twenty years ago, he would have been eighteen, the younger end of the profile spectrum but still in the realm. He's moody when he returns from his trips. A couple of months ago, he was especially distant—which coincided with the kidnapping of Skyler Jane Kipniss. Not to mention, he's been elusive since. Could he be popping in and out of my life because he's tending to a little girl he's holding captive?

Skyler was taken from the Indianapolis area. Sterling's brother lives in South Bend. How far apart are the cities?

I open my laptop to search for the answer. My mother's password-retrieve questions are still displayed on the monitor.

Monet. My mother's voice sounds in my head. *The cat's name was Claude Monet.*

It's like Psychic Yanneth said—it's an echo of the past.

I type it in—*Claude Monet*—and much to my surprise, I suddenly have access to my mother's email.

I scan through the senders in her in-box. Most emails are from vendors, and as she's been asleep for nearly two months, she has more than two hundred unopened messages. I don't see any evidence that she's been corresponding with a man other than Dad.

Unless she's hiding the messages elsewhere, or instantly deleting them, Guidry was way off base with his assessment Mom may be having an affair.

My eyes go directly to the dock on the left side of the page, where a folder is labeled with four question marks.

I click on it, and a list of messages appears. Each has a nondescript subject line: *FYI*, *Seen this before?*, *Thought you should know . . .*

They're all from different addresses. I click on one, and a picture fills the screen.

I cover my gasp. I'm looking at a lock of hair, blonde, tied with a pink ribbon. The text accompanying it reads, Are you going to do something about this?

I click on the next message. Another lock of hair. Are you going to do something about this?

The next, and the next, and the next . . .

In all, there are ten pictures of locks of hair, most blonde, some brown. Exactly like the list of girls in the manifesto. The most recent is a white blonde. It was attached to an email sent to my mother a day after Skyler Jane was taken.

I open another window and pull up a picture of the missing girl and confirm the hair color matches.

Whoever sent them either followed my case closely and wanted to taunt my mother for tampering with my hair twenty years ago, or has direct knowledge of each little girl named in the manifesto.

I pick up the phone and dial.

"Detective Guidry? It's Holly Gebhardt. There's something you need to see."

CHAPTER 21

Holly

June 8

The detective arrives armed with information.

"For several years, your mother reported these emails." He pulls out a stack of copied reports dating back twenty years. "Nothing ever came of the reports."

"How is that possible?"

"First, you have to understand the cases weren't linked, and very often when tokens like these locks of hair are sent, it isn't something we're broadcasting over the news in active investigations, so there was no way for Lake County PD to link your mother's reports with what was happening in cases in other municipalities. Looks like they traced the first couple of emails to public libraries, but there was no link between one message and the next. Different addresses, different libraries, different cities. The general consensus is that someone was bothering your mother. The emails didn't come often enough for anyone to take her complaints of harassment seriously, I'm afraid, especially considering her general condition when she reported the emails."

I glance at the report: *Complainant is intoxicated, slurring.*

I draw my own conclusion: they all thought she deserved the harassment.

"But now that we know . . ." Guidry's intentions hang in the air.

You were onto something, Mom, I silently tell her. *I'm sorry no one listened to you.*

"We're working on cross-referencing the emails. The first came from the Hammond Library, downtown Chicago."

I wonder aloud: "Did any of the other girls' mothers receive emails like this?"

Guidry shakes his head. "Some investigators still think there's a reason Cecily was the only one."

"You don't mean you think my mother's involved in all this? That she knew not only about *my* kidnapping but all these others?"

Guidry clears his throat. "*I* don't necessarily subscribe to the theory. Why would she report it if she were involved? But some cops think she reported as a measure of remorse. It happens often, with female subjects accused of aiding and abetting." He gives the stack of reports a shove closer to me, as if in invitation to read them.

I've seen enough. Regardless of my mother's addiction to alcohol, these are tall accusations, and she doesn't deserve it. "And what about Sterling? Am I completely off base?"

"Well, here's where it gets interesting. Do you know where Sterling was the day you were kidnapped?"

"He once told me he and a friend came out to Lake Bluff to help search for me."

"He was a freshman in college at the time. Do you know where?"

"UIC."

"That's right. Not far from the Hammond Library."

My heart sinks and splashes in my empty gut. I wonder if he's been drugging me. I open my mouth to raise the possibility just as Guidry opens another file. What I see there silences me.

"I think you'll agree that there are similarities to our composite sketches of the kidnapper." He lays out color copies of pictures of my ex-boyfriend's driver's license photos dating back twenty years. "This is the sketch our artist rendered after speaking with Katherine Hershey after you were taken, and this"—he points to one of the photos—"is Sterling at the time. The hair in particular . . ."

There are similarities, for certain, but lots of guys wore their hair in haphazard spikes with frosted tips back then. My dad, at thirty, did. Matt did, too.

"Here's our second composite sketch, a few years later, after Enna Scotsman's abduction. Longer hair." He points. "And here's Sterling at twenty-one."

His hair, and there's a lot of it, swoops down over his forehead, just like the suspect in the sketch.

"And, Holly . . ."

"Yeah." I meet the detective's gaze.

"He fits the profile. We've always thought whoever took you returned to the scene. It's one of the reasons we centered on Kohlbrook. Given you're the only survivor, thus far, in the lot, it makes sense he'd insinuate himself into your life now."

The thought is positively chilling.

"The last time his phone registered wasn't far from here. He could be watching you even now. Maybe he'll respond if you invite him for a drink."

Just as I'm about to protest, Guidry continues: "You won't actually go. *I* will. We need to draw him out."

"He hasn't been responsive lately, but . . ." I dial Sterling's number. It rings a few times, then goes to voice mail.

"When was the last time you saw him?"

"I think I saw him last night. At the ravine." The blurry events flash in my mind again: Sterling at the ravine, Vellerman . . .

And that's another conundrum altogether. What was Vellerman doing there? And was it coincidence that he showed up at the jazz club? "My foreman hasn't called to see why I'm not on-site. I should've been to work hours ago." I fill Guidry in on the recent messages asking me to go for a drink, the inquiry about the scar on my arm, and his strange appearances. "And lately, I've been waking up with blackouts—pieces of the night missing. I think someone might be drugging me. It could be coincidence, but it's strange."

"You think it's this Vellerman?"

"I don't know *who* it is, but—"

"First, let's get your blood drawn today." He scribbles *flunitrazepam* into his small notebook, then tears out the sheet and hands it to me. "Have them check for this drug and variations of it. Once we learn *if* it's happening, we'll concentrate on who. I'll put someone on Vellerman," he says. "But I'm going to track down Derrion Sterling."

"You'll let me know when you find him?"

"Of course. In the meantime, you shouldn't be alone. Is there someone who could go with you to get your blood drawn?"

I look across the fields to Susan Hershey's place and hope her son and I are still friends after last night. "Yeah. I'll call Matt."

"Will you do me a favor? Share your location with me."

I meet his gaze.

"Someone's been following you, maybe even drugging you. I don't want to take any chances."

CHAPTER 22

Holly

June 8

I load my firearm, strap it to my ankle in a holster, and yank my denim pant leg over it. Like most people with a carry license, I pray to God I don't have to use it, but I'm not taking any chances. Next, I hook a leash to Dog's collar and head out to my truck.

I park the truck at my parents' place. If Sterling happens by, he'll think I'm inside the house. And if Sterling happens to be involved in this mess, I'm not interested in meeting him one-on-one.

But Dog and I head through the wildflowers to Susan Hershey's place, where Matt said he'd be packing.

I knock, then let myself in. "Matt?"

The kitchen looks nearly empty, if only because Susan isn't in it.

I follow the sounds of Led Zeppelin down the hallway to Matt's old room. Dog follows dutifully at my heels.

I knock on the open door.

"Hey." He looks up, does a double take. "Holly."

"Where's your mom?"

"Visiting yours, I think. Are you okay?"

"I don't know, exactly."

"What happened?" He relieves me of Dog's leash and offers me a seat, which I take on the edge of a moving box.

"I don't remember last night. I didn't remember your first night back, either."

He perches on the edge of his dresser. "Kitten's worried about you, you know. You're drinking . . ."

"I obviously had a bit to drink on both nights." Nerves kick up. My fingers close around an article of clothing in the box next to me. "But not enough for me to black out like that."

"You were drinking fast."

"But two nights ago, at Kitten's black-and-white party, you *didn't* have much to drink," I remind him. "You finished my whiskey, and your head was pounding the next morning. Seems severe for one whiskey, don't you think?"

"It was cheap whiskey. I hadn't had much to drink in a while." He chews his lip. "I don't want you to get defensive, Holly. I care about you, is all I'm saying, and I think you need help before this gets out of hand."

"It's already out of hand." But I'm not talking about my drinking. "I just need to know what happened last night. Did you see me with anyone else on the bluffs later on?"

"No." His brows knit together.

"So you don't know how I got home?"

"I assumed you walked the loop of the property and got yourself home."

I'm shaking my head.

"You left with the dog, heading south, and you didn't cross back. You were home when I checked on you about an hour later. Passed out in your clothes."

"You didn't see anyone with me? Sterling or . . . anyone else?"

"Why? What's going on?"

"I think someone might be following me. Drugging me. Waiting for me to pass out. There are a lot of nights I don't remember."

Every incident involved some sort of bourbon, maybe an energy drink, and an amnesia effect with blackout moments.

"Will you go with me to get my blood tested?"

"You really think someone's drugging you?"

"The detective I've been talking to seems to think whoever took me twenty years ago might still be out there," I explain. "Taunting me."

"Not on my watch." He's on his feet and closing the gap between us.

He crouches in front of me, his hands cupped on my knees.

Suddenly, I'm overaware of the heat emanating off his suntanned skin, the scent of his cinnamon gum. His voice softens. "I'm sorry I upset you yesterday."

"You didn't upset me."

"I did. I know you're capable of taking care of yourself, and if Sterling's what you want, I support that. It's just that lately, I've been thinking that if you're ready to be with an older guy . . . why shouldn't it be someone who's known you your whole life?"

My breath catches in my throat, and I grip more tightly to the garment I'm holding. "Matt . . ." It's hot in here. "Are you saying . . . What are you saying?"

"We can start small. Simple. I'm invited to a wedding next month. You free?"

"I think I'm invited to that wedding, too." Finally, I exhale. I laugh.

He laughs and embraces me.

I wrap my arms around him, pulling the item out of the box in the process.

"Now that that's out of the way . . ." He turns to gather another armful of pre-army clothing and in the process pulls out of my arms.

My eyes widen when I see what I'm holding.

Matt's still talking, but I can't hear anything beyond the beat of my heart deep in my ears. I can't breathe. I can't speak.

It's a child's romper. *My* romper. The one I was wearing the day I was taken.

I get to my feet.

I silently back into the hallway.

Why else would the romper be there, in a box in Matt's teenage bedroom, if it hadn't been there since the day I disappeared?

And it hits me . . . Who knows how long Matt's actually been in town? I already know he lied to Kitten and Susan about when he flew in; maybe he's been in town for months. He was there the night before I woke up wearing his T-shirt, and he was there the night of the black-and-white party, and at the bonfire last night. All nights I don't fully remember.

What's more, Matt already admitted he thinks Kitten lied about what she saw the day I was kidnapped. What if she lied about it being Kohlbrook because she couldn't comprehend her brother doing such a thing? He would've been young at the time. Almost seventeen. But he had a driver's license and access to his father's hunting cabin. I might have gone with him, stayed with him, willingly.

And according to the medical examiner reports, the kidnapper didn't lay a hand on me. Neither has Matt. Ever.

It doesn't make sense.

Why? Why would he do it?

Matt looks at me over his shoulder.

I glance at the romper in my hand, then back at him.

"Holly—"

I bolt.

Cecily

The package arrived the morning before Holly was taken.

Thick.

Stuffed with cash.

And a letter, unsigned, which the police later got ahold of. I don't remember what the letter said, exactly, but it alluded to schemes and revenge.

It helped paint me as a mastermind.

They thought I was hiding something.

I was, but not what they thought.

The day Holly was kidnapped, I'd planned to tell Trevor everything.

But something happened that morning that threw me off course.

Susan arrived at the doorstep with Kitten and invited us to go to the park.

There was something in her voice that impelled me to accept the invitation, and I knew before she pulled the sunglasses from her eyes that she was crying.

"Come in," I said.

"No, we'll wait out here."

I don't know if she felt funny entering my house because she was about to tell me that she'd been sleeping with my husband for the past however-many years or if she wasn't about to set foot in the house of a woman who'd screwed hers.

I didn't know what she knew or if she knew what I knew.

But I scooped up Holly, wrestled her tangled hair into a ponytail.

"It *hurts*," she said as I pulled at her snarls. "I want my doll."

"No, sweetie. We're not packing a bag. We won't be there too long."

"I'm hungry."

"Here." I shoved a sleeve of crackers into her hands, and before she told me she was thirsty, too, I found the juice box I had recently opened and gave her that, too.

I grabbed my keys.

I didn't have a pocket, and I was nervous with what was coming. I didn't want to bring a purse and a go-cup, so I pulled the house key off the ring of car keys without knowing what I'd do with it or where I'd carry it.

"Mommy? What's wrong?"

"Nothing." Between thoughts of Susan and Trevor, memories of what I'd stupidly done with Paul somersaulted through my brain. Tears sprouted in my eyes. *Calm down.* I braced myself against the counter and tried to take a deep breath. I pinched my eyes closed, and when I opened them, I saw a safety pin among the clutter on the countertop.

"Come here, Holly. Can you help Mommy today?" I turned out the pocket in Holly's romper and pinned the key there. "This is a very important job. You're the keeper of the key."

She grinned up at me, and I kissed her on the nose. More tears escaped me.

"Mommy? What's wrong?"

"Nothing." I splashed vodka over my lemonade.

Just a bit.

The cops' report made it sound like I was drunk the day it happened.

I wasn't.

But when they asked for the third time what I was drinking, I told them honestly: it was lemonade splashed with vodka.

The newspapers had a field day with that.

Negligent mother.

Drinking at the park just after noon.

Wasted and chatting while her daughter was plucked away at the hands of a psychotic predator.

I never set the record straight.

I never told them about my husband and my best friend.

I think that if they'd known the rest, they might have understood my negligence that day.

I should have told them about Susan and Trevor. Maybe I should have told them about Paul and me, too. But when the bottom fell out of my world, I couldn't bear sharing our private horrors with anyone.

We needed each other then, the four of us. Suddenly, the disintegration of two marriages wasn't nearly as important as keeping everyone focused on finding my daughter.

The only lie I told that day was that Susan and I were discussing Holly's fifth birthday party. I wanted to spare her the humiliation of the truth. She told me I was being a good friend; she didn't know I had my own selfish reasons for bending the truth.

It didn't really matter. The minds of the public were made up: I was an asshole.

Here's what people don't understand: the girls were fine.

Susan said very little on the walk to the park, but the moment we took a seat on the bench and the girls scampered to the pavement not fifteen feet away, she burst into tears.

"He wants a divorce."

"Why?" I could have guessed the answer. My head was spinning, and I kept waiting for it to come: the admission of guilt about her and Trevor, the accusation about Paul and me.

"He left this morning. He'll stay at the lake house for a while. He wants to finish remodeling it. I told him Trevor could help, but he said he already had someone else in mind. Can you imagine? It's like he's not only leaving me. He's leaving all of us."

I felt betrayed.

He was leaving me to deal with it all on my own and all because I'd decided one roll in the hay with him was one roll too many.

"He already left?" I asked for clarification. "Did he explain himself to the children? Matt will be devastated."

She squeezed my hand. "I'm grateful Matt has Trevor."

"What about you?" I asked. My words had an edge to them. I was challenging her to tell me that she, too, had Trevor to help her make the transition, but I instantly softened. "Maybe someday you can move on. You'll find someone else."

Silently, I prayed she'd do it quickly. *Find someone to replace my husband in your life.*

"I can't even think of dating right now! Cecily. What am I going to do?"

And then came Kitten's scream.

CHAPTER 23

Holly

June 8

Dog is far out ahead of me now, barking up a storm and causing a general ruckus. But Susan is gone to visit Mom in the ICU, and my dad's at work; there's no one to hear for miles.

I'm almost out of breath, and I keep tripping on the stems of the wildflowers as I part them, but I'm scrambling to my feet every time.

"Holly!" Matt grabs my arm, catching up to me.

I come back swinging.

He blocks and dodges and blocks again, but I keep coming at him until soon, we're all out grappling in the field.

Dog must sense the turmoil, because she's in on it, too, coming between Matt and me. Growling. Pushing me back and putting distance between me and him.

I don't know if it's survival instinct or anger or frustration or a mix of all three, but I keep advancing, punching, kicking.

"Holly! Stop!" After half a dozen blocked shots, Matt's arms go down, and he takes a hit on the right side of his jaw. *"Fuck."* He rubs the already-blossoming red spot.

I take advantage of the moment, crouch down, and place my hand on my ankle holster, ready to draw. I speak between heaving breaths: "You know I know how to use this."

He takes a step back and puts his hands in the air. "You won't have to. Holly, it's *me*. What's—"

"You were there," I say. "There when I was taken. It's why Kitten ID'd the wrong guy . . . she adored you and couldn't possibly tell the truth about it. Did your dad know? Is that why he's gone?" In my mind, they were all in on it—all the Hersheys, maybe even my dad. Thoughts race through my head at a speed so uncontrollable, I'm stumbling over them the way I tripped over the wildflowers. There's no time to determine what's real or perceived, possible or probable.

"I was a kid at the time, Holly."

"Just a year outside the profile."

"Holly." He takes a step closer.

I draw my firearm, but I don't yet aim. *"Don't move."*

He stills. "I loved you like you were my own sister. I didn't—"

"I was wearing a green-and-white romper the day I was taken." I scan the area for it when I realize I must have dropped it. It must be in the field somewhere.

The crease in his brow melts away, and his shoulders go lax. "Oh."

"And you just happen to have it in a box in your room for no reason."

"It's *Kitten's* old romper, and my *mother* put it there after coming across it in an old box in Kitten's room across the hall. She's making a quilt of all Kitten's favorite childhood outfits, costumes, even her prom dresses."

That sounds like something Susan would do.

"A wedding gift," he punctuates. "She didn't want the box to get mixed up in the stuff that's going to Goodwill."

But you never can be too sure when your life is on the line. His hands are up. His blue eyes plead with me.

"And now I'm remembering why we still have the damn thing," Matt says. "We gave it to the police. An exact description of what you were wearing . . . that day. They brought it back in a box, and it's been sitting there for twenty years."

I reholster.

His breath comes out in a relieved exhalation. "Jesus, Holly."

"Stay there." I put up a hand. It's a likely story, but it's equally probable and false at the same time.

"Holly. We can call my mom. She'll clarify."

"Stay there," I say again. "I'm gonna go. You stay here."

"Wait." He takes a step in my direction.

"No." I put up my hand again and back toward my parents' house. Dog scampers, leading the way. "I need you to stay here."

This time, he listens.

Tears burn my eyes by the time I arrive at my truck.

Dog jumps in, I follow, and I lock the doors.

A glance out the window confirms that Matt's planted right where I asked him to stay. Even when I drive away, he doesn't move.

"Mom. I don't know what to do," I say. "Do I believe him?"

In my mother's absence, I look to Dog, but she's no help.

"Well, when all else fails, why not ask a psychic?"

Dog lies across the bench seat and props her chin on my lap.

I dial.

"Yanneth, this is Holly Gebhardt. We met at the 7-Eleven?"

Cecily

"I don't understand how it happened right under your nose."

At the time, I figured Trevor was blaming me for losing Holly, as if I'd simply misplaced her when I went to the supermarket. Looking back at it, however, now that I've lived decades after something no mother thinks she can survive, I understand that Trevor was desperate for answers.

I'm still looking for answers, myself. When you survive an ordeal like that, it never leaves you.

Last Christmas, I dropped by Dew Point Park and found a doll abandoned near the slide.

The doll, not unlike the one that had been lying around the same park in the days before Holly was taken, appeared to be new . . . and it was clothed in a white nightgown and ruffled panties.

Exactly what Holly was wearing when we found her.

It wasn't the first doll to appear since her recovery, but it was the first I'd seen in years.

I hadn't been to Stateville prison to visit Kohlbrook for a long time, but I went that afternoon.

"I keep seeing these dolls," I told him. "It's been long enough, twenty years. Tell me honestly: Did you do this? Did you take my daughter?"

"I know you didn't have anything to do with it, Ceci, but the cops wouldn't leave you alone."

"Do you know who's leaving the dolls? The cops won't help. They think I'm a crazy drunk, a nuisance. But they're not paying attention. Things keep happening in the outside world, Al. Things that shouldn't happen because *you're* in *here*. Admit it once and for all: you didn't take my daughter twenty years ago."

He stared at me for what felt like minutes on end. Finally: "No."

"We have to do something, then. You're up for parole again next fall."

"I belong in here."

I'd known since the day they put him in that cell that Kohlbrook felt safer behind bars, where he couldn't act on his pedophiliac tendencies.

"The trouble is," I told him, "someone *else* belongs in here for the abduction of my daughter."

"I have a lawyer." He shrugged a shoulder and half smiled.

I softened to see the first glimmer of hope I'd seen in the man in twenty years.

"He's a young, hungry thing. Someone mailed him a manifesto detailing all the reasons I can't possibly be the one who did it."

"A manifesto?"

"It's gruesome. And the cops don't give a shit, anyway. They might take notice if the prediction at the end of the manifesto comes true. Another kidnapping. Let it be," Kohlbrook said. "Don't get involved."

But there was one detail hammering at me that made his advice impossible:

The dolls kept appearing on anniversaries of Holly's abduction, anniversaries of her return. And then, at random. The emails containing pictures of curls cut from little girls' heads kept coming, too, sometimes coinciding with sightings of the dolls. Every time, I'd call the police, but they paid me little attention. When a new picture would appear in my in-box, I'd conduct an internet search for missing girls, and every time, a new case popped up on the screen.

Who was sending the emails? Was it someone who simply hated me and wanted me to suffer? Or was it the man responsible for it all?

If the latter was the same party responsible for kidnapping Holly, Alan Kohlbrook shouldn't have spent a day behind bars . . . at least not for the abduction of my daughter.

But if he didn't do it, who did?

I kept coming back to one name: Paul Hershey.

The day Holly disappeared, Kohlbrook was on my doorstep, ready to help locate a child he was later convicted of stealing.

The whole town came together, but Paul scarcely made an appearance the entire time she was gone. He came twice—once the day I received Holly's hair and once more after that.

Could it be he was busy tending to Holly when the rest of us were attending candlelight vigils?

I didn't want to believe it, considering our history, considering the secrets I still harbored about the month before Holly was taken. I was hiding things for Paul's sake as much as mine. We were interlaced in our guilt, and if he was somehow responsible for my daughter's disappearance, it meant I was responsible, too, given our closely yoked pasts.

The police had long since stopped badgering me about what I knew; that stopped the moment suspicion fell on Alan Kohlbrook. But they still didn't know what I've been hiding for two decades.

Maybe if they knew, they'd consider Paul might be hiding more than I am.

Paul was gone when Holly was gone. He was gone, and other girls were disappearing.

And the prediction in the manifesto came to pass.

About a week after Skyler Jane Kipniss was kidnapped from a town near Indianapolis, a doll appeared at Dew Point Park.

I suppose that's why I was rattled when I encountered the psychic at the park that day.

"I see her," Yanneth said. "And I see *him*. Right here. This is where it happened, yes? Echoes of the past. I can help you find him."

She handed over a business card. "Please call."

I did make a call. I called the police, who assured me they'd look into it.

That night, I refrained from pouring a drink.

When Trevor arrived home after work and realized I was sober, we cried together for the disaster our marriage had become, for lost hope and crushed dreams.

He held me, torso to torso.

He kissed my head, then the tears from my eyes, my nose, my lips. And soon, passions ignited between us, and for the first time in a long time, I wrapped my legs around him.

He said that night, in the aftermath of sex, in a voice gravelly with sleep, "I know your secret."

I tensed in his embrace.

"I know you were pregnant when Holly was taken. I know about the baby."

"Trev."

Twenty years had passed, and not once had we discussed the pregnancy. I'd driven myself to the hospital. I delivered her seven weeks early, and I passed her to a nurse, who introduced her to her parents.

"I understand why you gave it up," he said. "We needed to be present for Holly."

I curled into the crook of his arm and let my tears fall onto his chest.

"It tore me up inside to think you'd decided to do it without asking me," he said, "but we weren't exactly a team back then, were we?"

I shook my head. "No, I guess we weren't." Confessions about Paul danced on the tip of my tongue, and as I looked at the love of my life, I decided he deserved to know everything. "Trev—"

"There's something about feeling like dying that makes me want to keep living. That's why we're still here together."

"I disagree." I looked up at him, but I was only watching him fall asleep. "Trev?"

His breathing was even, and he was out.

I snuggled in his side and whispered, "There's something about not knowing the truth that makes me want to disappear all over again."

CHAPTER 24

Holly

June 8

Matt called, but I didn't take the call.

Dad called, too. I've dumped calls from him to voice mail at least three times already. I can't explain to Dad right now why I didn't go to work, and I can't handle him trying to talk me out of keeping my appointment with Yanneth.

The address she provided me with is about an hour away, and by the time I near my destination, the weather has taken a turn.

I stop on the way for a deck of tarot cards and drive south of the city and down a winding path marked with a sign: **Xanadu Farms**. At the end of the path is a good-size cottage overlooking a pond. In the distance, the fields are dotted with outbuildings—stables, a barn. Psychic Yanneth sits on the covered front porch, knitting needles hard at work.

I park the truck next to a beat-up sedan. The rain is a heavy mist, the kind that this time of year hangs on your skin and doubles as sweat. But Yanneth seems unaffected and perfectly comfortable in another ankle-length dress and her skeins of yarn slowly weaving into a blanket in her lap.

Even when I get out of the truck, with Dog in tow, she continues to knit, acknowledging me with only a raise of a brow.

Dog and I climb the steps and find shelter at the far end of the porch.

"So you're finally ready to see shades of gray. It took your mother a while, too."

"You know my mother." May as well jump right in. "Why didn't you tell me that?"

She glances up at me. "Sit."

Dog, in a rare moment of obedience, listens. I don't.

A teenage boy appears at the doorway. "I'm out of minutes again. Can I *please* charge my normal phone?"

"You know better, and you know why."

"Jeezus."

"Read a book." She doesn't look up from her yarn. "Or better yet, write one."

"God. This fucking sucks," he mutters. "There's no internet out here without my phone as a hot spot."

"Language," she says over her shoulder. "Would you prefer to muck the stables?"

"Oh man." The teen walks away, swearing under his breath as he goes.

She then turns back to me. "Normally, I'd send him out to the fields to burn off some energy, but not in this rain. Will it ever end?"

"Raining cats and dogs," I say.

"Now, Holly, what can I do for you?"

I lean against a post on the porch, just out of the weather. "I'd like a reading." I take the cards, unsheathed and bound by a rubber band, from my bag and toss them to her.

She fumbles them but ultimately catches them. "I have my own cards, dear."

"Oh." I shrug. "I didn't know how it works, so—"

She smiles and extends them toward me. "Quite all right."

I open the bag they came in, and she slides them in. "Great place you have here."

"I grew up here. There's nothing like coming back to nature, don't you agree?"

"I grew up on acreage as well." After a moment, I get right to it: "I need to know who I can trust."

"It's all a question of faith, isn't it?"

"I don't have time for faith. And neither does Skyler Jane Kipniss."

"Skyler Jane Kipniss." Her eyes slant downward.

"She was taken March eighteenth, and the police seem to think that whoever took her might have had something to do with whoever killed that other little girl from Memphis."

"Oh my." She stands. "I think you'd better come in. You'll leave your dog on the porch?"

Cecily

By now, everyone knows how the investigation went.

High hopes dashed into harsh realities.

Crowds of people held candlelight vigils at the park.

A pile of stuffed animals and flowers and dolls grew to a mountain at the foot of our driveway.

But people have lives of their own to get back to.

Eventually, there was no news to report.

Eventually, there was nothing left to do but wait. Believe. Hope against hope.

Eventually, we emptied the casserole dishes, sure as our house emptied of visitors, as well.

Paul showed up alone in the sixth week after Holly's disappearance. He came during the day, when his kids were at school, when Trevor was on a site, when Susan was probably bringing a hot lunch to my husband.

"This package was on your doorstep."

"Thank you." I took the padded envelope from him.

My best friend's husband drew me into a long, warm hug. "You're a tower of strength," he said.

"I don't feel like one."

He pulled me in a little more tightly, then sharply pulled back. He took one look at my slightly protruding belly and knew what Trevor hadn't noticed in months.

"How far along are you?"

The secret wasn't mine anymore. I broke down in tears.

I hadn't realized I was pregnant until a couple of weeks after Holly's abduction. I hadn't had time to think about what I might do. My daughter's disappearance took my focus, gripped it with angry, frustrated hands, and wouldn't let go.

There wasn't time for me to deal with the pregnancy and all the drama that would come with it.

I was creating new life.

Something worth living for.

But I only felt like dying.

"Does Trevor know?" Paul asked.

"No one knows, and you can't tell a soul. The police already assume I wanted a way out of this life, and if they find out . . ."

The realization came to him: "It's mine."

"It doesn't matter." I would have the baby, but I wouldn't raise it. Mothers like me didn't deserve the blessings of children. "My family is all that I have. This secret will tear us apart even if Holly comes back. I can't survive that, do you understand? I can't keep this child."

"It doesn't have to be this way," he said. "We could make a life together. You, me, this baby . . ."

"Paul. No."

"And Holly."

At the time, I figured he was thinking positively, assuring me she'd come home. But in hindsight, maybe it was a hint. Did he know where Holly was?

I opened the package, and out fell a snapshot of my daughter, posed lying on her left side, with hands folded beneath her cheek.

I screamed.

CHAPTER 25

HOLLY

June 8

Five minutes later, Yanneth and I are leaning over a table with Guidry's time line spread out before us.

Yanneth counts the number of kidnappings. "Eleven. I told you something about that, didn't I?"

I nod.

"I don't often know why I see things, but it's always explained in the end. I can give you a full reading."

"Did you provide my mother with a reading?"

"Oh yes. I think it was good for her."

"How does it work?"

"I verbalize what comes to me," Yanneth says. "You listen. You might want to record the session. It comes to me quickly sometimes. That way, you can transcribe it later. Less chance of missing something, in that case."

I'm turning on the recorder on my phone when she asks, "May I hold that ring? It's important to you, yes?"

Instantly, my fingers go to the ring on my pinkie finger. "It's my mother's." I twist it and pull it off and place it in her hand.

"There it is again," the psychic says. "The *P* and the *H*. Eleven." She makes a show of closing her eyes and pressing her lips together. "Okay, I have a feel for you now."

She presses the ring back into my hand, then produces a deck of cards from the pocket of her caftan.

She shuffles and instructs me to cut the deck three times.

I do so.

She lays out the cards in the form of a cross.

She flips them over, revealing their odd markings, and again pinches her eyes shut. She points to a card. "The suit of cups is dominant here. Something happened to you near water. Near the confluence of two rivers. There's a small lake. I see a body being pulled from the water. She's been in there a long time, tangled in the brush, and when they pull her out, a branch snags on her, cuts her arm. It's a mark like yours. He's watching. He's scared. He feels responsible. He's re-creating it with these girls. He re-created it with you."

"So the girls . . . he drowns them?"

"He's trying to save them. Trying to help them survive and taking care of them. But the other side of the suit is that he's detaching. Killing them is just an exit strategy, but it doesn't happen in the water."

"How do they die?"

"The suit of swords says peacefully. It symbolizes air, so we're looking at air being deprived. Pentacles symbolize the earth. They're all buried. Somewhere."

"Yanneth, where is Skyler? Is she still with us? Is she alive?"

"Pen. Hook. Near Penhook, is what I see."

Yanneth's eyes slowly open.

"Penhook?" I ask. "Where is Penhook?"

"I'm seeing . . . south. On a small lake." She sighs dramatically and points to another card. "He's still in your life, you know. He comes and goes. On the fringes. Watching. Waiting. He won't quit until he finishes what he started with you."

"Tante?" The teenager appears now, this time holding his open laptop propped on an arm. His ears are covered with headphones, and he speaks a bit too loudly. "Who is Alan Kohlbrook?"

I gasp when I hear the name.

"I'm in the middle of a reading."

"Someone's been fucking with my files. There's a whole paper here about this guy, Alan Kohlbrook! It's taking up a lot of fucking space!"

"I'm in the middle of a reading," she says—more succinctly this time. "And *language*!"

The kid rolls his eyes and, with a huff, sinks to a chair at the table across from me. The music from his headphones is loud enough that I can hear the bass.

I take a step around the table, toward him. "Can I see that?" I ask.

Yanneth darts between us and turns me by the elbow toward the door. "That'll be all for today."

"What did you say I owed you?"

"Nothing. On the house."

We stare at each other now, a test of wills.

"Why is there a paper about Kohlbrook on that computer?" I ask.

Yanneth sighs and closes her eyes tightly. "Not as important as the rest of what you've learned here."

"You know him," I realize. "You're afraid of him."

"Thank you for stopping in to see me."

"You're not psychic," I say. "You know things because . . . you *know* things. It's the manifesto on your son's computer, isn't it? How did you get it?"

"Turn off your recorder," she says. "The reading is complete."

Psychic Yanneth indicates toward the door.

I pick up my phone and the time line from the table. I pretend to turn off the recorder and push my phone into the front pocket of my jeans.

I follow her back to the front porch, where she resumes her seat and rests her head in her hands. It occurs to me . . . "Did you write the damn thing?"

I wonder if her prints will match whatever prints were left on the manifesto and letters.

"It came to me," she says.

It's a cryptic explanation. *Came to me* could mean that she saw it in a vision. *Came to me* could mean she received it in the mail.

"I went to the police with the information, but my sister and I . . . she gave a bad reading once, many years ago, and they charged us with fraud. They don't listen to psychics with criminal records. I knew they wouldn't help, so I went to the lawyer."

"Who's doing this to these girls?"

Her lip quivers.

"Your secret is safe with me," I say. "I won't tell anyone you're a fraud. I just need to know, for the sake of Skyler Jane, if what you're telling me is an absolute truth."

"I'm not a fraud. I see things. Just not on demand, not about *this.* I keep trying . . ."

"So the little boy in Guatemala?" I ask.

"I read about him, about how a psychic intervened. No one ever researches to see the name of the psychic. People just like the story, and it's a living. We need the money."

"So someone else's triumph gives you credibility."

"I know who you are," she says. "I know what happened to you. I know things."

"Fine. Who are you?"

"I married William Wright."

Words from the Deanna Renee Rhine letter come back to me: *You're not looking in the Right Place(s).*

"Your husband is responsible for what happened to me? For what happened to all the little girls in the manifesto?"

"*Ex.* And I think so. If he isn't, he knows who is."

"Where is he? Can we talk to him?"

"I haven't seen him in over fifteen years. We weren't married long. We were so young."

"Yanneth. Please."

"He was a good man. But something used to overtake him, and he just couldn't stop the restlessness."

Before I can ask her to explain, she's spewing it all out:

"He would buy dolls, three, four at a time. I would wake up in the middle of the night to find him playing with them. Posing them, talking to them, saying, *Wake up, Amy. Wake up.* It scared me."

"My mother reported seeing dolls around town."

"Someone else was arrested for kidnapping you, but when they found Gretchen Klemm, I wondered to what extent he knew you. That's when I found your mother. Your mother's the one who put it all together. All the other girls. Their names, their hometowns . . ."

I think of the emails she received, the photographs of hair snippets. "Did my mother help you write the manifesto?"

"She didn't *help* me; she wrote the whole thing, but I'm the one who put it in the right hands. The cops wouldn't listen to her, either. We needed a way to make him stop. She wanted a way to help her friend. The innocent man who's in prison."

"When did you start to suspect your ex—"

"When they found the Alleyway Angel. I read about her. Saw the way she was found."

"I didn't think those pictures were released to the media."

"Pictures." She taps her head. "I saw them *here*. The scar on her arm . . . it's like yours, yes?"

I confirm with a nod.

"And once, a while before I left him, I found pictures of a child. Dressed in white. Sleeping. Posed just like the Alleyway Angel. He got very agitated when I asked, but he said they were pictures of his sister, who'd died when they were young. But after comparing notes with your mother, I'm sure the pictures were of you. I left him fifteen years ago, and I haven't seen him since. Rarely thought of him, either, until Gretchen."

The hair on my arms stands up, and it feels like slivers of ice shoot through my veins. "Then you understand the urgency with Skyler Jane Kipniss," I say. "The police seem to think my captor knew the family. Did your husband know my mother?"

"*Ex*-husband. And it doesn't appear so."

"Would you happen to have a picture of him?"

"Of William? It was a long time ago."

"Facebook page, Instagram? Maybe your son's page might have a photo?"

She shakes her head. "He's my sister's son. Not mine. He never met his uncle. William wasn't part of my life for very long."

"Do you know . . . Where is your husband now?"

"I don't know."

"I need more than that. You want to help, don't you? That's why you went to my mother, why you came to me."

She covers her mouth with her hand and nods. "He was part of my life such a long time ago."

"What did he do for a living? Let's start there."

"Lots of things. He ran errands, worked construction, odd jobs."

"Construction?"

"But he was *smart*. So smart. He really could've been something if he had help, if he had confidence, and if someone had believed in him when he was a child. But he didn't know he was smart. He kept trying to prove it."

"How tall was he?"

"Taller than me, but who isn't? Five ten, maybe five eleven."

I queue up a picture of Sterling and me. "Is *this* your husband?"

She narrows her gaze at the image. "It could be. It's been so long. But there's something about the eyes, there. Grayish green, am I right? Maybe that's what he'd look like now. I'm sorry I can't be more help. I haven't seen him in a long time, and he's probably changed."

I make a mental note: *Maybe on suspect number one.*

On to the next: "Yanneth, did he have a scar on his hand?" I tap the area on mine where Vellerman's scar is. "Right around here?"

"He didn't back then. But so much has happened. He might by now."

I flip to a picture of Matt, just to cover all bases. "How about this guy? Is he the guy you married?"

"I only wish."

I crack a smile.

"He had chameleon eyes, my husband. Sometimes gray, sometimes green or blue. I keep trying to see what's happening, where he is . . . I thought I saw him last spring. I thought he was following you, but it turned out . . ." She shuts up. "It wasn't you, and it wasn't him."

I think for a second. "Did you follow my SUV on April sixteenth?"

"I thought it was you." She lets out a whimper. "It was your mother. The roads were slick."

My heart feels as if it just plummeted into my stomach.

"I saw the accident. She tried to stop. He tried to stop, but . . . he slid. She went over the edge."

"Yanneth."

She looks up at me.

"This cryptic bullshit stops right here," I say. "You're going to have to tell me everything you know. What kind of car was it?"

"A blue utility vehicle."

"Anything you can give me about where you lived with your husband—"

"It was a tiny studio apartment near Chicago."

"That narrows it down to about a million places. Any idea where else he might be right now?"

"If I knew, I never would have let him take her, or any of them. I met him and married him quickly. He had no family, and when we split, I never heard from him again. I don't see him, if not in an echo." She takes a deep breath. "I see the number eleven. Lovely energy." A smile slowly appears in her lips. "And you feel the echoes of the past, don't you? Lovely energy. Pay attention to it. Pay attention to the signs, and you'll be able to stop him."

CHAPTER 26
Holly

June 8

Pay attention to the signs.

I keep seeing the sign in my mind. Letters worn off. An *H*, and a *P*.

The police thought my kidnapper knew my parents, but it appears, if Yanneth's theory is correct, that they're wrong in that assessment.

"Did you know him, Mom?"

Rain beating down on the roof of my truck answers me in my mother's stead.

"Let's see what Dad knows." I dial my father.

"Holly?"

"Dad, did you know a William Wright?"

"Are you *driving*? You aren't at work?"

"No."

"Vellerman didn't tell me."

"Listen, Dad. I need to know if you and Mom knew someone named William Wright."

"Is everything okay? I talked to Matt earlier, and he said—"

"Dad! William Wright. Maybe someone who worked for TrevCon?"

"I don't know, Holly. I don't think so, but maybe. We had a lot of turnover in the early days."

"How about the town of Penhook? Do you know anyone who lives in Penhook?"

"Hmmm. Not anymore, but I think the Herseys had a place out there for a while."

Pay attention to the signs.

"Hershey's Place," I whisper. I think of the sign I keep seeing in my almost dreams. The peeling, white paint and the *P* and the *H*. Could it be the lettering on the shingle pointing the way to the Hershey family's lake house?

Yanneth said if her ex wasn't responsible, he knew who was. Did William Wright know Paul Hershey? Did they work together to abduct me?

It's possible, I suppose. Maybe one was the abductor and the other was the voice of reason, which landed me in a park at midnight alive, when so many others have yet to be found. The world starts to tilt.

I pull over to the shoulder of the road until the sensation quits.

"Holly?" Dad asks, "Did you hear me?"

"Dad." I breathe through the dizzying effects of all I've learned in the past half an hour. "Did Paul Hershey ever mention a William Wright?"

"Holly, I haven't talked to the man in almost twenty years."

But Paul Hershey and my mother were in contact before the accident.

He knew my dad.

He knew my nickname. *Drink your juice, Holly-Dolly.*

"Dad? Paul Hershey virtually disappeared from our lives after I came back. Could he have been the one who took me?"

"Holly, no."

"I'm trying to put these pieces of the puzzle together, Dad, and—"

"Where are you?"

"I went to see Psychic Yanneth, and, Dad—"

"Is that where all this is coming from? Promise me you'll come home. I'll meet you there. We'll talk this out."

I don't reply right away.

"Holly Adryenne."

"Okay. Okay, I'll come home."

"Promise?"

"Promise." It's a promise I know I can't keep, but I hang up, anyway.

I consult with my mother, who's a better listener these days than my father:

"It could have been Paul. Only you know. Did you figure it out, Mom? Is that why you brought the gun with you that day? Did he follow you around the ravine and nudge you over? To silence you?"

I mull it over, and while I don't want to believe it, I decide it's possible that Paul Hershey might have had something to do with my abduction. I don't know what his motivation might have been, but he was gone afterward.

And maybe what I said earlier about Kitten not wanting to implicate someone she adored in the crime holds true. Would she, subconsciously or otherwise, point her finger at Kohlbrook if it meant saving her father?

I merge back into traffic and call the detective.

"Holly, hello. We've yet to locate Derrion Sterling. Are you still safe? With Matt?"

"Not exactly. I *was* with Matt, but he had a romper exactly like the one I was wearing when I disappeared, and—"

"Slow down. He had an article of your clothing?"

"He had an explanation for it. He said it was Kitten's, and maybe it was, but . . . Detective, can you tell me what kind of car Paul Hershey drives?"

"It'll take me a minute, but sure. Why? *Tell me what's going on.*"

I fill him in about Psychic Yanneth's visions of Gretchen Klemm, the scar on her arm, the number eleven . . . and the possibility that it was Paul Hershey driving a blue vehicle and following Mom the night my mother was nudged over the edge of the ravine.

"And I have that glimpse of a memory I was telling you about . . . the sign with the peeling paint. I remember two letters. *P* and *H*. I don't know the address of the Hersheys' place, but I remember it's somewhere in the Illinois valley, on Evergreen Lake. Matt or Kitten would know. I'm going to call them next."

"You can't mean . . . no, Holly. Go home. This isn't your job. We still don't know what Derrion Sterling may or may not have to do with this. We don't know if someone's been drugging you or for what purpose—"

"Evergreen Lake is *hours* from Lake County, Detective. I'm halfway there. If he's holding Skyler there, someone has to get there. We might not have the luxury of time."

"I have a man who can get there fast," Guidry says. "Go. Home. Go get your blood drawn."

"I have to do this. If I'd remembered when I was a child what happened to me, none of this would be happening now. If I'd been able to help back then, no other girls would have gone through this. I was the first. I could have been the last."

"Holly, this isn't your job, and no one thinks it's your fault."

"I have to do this."

"Do I have to send an APB out on you?"

"Probably."

Before he can deter me, I hang up and call Kitten.

When she doesn't answer, I dial Matt.

"Holly, thank God," he says without saying hello. "I've been worried about what happened. I—"

"We'll get to all that later," I promise. "But first, where's Kitten?"

"I don't know. She texted earlier that she needed to talk to me about something, but she didn't answer when I called. Weren't you supposed to be at the tailor for final fittings right about now?"

"Fuck." She's going to be pissed at me again. "I'll make it up to her. But I need some information."

"What's going on?"

"I need the address to your family's lake house in Penhook."

"Why? No one's used it since we were kids."

"I'm not so sure about that."

Cecily

"It's Holly."

I bolted upright in Holly's bed.

Moonlight poured through the window, highlighting the outline of my husband's body in the doorway.

"Someone spotted a little girl in the park, and the police are on their way."

After hope upon hope being dashed away, I didn't know if I could be optimistic again, but I tossed on a coat, and Trevor and I drove to the park.

Blue-and-red lights flashed against the snow.

And there she was, nothing short of a miracle, wrapped in a police blanket. A blank expression painted her face until the moment she laid eyes on her father, at which time her eyes brightened, and she reached for him.

"You're all right, Holly-Dolly. You're all right."

Later, at the hospital, we learned that except for a cut on her arm, she seemed to be fine, virtually unscathed. The medical examination didn't show signs of sexual trauma, but I wasn't so sure; there were other ways to violate a child.

And she wasn't saying much about the time she was gone. It was as if she were in denial about the fact that someone had snatched her away from us.

"Who were you with?"

She looked up at her father when he asked. "My brother."

"She doesn't have a brother," Trevor told the police. "Matt Hershey is the closest, but he didn't do this."

The child psychologist, Dr. Simone Parrish, explained that whoever had taken our daughter likely identified himself as a brother figure, which was more good news, if we were to believe that her captor had treated her like a sister. Then again, anyone deranged enough to take a child wouldn't necessarily respect the brother-sister dynamic.

Parrish went on to explain that Holly's lapse in memory was an effect of post-traumatic stress disorder. PTSD, in conjunction with her captor's drugging her, meant she might never talk about what she'd endured.

"How do we help her unless we know what she's been through? How do we know what she's been through if she can't tell us?" Trevor asked.

"She may remember in time," Dr. Parrish said. "Or . . . there's always hypnosis."

"No." I spoke the word sharply and quickly. If Holly didn't remember what had happened to her, I counted it as another blessing. I didn't want her to remember. I didn't want her to have to live with it.

"He's still out there," Trevor said. "We know what he may have done. We have to put the bastard behind bars, and if hypnosis is the only way, so be it."

"No," I said again.

"Are you hiding something?" Trevor asked later that day. "Are you afraid of what she might say if we put her under?"

"Yes," I told him. "I don't want her to remember."

CHAPTER 27

Holly

June 8

As soon as the horizon clears, I see the house . . .

My fingertips tingle when it's instantly familiar.

This is it.

This is the place that's been just out of reach my entire life.

Suddenly, I'm four years old again, bumping down a gravel road in the extended cab of a truck. It's dark outside, and I'm crouched on the floor, hiding behind the driver's seat. Just like I was told to do. *Drink your juice.* I'm sleepy. The truck bumps to a stop on a gravel lane.

I hear a familiar voice.

I'm not afraid anymore.

Whose voice was it? Paul Hershey's? Someone else's? It's been so long that I don't remember what Kitten's dad sounded like.

A two-story home, in great disrepair, stands as if forgotten about thirty feet from the shore and surrounded by overgrown prairie grass. All the windows are boarded up, and half the siding is rotted away.

There are no neighbors, and the lake appears to be private, perhaps completely encompassed by the property lines.

I park and crack the windows for Dog. I don't know what I'm walking into, but if someone drives up, I'm sure the dog will serve as an alarm system.

My firearm is at my ankle, and Guidry's man should be here soon. I'll be fine.

Through the rain, I walk around to the lake side of the house and find the door unlocked.

The place stinks like mildew and urine.

I pass through a closet of a kitchen and spy an old tube television with an antenna in the room beyond. There's a ladder against the far wall. I look up. The ceiling is missing. I look down. So is the floor.

A stack of plywood sheeting is propped against the wall nearest me.

I swallow over a lump in my throat. This is really it. The image that's haunted me since I nearly fell on the construction site—a dark frame of a space, no light filtering in, and a great sense of loneliness. Nothing to see if you look up, no ground to feel below you.

Next, I open a door I know will lead to a bathroom.

Orange shag carpet covers the bathroom floor.

Rust stains drip down the harvest-gold toilet and tub.

A memory zaps me:

A man is sitting on the closed lid of the toilet. I see his large frame, not nearly as big as Dad's. I cannot conjure his face. Maybe I never looked at him. Maybe he told me not to. But who was it, if not Paul Hershey?

Perhaps someone he knew? Someone who knew about the lake property he owned?

In my memory, I'm just out of the bathtub, wrapped in a thin towel.

I'm cold.

Always so cold.

I push at my loose tooth with my tongue, the taste of blood bursts in my mouth, and the next I know, I'm staring at the tooth in the man's hand. His fingers are scratched and calloused—fingers of a laborer.

You lost your first tooth.

Want to hold it?

He places it in my hand and pats me on the head.

I try to bring it closer.

I drop it.

It's all so vivid now that I'm here, now that I'm seeing this place.

I shine my phone's flashlight down to the basement and see vermin scurry to get away from the light.

It's then I hear her: the whimper.

"Skyler Jane?" I say.

I listen hard but don't hear her again.

"Skyler? My name is Holly. I'm here to help you. I'm here to take you back to your mom and dad."

No reply.

"Skyler?"

I wonder for a breath or two if I only imagined her cry, if the echoes of the past are haunting me.

I shine the light up. From this vantage point, I can't see anything beyond cobwebs hanging from the old wood.

But I'm not going to leave without checking every square inch of this place.

First, I walk the joists to reach the ladder, drop a sheet of plywood down, and prop the ladder against the upstairs joists.

I climb, gripping my phone at the ready, and as soon as I reach the top, my flashlight passes over the expanse of the rotting frame of the second floor to a small section of cupping plywood, the only floor remaining in the space, just beyond the remains of what probably used to be a doorway to a bedroom. Centered on the plywood is a thin twin mattress, soiled and old. Her tiny body, draped with a white blanket, lies atop it, stashed here on an island of a bed with the skeleton of a floor, nail ridden and open to the basement two floors down. Whether or not this is the place I was hidden for ninety-four days, it's clear Skyler's been here for eighty-two.

And he probably kept Enna, Selena, Jenny, Alyssa, Deanna, Bethany, Sophie, Lauren, and Gretchen here in the interim.

"Skyler?" I whisper.

She's not moving.

Dog barks.

I freeze.

Someone else is here.

CHAPTER 28

Holly

June 8

I pull myself up to the second floor and shine the light over the nail-ridden joists, then down at the basement below.

I look across the expanse at Skyler's motionless body.

"Skyler?" I whisper.

Still, she doesn't move.

I dial 9-1-1, but the call fails.

No service.

When I close my eyes in silent prayer, I see the little girl in my mind: blonde with blue eyes.

"Don't cross."

Did I imagine the mumbled words, or did they come from the mattress across the way?

But I can do this.

I don't have a choice if I want to get both of us out of here alive.

I look to the stack of plywood. There's no time to sheet the floor.

I'm going to have to go get her and balance with her on the way back and hope we make it to the ground floor before anyone interrupts me. I don't know if I can do it in the dark, with my firearm drawn. I hope I can get to her and back before I need to draw it.

Dog is barking like mad now.

I take a step.

The trick, which I learned after half a lifetime on sites, is to avoid using an inch-and-a-half-wide joist as a balance beam. Instead, I think of the skinny lengths of wood as an entire supportive network. I use more than one run and place my foot diagonally with each step so that more of my foot is in contact with more of the board.

The trouble is that this network is old and defunct. Rotting in certain places and cracked in others. Adding to the challenge is the leaking roof above. Rain patters down and drips in cadence throughout the space. *Drip, drip, drop.* The joists are going to be slippery.

If I were on a site, no foreman would condone working under these conditions.

I walk the length of the room, choosing each step with care, and the moment I reach the filthy mattress, I place a hand on the child's back.

Thank God, she's breathing. It's shallow, but breathing is breathing. I roll her toward me.

She meets me with a blank stare. "Skyler?"

Her pulse is weak.

The mattress is filthy and wet with rain and probably urine.

I scoop the limp child into my embrace.

I hear the latch of the door downstairs.

Someone else is inside the house.

I'm running out of time.

"Hold tight," I whisper. "I'm going to need my hands, so you have to hold on to me."

She blinks and tries to grasp my hand, but her grip is weak.

She can't do it.

I think fast and wrap her in the thin blanket, then wrap and tie it around my body, like a sling.

I start back toward the ladder, only I'm too late. Someone is climbing up.

CHAPTER 29

Holly

June 8

I crouch to the joists, each foot planted on a separate plank.

Crack.

I feel the board under my right foot give a little. A quick inspection tells me it's split. It won't hold me much longer.

If it were only my own weight, I could swing down between the joists, perhaps even undetected. But with the added forty-odd pounds of a frightened five-year-old throwing off my center of gravity, odds of a successful dismount are slim.

A hand appears first.

My heart beats double time.

I know that hand.

The scar on the back of it.

Next, a head peeks over the top of the ladder.

My breath catches in my throat. *Vellerman.*

Just as familiar with a house under construction as I am, just as adept in traversing through a roughly framed structure, my adversary pulls himself up, and while he scans the space, it's dark enough that he doesn't see me—at least not right away.

I balance and say a quick prayer.

Feel for my pistol with a sweaty hand. But when I was trained for concealed carry, I never ran drills like this: balancing with a child fastened to me with a thin sheet of fabric in a dark, dank house with a thirty-foot fall past rusty nails and slippery, rotting wood.

Finally, I get a grip.

I draw.

Aim.

"Stop right there."

He's only about five feet away now. He looks at me, finally acknowledging my presence. "Don't shoot."

I keep him in the crosshairs.

"One more move, I'll put a bullet in your head."

"You're going to have to trust me."

"And *you're* going to have to trust *me*. I'm a good shot from a distance, but from five feet away? Move just an inch. That's all I need."

"I'm not your guy. Skyler will tell you."

"She's not saying much. Back down the ladder."

"Give her to me," he says. "Let's get her out of here."

Skyler murmurs, "No, no, no, nonononono."

If she moves, we're both going down.

"Stay still, Skyler," I whisper.

"We don't have time," Vellerman says.

"Down. The. Ladder."

He begins.

I inch closer.

With every rung he descends, I move another few inches across this expanse.

About two feet to the ladder now.

The joist cracks.

The child gasps.

We're going down.

CHAPTER 30

HOLLY

June 8

Vellerman rips Skyler from my body.

I'm dangling over an open basement, one hand gripping a failing joist and the other holding tight to my firearm.

Vellerman puts the child aside, then grabs me by a belt loop.

He pulls me to him, and soon I'm safe on the small square of plywood.

I recenter and train my gun on him.

It's then I see a glint of metal at his belt: a badge.

His hands are up. "Guidry did tell you he was sending someone, right?"

I lower my firearm.

CHAPTER 31

HOLLY

June 8

The place is swarming with uniforms and members of the press now, and Skyler Jane is not only safe but becoming more alert. She won't leave my arms, so I'm sitting in the back of the ambulance while the EMTs check her vitals and bandage the arrow-shaped cut on her arm.

"Save her," she whispers to me.

"You're safe now," I tell her.

"No. *The other girl.*"

I look to Guidry. "Is there another little girl here?"

"No."

"Are you sure?"

"We've swept the place."

"She's here," Skyler says.

Guidry turns to a uniform officer. "Has there been another kidnapping? Check the database. And for *Chrissake*, someone tell me we've located Paul Hershey!"

"Soon, Lieutenant. Just arrived at his main residence."

"She's here," Skyler says, more succinctly.

"Who's here?" I ask.

"She says, *Don't cross, Skyler. Don't cross.*"

A chill races up my spine. "What does she look like?"

"She looks like me."

"Blue eyes?" I swallow hard. "Blonde hair?"

"Yes."

"Is she little like you? Or big like me?"

"Amy is little."

My fingertips go numb. I'm convinced more than ever now: I wasn't here alone, and neither was Skyler. There are more victims. Guidry just hasn't located them all yet.

Someone sweeps in and pulls Skyler from my arms.

"Mommy!"

The sight of it brings tears to my eyes. My heart aches to have that sort of connection to my own mother. I imagine the turmoil she must have been in not only while I was gone but since. She'd reported evidence that was ignored for years, harbored a belief that the police put the wrong man in prison, and probably agonized over the fact that justice was never served for my ordeal. To think of her suffering alone . . . to think Psychic Yanneth was the only one who listened to her, that she resorted to writing a manifesto . . .

I'm coming home, I tell her in my head. *And I want you to wake up when I do, so we can start over. So we can share life. It's not a second chance. It's a third. And I won't waste it this time.*

"She's safe," an officer says to Skyler's parents. "That's the most important thing."

It's what everyone says. It's what everyone said when I turned up in that park twenty years ago. But I know better now. Because it's not just about me, and it's not just about Skyler. It's about at least nine other girls, their families, and whoever is responsible for this storm of grief.

Was it Paul Hershey?

Or William Wright?

Or someone else altogether?

The man I know as Craig Vellerman, foreman at TrevCon, approaches with a hand extended.

"Let me guess," I say as I shake his hand. "You're not really a carpenter."

"Christian Brown, PI. I came out of retirement to help an old friend."

Guidry approaches. "Chris."

The two shake hands.

"Holly," Guidry says, "Chris, here, has been keeping an eye on you, and once he suspected someone might have been looking to incapacitate you, he's been keeping a closer-than-usual watch."

"Sorry if I scared you," he says.

"No, that's all right," I say. "Were you, by any chance, on the bluffs last night? I got dizzy, and—"

"I got you home safely."

I'm still rather creeped out, but I thank him, anyway.

"Thanks for your help," Guidry says to his undercover man. "I'm sure you're anxious to get back to Key West, but I need you for one more task."

I'm about to excuse myself. They obviously have police business to conduct.

But Guidry stops me. "Holly, wait. Would you mind weighing in? I know it's been a long time. But can you have a look at this guy's picture?"

He produces a tablet. "Is this the man who abducted you twenty years ago?"

The picture is an old image from the department of motor vehicles. He looks familiar, but . . . "It's Paul Hershey, I think." I swipe and see an updated image. He's aged. His hair is almost completely gray, and his skin looks weathered. I return the tablet. "I still don't remember it, but this is his place, so—" And now that I've been in the house, dim, dark, I understand that the drugs are only part of my amnesia. The house is so dark, and if all the windows were boarded up back then, which is possible if they renovated, I probably never got a good look at the man who kept me.

"Skyler says no," Guidry says. "This isn't the man who took her. The man we're looking for is younger. She didn't recognize Derrion Sterling, either."

Guidry frowns. "Is there anyone else who had access to this place?"

"Matt," I say quietly. "His son, Matt, knew the address but claimed no one had used the place in a long time. Judging by the state of disrepair, I guess we know why, but . . . Here's a picture of him." I call up the most recent on my phone. "Maybe Skyler can rule him out."

I'm a little dizzy with the thought of the possibility that the man I've loved most of my life could have been the one to take me. But I think of the romper I saw in his bedroom. I'm not even sure I believed his explanation.

Guidry takes my phone to the little girl.

The earth starts to slant, and I ball my fingers into a fist. But there's nothing I can hold on to to steady myself.

I hold my breath until I see the definitive shake of her head.

"The trouble is," Guidry says when he returns my phone, "she's obviously been given a fair amount of sedatives, maybe the same situation as you. I'm not sure she'd recognize anyone."

"What about William Wright? The psychic's ex-husband? She claims he had a picture of me that must have been taken when I was gone. No one seems to know where he is, but it's just possible, isn't it, that he was involved?"

"Holly." Guidry pinches the bridge of his nose. "I have reason to believe that psychic wouldn't see the truth if it was published somewhere—if she's the same Psychic *Janet* who took thousands from residents of the Fair Oaks Assisted Living tower. We need her prints to determine, and—"

"Prints?" I think of the deck of tarot cards in the cab of my truck. She handled them. "I can give you her prints right now." I explain how and relay what Yanneth told me about her sister's bad reading.

"She has a criminal record, history of fraud," I say. "I get it. But in a case like this . . . in a case like *mine,* don't you think we have to turn over every stone? There's something else happening here, and I can't help but think you people want to *once again* wrap this up with a neat and tidy bow. Yes, we're at Paul Hershey's house. Yes, it's plausible he's responsible. But isn't it also possible that someone else realized no one ever used this place and decided it was isolated enough to pull off hiding someone here? Are we going to be back here in twenty years? Talking about leads we never pursued? Or are we going to look back and know we were thorough? We still don't know how Wright's involved, or Sterling, and as a matter of fact, you're even wrong about who wrote the manifesto!"

I shut up.

Two seasoned detectives, a handful of uniformed cops, and one private investigator from Key West are staring at me.

"Sorry if I'm out of line," I say. "I'm just frustrated."

"It's okay," Guidry says. "We all are."

If I've never remembered what happened to me, it means Skyler might not remember, either.

This means, of course, that if whoever is doing this manages to elude the cops *again,* he can keep abducting little girls.

"I'm ready to remember," I say.

I'm ready, Mom. I want to know what happened to me.

Cecily

"Where's Derrion?"

I stopped before entering Susan Hershey's kitchen when I heard her speaking to my daughter.

"I thought he was going to be here," Susan said. *Here* was Kitten's engagement party, which Susan hosted on a frigid Friday in early spring. "We'd like to get to know him a bit better."

From my position, undetected, in the hallway, I watched Holly's lips turn up in a half smile. "I think it's about over between us."

"Oh, honey. What happened?"

"I don't know." Holly shrugged. "I sometimes get the feeling that he found me interesting at first because of what happened to me when I was a kid. But now that he sees the real me, and that I don't even remember what happened to me, he's over the novelty of it all."

"Kitten says he actually was here helping to canvass the neighborhood after you were gone?"

"That's what he said."

"There were a lot of volunteers in the first few days. A boy who'd do that isn't disappointed that you've become a well-adjusted member of society, Holly. Maybe you're pushing him away because you're afraid to get close to anyone?"

Bravo, Susan. It was a good observation, and while there was a time I might have resented the fact that Holly chose to confide in Susan what she had yet to share with me, I'd mellowed over the years to appreciate the blanks Susan managed to fill in. Holly had become a well-rounded woman because of it.

"Or maybe I'm just incapable," Holly said. "I still feel as if this enormous part of me is missing."

"We don't have to talk about it."

"That's the point. We *never* talk about it."

"Because none of us know what happened. Kohlbrook took you, and he's in jail. Open, shut."

"I've been thinking I might agree to be hypnotized. Just to see if I remember anything."

I held my breath. Whatever she went through, I was glad it was over and gone and hidden in her mind. I didn't want her to remember.

"Are you sure you want to scratch that itch?" Susan asked. "There could be worse things than not remembering."

Bravo, again.

Without Trevor coming between us, Susan and I had managed to get back to good, and over the years, we'd become a team again. I had to let go of the past, let go of the hate, and I had to find a way to trust Susan and Trevor together again.

"Ceci!"

I'd been spotted.

"Get in here and have a drink with the maid of honor."

"I've got one." I raised my glass of ice water. "Maid of honor." I smiled at Holly. "A big deal."

"God, that clan of bridesmaids is already talking about the bridal shower. But not just one. One for the ladies and one for couples. I mean, jeez. Let's all take a breath. This engagement *just happened.*"

"I'll help you plan it," I offered.

She laughed a little. "Who's going to help you?"

Valid. "I think I know someone."

Susan and I shared a smile. Things we'd left unsaid at the park the day my daughter was kidnapped remained unsaid.

It's as if we realized that none of it mattered anymore. Life as we knew it no longer existed.

I leaned against the windowsill and stared across the field at the house Trevor and I had built. We were happy there for such a short time before the turmoil, before the horror. And my daughter, for all she's overcome, is still a shadow of what she might have otherwise been . . .

One of the hardest things about being a mother: watching your kid trip on the same cracks in the pavement you stumbled on.

Looking at her, I longed to be able to open a conversation, but all I managed was: "Can I take your Explorer tomorrow? I have some errands to run."

She didn't even look up from her phone. "Sure."

Always a struggle.

I'd been keeping a secret from her and her father. I had recently met the baby I gave up for adoption shortly after Holly was recovered. Her name is Avery. I flew out to Vermont in March, and we spent a nice week together.

We've been in contact ever since, and it's funny how close a mother can feel to a daughter she's barely met. Yet the one who grew up under my roof? There's darkness between us. It's as if the kidnapping is still ongoing, at times. Even though she's back, he took parts of her she's yet to regain.

I took a breath and tried again: "What do you think of Eliot?"

Holly jumped on the question. "I think they're moving too fast. And his place looks like Miami threw up a condo and placed it across from Lincoln Park Zoo, but other than that . . . I don't know."

"He's a little old for her," I said.

"You think?"

Rare common ground for Holly and me. She smiled.

"Oh, what's age but a number?" Susan asked. "Kitten says she feels like she's known him forever. And I'm glad she found a good, stable man, which is quite a feat, considering the ghost her father's become. You notice that asshole didn't make it in for the party."

"Hmm." The very mention of the man carves a sense of guilt in my heart. Avery is Paul's daughter, too, after all, and I know that before long, she's going to ask about him.

"I swear, if I'd known he'd ignore a kid simply because his swimmers no longer worked—"

Holly shifted in her seat.

Susan continued, "I probably wouldn't have suggested a donor at all, if I'd known he'd feel absolved of all parental responsibility."

"I'm sorry . . ." I tried to repeat the words in my head to ensure Susan had said what I thought I'd heard. "Can you say that again? Something about . . . his swimmers?"

"I thought you knew: The car accident when Matt was a toddler. You know . . . the one that gave him the scar by his left eye. Paul didn't walk away unscathed, either. We tried for years, but the only thing that did it was the donor stuff. That's how you end up with twelve years between kids."

Stunned, I stood there with what I'm sure was a stupefied look on my face. "I never knew . . ."

"I swear I told you." Susan propped a hand on her hip and drummed her fingertips against her pink leather belt. "Anyway, it's why I'm so thankful for you and Trevor. Without you, my kids might not know what a father is supposed to look like."

"Uh-huh." But nothing made sense. Paul and I shared one night together, and I got pregnant. "He's *sterile*?"

"Very low numbers and low motility—" Susan chattered on, but I couldn't listen. "He used to go to those support groups for men who couldn't conceive . . ."

Everything hit me at once like a bolt of lightning.

Paul let me believe the baby was his! Let me believe Kitten was the product of my husband's affair with his wife!

That meant one thing: Avery wasn't likely Paul's child.

Avery was Trevor's, and I'd given her away.

If I'd kept her, maybe I would have gotten my act together sooner. I might have stopped drinking years ago. Maybe a baby would have united us, given us another reason to carry on.

And Holly . . . maybe being a big sister could have given her a sense of purpose. Certainly, if Trevor had another baby to consider, maybe he would've given Holly some air and room to move and breathe instead of treating her as if she were his very own unearthed treasure. The family dynamic would have changed, had Avery grown up with us.

Paul's deceit was inexcusable and incomprehensible, and I started to wonder . . . I'd never seen the pictures of our spouses in flagrante delicto. I'd taken him at his word. If he'd slanted the truth about Kitten's paternity, what else had he lied about?

It was time I paid Paul Hershey a visit.

CHAPTER 32

Holly

June 9

After doctors gave me a once-over, a discharge, and a bill, I spent the night in the waiting room at the hospital, just in case the police, or Skyler and her family, needed me. The local police department kenneled Dog at my request. She's not mine, and until her owner is located, the authorities will care for her.

But I miss her.

I text Kitten for the thirtieth time asking her please to call me. I want to explain why I missed the fitting yesterday, but she must be really angry with me, because she isn't responding.

Maybe I'll swing by her place on my way home and make her understand.

"Holly." Guidry takes a seat across from me. "You can go home. We know where to find you if we need you. We're questioning Paul Hershey, a team in Lake County brought Matt in for the same . . ."

"How about Sterling?"

The detective pauses for a moment. "MIA."

"Did you check his brother's place in South Bend?"

"Left two days ago. Hasn't reported to work. His vehicle was found parked in a garage in the Edgewater neighborhood. The ticket on the dash indicates it's been there since early morning on the eighth. Has this ever happened before?"

"Unfortunately, yes. All the time. And I told you about his moodiness and going off radar around the time Skyler was taken."

"Circumstantial. But we'll see when we find him."

"How's Skyler?"

"An arrow was cut into her arm. Just like yours. She'd obviously been given sedatives. Let's hope that will prove to be the extent of her physical injuries."

I agree.

"She keeps talking about this Amy," Guidry says.

The name of the other little girl Skyler mentioned—Amy—is puzzling. There are no Amys reported missing, and there is no Amy compiled in the manifesto my mother put together. Guidry and his team found no evidence of another little girl anywhere on the premises, although they found a doll—the same poseable sort—on the rafters near the mattress Skyler slept on.

But why does Skyler remember seeing another little girl? Why do I? Especially when it seems we don't remember anything else?

Psychic Yanneth once told me to pay attention when I saw someone who looked like me. She called her an echo of the past. Maybe the little girl is a coping mechanism, a playmate Skyler conjured to help her get through the horrors of being alone in such an awful place. But is it then coincidence that I did the same thing?

"If you think of anything that might help explain the Amy factor—"

"I'll let you know," I say.

Guidry stands. "Want a coffee or anything?"

"No, I'm probably going to head out soon. But thanks."

Once Guidry begins toward the cafeteria, I open the browser on my phone and type in the address of the property.

Already, stories about Skyler's rescue have been published online.

I jump from link to link, but I don't learn anything I don't already know.

Then, I add the name *Amy* to the search.

My jaw drops with what I see: *Pastor Wright Commemorates Daughter Amy.*

I rush to find the detective.

—

"There's not an Amy on the list," I tell Guidry. "But an Amy drowned on that lake. The Wrights sold the property to the Hersheys the following year."

"You're telling me the house is haunted?" Guidry asks. "I can't build a case on tarot cards and ghosts, Holly."

"I can't explain it, but I just read that a few years before I was taken, a little girl, *Amy*, drowned on the property. Her brother, *William*, was fifteen at the time and is named in the article. I think this is the same William who went on to marry Psychic Yanneth. And if you do a search on the property, you'll see that the Wrights sold the acreage, I assume to the Hersheys, shortly after Amy died."

I continue: "Pastor Wright used to be the pastor of the church at United Methodist. That's probably the church the Hersheys went to when they were vacationing at the lake house—I know they're Methodist. Kitten said she remembered the person who took me was someone from the church. No one asked her *which* church—if it was church at home, or church at the lake. It's possible, right?"

"I'm listening."

"The letter you told me about . . . the one that referenced the Right Places? Maybe this lake house used to be known as Wright's Place. Maybe you'll find other girls buried there, or at other homes the Wrights might have owned."

"Worth looking into," Guidry says.

"There's more." I pull up a screenshot of the article on my phone and hand it to the detective. "The pastor mentions seeing divers pulling his daughter's body from the brush. On her left arm was an oddly shaped cut, likely caused by something in the water. He interpreted it as an arrow, as if God were showing him the way to forgiveness and absolution. I'm guessing that if you can get your hands on the autopsy photos of this girl, you'll see that my captor, and Skyler's, cut us in the same fashion. It's like Psychic Yanneth says: whoever is doing this is re-creating a traumatic incident in his life."

"How do you explain Skyler's seeing a girl who died?"

"I don't believe in ghosts, either, Detective," I say. "But I have similar visions of a little girl, saying virtually the same thing to me—*Don't cross*." I don't speak my next thoughts aloud: *I don't think Amy is a ghost. I think she's an angel.*

CHAPTER 33

Holly

June 9

Kitten still hasn't answered my calls or texts, but her condo isn't too far out of the way. I swing by on my way home. Once she realizes why I skipped the fitting, I'm sure she'll understand.

The moment the door opens, I force a smile. "Eliot. Hi."

"Well, hello," he says. "If it isn't our maid of honor. Come in." He holds the door open with one hand and shoves the other into the pocket of his khakis.

He looks different somehow. Disheveled and unkempt. His hair is unruly, like it hasn't been brushed for days, and his clothing is wrinkled. He isn't wearing his glasses.

"Is Kitten here?"

"She'll be home soon." Eliot locks the door behind me.

The world tilts, and I feel light-headed. I should've excused myself the moment he told me Kitten wasn't here. Now I'm going to have to talk to him, face-to-face, alone.

Eliot turns a chair toward me. "Have a seat."

"Maybe I should just . . ." I thumb toward the door. "You'll tell Kitten I stopped in? You'll have her call me?"

"We're going to be part of each other's lives for a long time," he says. "So let's lay it all on the line, once and for all: you don't like me very much."

I meet his glance. "If you love Kitten, and she loves you, it doesn't matter what I think—"

"Oh, but it does. This icy wall between us makes Kitten uncomfortable. She's important to both of us. Can we find a way to be friends?"

"I have nothing against you," I say. "To be honest, it's probably just that . . ." I sigh. "I've probably been a little preoccupied. The drama with Sterling . . . my mom . . ." *And the missing girls*, I think. "And maybe . . ." I take a deep breath. May as well say it all. "Maybe I've been jealous that Kitten's moving on without me. We've always been living parallel lives, and suddenly—"

"Understandable."

"I'm sorry, I'm just not very good at new people."

"It's all right. I understand."

"Maybe once we get to know each other—"

"How about a drink? Kitten'll be back soon."

I probably shouldn't, but after the day I've had . . .

"Bourbon?" he offers.

"Okay, thanks."

A few steps into the apartment, my eyes pass over a small pewter box, not unlike the one I stole from Kitten's bridesmaid's place. It's stationed on a glass shelf in a black lacquer curio cabinet. I wonder . . . Is it the same one I took the other day? I gravitate a few steps closer for a better look. It's a bit larger, I think, and there's a daisy embossed on the top of this one.

An echo revisits me now: I'm little, in a dark room. I grasp the box, open it, and see a lock of hair and a key inside. Instantly, a spank bites my backside, and the box is yanked away.

"Have a seat," Eliot offers again. "Rocks? Or straight?"

"Rocks," I say. "Thanks."

The moment he turns his back, I cross the room toward the box.

He's chattering from the kitchen as he fills a glass with ice. I reach for the box.

Suddenly, Eliot's there, extending the glass of bourbon toward me.

Busted. I offer a sort-of smile. "Sorry. It's just—"

"If you don't mind . . ." He exchanges the box for the liquor. "It's special. It was my sister's."

I look into his gray eyes, usually masked with the amber-tinted lenses of his round, wire-framed glasses, and suddenly, I see those same eyes looking down at me: *You lost your first tooth. Lucky girl.*

I cough over the anxiety rising in my chest. "I didn't know you had a sister."

"She died when we were young."

"I'm sorry." I swallow hard. My throat suddenly feels as if it's stuffed with cotton. I tighten my grip on the glass when I feel my fingers tremble with nerves.

"I know you thought Kitten and I were rushing things, but she told me about the day you were taken, and I told her about my sister. I proposed to her the next day. We bonded over shared experiences. We both understand how it feels to lose someone."

"I'm glad you have each other." I steal another glance at the box. My fingers twitch. I have to hold it. I bring the glass of bourbon to my lips—purely habitual. I remember too late the possibility that someone's been drugging me. And Eliot has a box I may or may not have held as a child. And he has a sister. I wince as the bourbon goes down—*Don't take another sip*, I tell myself—then force a smile.

"Eliot, would you mind . . . just a splash of water in this drink? Strong bourbon."

One hand emerges from his khaki pocket. "Of course."

The moment he disappears around the corner, I rush to the box.

I flip the clasp on the lid and gasp at the sight of curly locks tied with pink ribbons. I blink hard to ensure I'm not imagining what I see, but the curls are still there when I open my eyes. Mostly blonde. Some brunette.

In an instant, it all floods back to me: the chloroform-soaked rag he used to incapacitate me, the funny-tasting juice, the cold nights on a mattress, waking up soaked in my own urine because I'd slept through the urge to go, the baths in freezing water . . .

My heartbeat fills my ears, and the world goes askew. But I have to hold it together. I clear my throat. Put the box back on the shelf. "Was Kitten pissed that I didn't make the fitting yesterday?" I say loudly, so Eliot will hear me in the kitchen. I turn around, only to see he's standing a few feet away. Did he see me open the box? "I didn't mean to miss it. Something came up."

"I'll say. You rescued that girl. It's all over the news. Former kidnap victim rescues abducted girl."

"Survivor," I say. "I prefer *survivor.* Not victim."

"You remind me of Amy," he says. "We never went back to the lake house where she died. They all blamed me. It was my fault. I was supposed to be keeping an eye on her. She wandered into the water when I turned my back."

When Cupid shoots an arrow through your heart, it means you found true love. Your brother loves you.

I remember now: he drew a heart on my arm, and when I awoke the next day, there was an arrow cut into my arm.

My heart kicks up a gear. "I know who you are," I say. "Isn't that why you left Skyler's tooth at the Moonbeam? You wanted me to take it. You wanted me to remember."

I expect him to deny it, but he doesn't. "Blessed are the forgetful. I've been watching you for a long time, waiting for a way to get back into your life."

"Get back into my life? Or get attention? It's why you wrote the letter to the press. You need the world to know what you've done. It's why you kept tormenting my mom with those emails. You wanted her to know how many times you'd gotten away with it."

He looks unhappy, as if I've offended him. "No, Holly. You don't—"

"I do know." I'm backing toward the door. It's getting dark outside, and Kitten really should be home by now. I wonder if she figured out who he really is, too. "Where's Kitten?"

"I'll take you to her."

What does that mean? I take another step back. "Just tell me where she is."

For a split second, he smiles sadly. Then he lunges at me, rocks glass in hand, and cracks my temple with it.

CHAPTER 34

Holly

June 9

"You cut my project short. I have to finish, you understand. I have to prove what I can do. I have to finish."

My head aches, and I hear a recurrent tapping or thumping all around me.

I'm on the floor of a living room I've never seen before. It's a monument to 1970—orange-and-gold shag carpeting, wrought iron painted white. There's a strange odor here. Something like mothballs mixed with rotting meat. It's making me nauseated. I have to get out of here or I'm going to hurl all over this tacky vinyl sofa. I sit up, press my legs together, and still feel the outline of my holster at my ankle. I can't tell if the firearm is still in its pocket.

"Where are we?"

"This is my mom's house." Eliot—or William Wright, I suppose—crouches in front of me. "I brought you here when you didn't wake up. How's your head?" He touches my temple. I flinch away. "I didn't mean to hit you that hard."

"I'm okay."

"Good. Sweet girl."

The fluorescent light in the hallway is buzzing, and the thumping, I realize, is bass pumping from the room below me. I focus on a black object on the gold-and-glass cocktail table behind him. My firearm. He found it. He probably has my cell phone, too. I don't feel it in my pocket.

"I have a problem." He paces the floor in front of me. "You know I can't let you go again."

"Tell me about the problem, and we'll figure it out." If I stick out a leg at the right moment, I might be able to trip him long enough to take advantage, long enough to regain possession of my firearm. But my head hurts. It's hard to focus.

"Death should be beautiful. I make them beautiful, you see. The living dolls. When I squeeze the life out of them, they're still pretty. Amy wasn't. Amy was bloated and green and—"

"They don't stay pretty, though," I say, "after you kill them. You know that, right? They decay, just like anyone. Their skin turns gray and green just like Amy. It falls off their bones—"

"Stop." He covers an ear with his hand. "Stop."

"You keep their curls in that box, and—"

"And you want the box, don't you? I was pleased when you took the one at Vera's. I saw it earlier, the first time Kitten and I went there, and I wondered if it would make you think of our time together. You so badly wanted it back then. I knew you'd want it again."

"I don't want it. I just want to remember."

"You were the only project I didn't finish—until Skyler. Damn it, I was so close to finishing her, and then everything started happening with Kitten, with your boyfriend—"

"Sterling? What does he—"

"You can help me finish. You're *obligated.* I let you go. You *owe me.*"

"I can't do that."

"But you *have* to! You have to or I'll keep doing it."

"Is that why you wrote the letter about Deanna Renee Rhine? You want to stop, don't you?"

"I want to *finish.* I'll stop when it's all finished."

"My mom figured it out. Did you nudge her over the ravine? Because she was going to tell?"

"No, I didn't . . . I *wouldn't* . . ."

"I met someone from your past."

His eyes widen. He leans against a chair and tightens his fingers around its back. "Impossible. There's no one left."

"Does Kitten know you were married before?"

His knuckles grow white, and his jaw tenses.

"Yanneth said—"

"You don't know what you're talking about."

"I know everything. I know about the dolls."

He shoves off the chair—"You don't know anything"—and pulls at his hair. The second he turns his back on a pivot, I shoot out a leg, and he stumbles. A split second later, I scramble toward the cocktail table as he goes down.

He pulls at my leg, but I already have my firearm in hand. I aim it at his head.

My vision blurs for a second.

"Stop right there," I say.

He glances at me; only his eyeballs move. His hands are up. "You don't want to use that."

"I never aim unless I intend to shoot."

"Holly, put the gun down." He moves to get up.

"If you come any closer—"

"You and I both know you aren't going to pull that trigger. That's not who you are."

"You're a man who preys on little girls. You took me from my family for ninety-four days."

"I was good to you. I cared for you. I let you live once. I'm going to have to ask you to return the favor."

"I can't do that. You killed nine little girls."

"I watched you your whole life to make sure you were happy. I left you presents where I knew you'd find them."

"The dolls."

"You loved those dolls. And your tooth . . . you lost it. I wanted to give one back to you, but I couldn't bear to part with it. I gave you Skyler's instead."

"How did it happen? Why did you take me?"

"Give me the gun, Holly." He takes another step.

"Sit down," I say. "On the floor. We're going to get all of this sorted out."

"And we'll be friends?"

"For Kitten's sake."

"Holly-Dolly . . ." He takes another slow step closer. And another.

"Stop."

He barrels into me, gets a hand on my firearm.

I squeeze the trigger.

CHAPTER 35

HOLLY

June 9

My ears are ringing with the gunshot, but I think I hear sirens in the distance. A split second later, I realize they might be coming for me. Before I left home, I shared my location with Detective Guidry, just as he asked.

When I get my bearings, I realize I'm on the floor with my back to the wall. Blood soaks the carpeting around Eliot's body.

Kitten's fiancé is still breathing. I register the rise and fall of his chest in rapid succession. His stare is locked on me, and he's clutching his right shoulder.

Every beat of the bass below jogs my vision, but out of the corner of my eye, I catch sight of something glinting in the carpeting . . .

I reach for it for a closer look, and I recognize it on sight. It's Kitten's engagement ring.

"Kitten!"

"I won't tell you where she is."

His words are muffled with the ringing in my ears.

Eliot laughs even as blood spurts between his fingers, which he presses to the wound in his shoulder. "But she's going through everything you went through, and I'll see the project to the end this time."

But her ring was discarded in the living room. Does that mean Kitten has been in this room? Did she take the ring off and drop it? Did it fall off her finger? Or did Eliot take it off her finger before he brought me here? Did it fall out of his pocket when we were struggling for the gun?

The periphery of the room goes fuzzy and black. I see her again: the little blue-eyed girl. *Don't cross.*

I blink hard.

But she's still there across the room . . . only I'm staring into a photograph.

Blue-eyed girl.

Blonde hair.

It's *her*. The one I've been seeing in my dreams.

The credenza is littered with photographs of the girl. My gaze flits from one frame to the next.

Pictures of Eliot as a boy holding his sister, hugging her, stand among the others. It's a face I recognize, a link between the man who held me captive twenty years ago and the man who changed his appearance, his demeanor, even the way others perceive him to wedge his way into Kitten's life, and thus mine.

"I loved Amy." He straightens against the base of a yellow floral sofa across from me, winces in pain. "I took the best care of her I could. It was just one of those things that wasn't supposed to happen."

"Neither was I supposed to be taken from my family, and neither were ten other girls—"

"It wasn't my idea. Not the first time. Not with you."

"Whose idea was it?"

"But once I had you, I couldn't let you go."

"Whose idea was it?"

"Your boyfriend was getting close. He figured things out."

"Sterling?"

"He was asking all the right questions, and the night of the bonfire, after the carpenter found you passed out on the bluffs, he found me watching you."

"Where is he?"

Eliot laughs.

"Where is he?"

"As Amy would say, *That's for me to know and you to find out.*"

"Eliot. *Where is he?* Where is *Kitten*?"

The sirens are growing louder now, and the flash of patrol car lights spins over the walls. I hold my breath. If the police are merely passing the house on their way to another call, the lights will pass right over us. But when they remain, I exhale.

It's almost over.

"I did the kindest thing in the world for you," he says. "I let you live even though I was dying inside. And even though someone else went away for the crime, I was still paying the price."

"You're not the only one," I remind him. "You've altered the course of life for eleven girls, and eleven families."

"I couldn't help it. It was the only way I could get a little bit of my sister back over and over and over again."

A loud pop sounds, and suddenly, the place is flooded with cops, all with weapons drawn. "Drop your firearm, ma'am."

I say a prayer and let it go.

I'm shoved onto my stomach and cuffed.

I'm staring across the orange shag at my offender, in a similar position.

His eyes fill with tears.

Now that I'm looking into his eyes, I can't imagine how I ever forgot them. I can't imagine I ever will again.

CHAPTER 36

HOLLY

June 9

When they had a minute to assess the situation, the cops removed the cuffs from my wrists and gave me an ice pack for the rug burn on my cheek, a result of their shoving me to the floor. They located my cell phone in Eliot's pocket, and they've returned it to me, even if they've bagged my firearm as evidence.

Someone's taking my vitals in an ambulance outside the house Eliot grew up in, and the ringing in my ears is beginning to subside. The dominant bass suddenly ceases, and I hear a call from within the house: "Gurney!"

Moments later, two EMTs wheel a body out of the house.

I jump out of the ambulance when I see the blonde hair spilling over the edge. "Kitten."

"She'll be okay." Guidry is instantly at my side.

"What's wrong with her?"

"High levels of flunitrazepam, likely. She's in shock, she's cold . . . but she'll make it. She's tough."

"Yeah."

"We should get you to the hospital," Guidry says.

"I'm okay."

"You're more than okay," the cop says. "You've been a rock star."

CHAPTER 37

HOLLY

June 12

Eliot, a.k.a. William Wright, is still in the ICU, under armed guard, suffering from complications of a gunshot wound. It's my hope that he survives, and not only because I don't carry a firearm to take lives. I want him to answer for what he's done.

Too many families have questions. Too many people have been terrorized with his actions. Dying would be too easy for him.

Kitten rests her head against my shoulder as we stare into a bonfire her brother tends on the bluffs.

"It was fine," she says of the questioning she underwent after her release from the hospital. "The detective just asked me when I figured it out . . . that Eliot was responsible for what happened to Holly when we were kids."

"Sounds like they were nicer to you than they were to me," Matt says.

"About that," I say. "That's probably my fault. I didn't trust anyone for a few hours."

Matt winks and throws another log onto the fire. "You trust me now?"

"Anyway," Kitten says. "I was looking through the proofs from our black-and-white party photo shoot. And there was one frame where he

was staring at Holly. *Staring* at her, and it started coming back to me. But I thought it was crazy. I mean, how could *Eliot* be the one who took her? So I started rummaging through his stuff, and I found a box labeled 'Pictures,' so I opened it. There were a ton of pictures of Holly as a little girl, posed on her side, in the same white nightgown she had on when she came home. And then I dug deeper and found pictures of all these other little girls in the same outfits. Just pictures of them sleeping. I went to call 9-1-1, and he was suddenly there, nervous, saying I didn't understand and he could explain. And he made me a drink and sat me down to talk about it . . . and that's all I remember. The lab results explained why."

My blood work had come back with traces of flunitrazepam, too. As unsettling as it is to know I was repeatedly drugged, it's also discombobulating to know I never considered Eliot a threat. I'd suspected Sterling, Matt, Vellerman, Paul Hershey, and even for a few seconds, my own parents. When I think about how close Kitten came to marrying the man who abducted me and thus shook up all our lives, I can't help but think I failed her.

"And next I knew," Kitten says, "I was in a dark place with all these boxed-up dolls lining the walls, and . . . it was creepy."

When they tore through Eliot's apartment and his parents' place, the police found all Sterling's notes, which they assume Eliot had stolen. The research concluded Alan Kohlbrook couldn't have been responsible for my abduction. But Sterling's notes never implicated Eliot. Sterling's still missing, and Eliot's not talking.

Kitten wipes a tear from her eye. "This is all my fault."

"Kitten."

"No, it is. I said it was Kohlbrook. I said, *It's one of Daddy's friends.* I recognized him from church, and I even told Dad that. And he said, *It's this guy.* And I knew it wasn't . . . I must have known it wasn't. Alan Kohlbrook doesn't look anything like Eliot, but Dad was so insistent . . ." She shook her head. "Why would he be so insistent?"

That's a good question. And I think my mom knows the answer.

Cecily

Paul and I met halfway between the Antiques Warehouse and the Indiana state line at a dive bar he frequented.

I didn't intend to bring the gun. But I grabbed it when I went to retrieve the thick envelopes of cash Paul had sent during Holly's absence. He referenced in his letter the plans we'd made together. I can only guess he was referring to leaving our spouses. I'd opened what I called a divorce fund account, but the moment the press got hold of the story—I'd received money from a mysterious source, and my own husband had ratted me out—I knew I couldn't possibly spend any of it. I tried to return it many times, but Paul became more and more elusive.

I even offered it to Susan once, for Matt's college expenses, but she's a proud woman. She refused my help. Still, *I didn't want the money.* I was hell-bent on returning the entire sum to him the day we met to discuss his lies. Maybe he would offer the money to Kitten and Eliot for their wedding. Maybe he would put it into a trust fund for his future grandkids. I didn't care what he ultimately did with it, as long as it was gone from my house.

Trevor's GLOCK was there in the safe, calling to me. The GLOCK was never part of the plan, but when I saw it, an addendum came to me, a contingency.

So I carefully picked it up and slid it into my purse and then into the glove box in Holly's car.

This was my plan:

First, get answers. Why had Paul misled me about Kitten's paternity? Why did he allow me to believe the baby I'd put up for adoption was his daughter? And most important: I wanted to know the truth about Trevor and Susan's affair. He said he had photographs of them together, but considering *his* reaction to the pictures, he'd made me wonder if I was too weak to look at them. I probably was . . . if that envelope contained the kind of pictures he said it did.

Second, relay the answers to Trevor and hope he'd understand the secrets about the child I'd never discussed with him. The night he confronted me about Avery, I let him believe he was Avery's father. I never told him the rest of the story—that I gave her up because I thought she was Paul's, and after Holly's abduction, in our family's fragile state, I didn't think we could survive the blow.

Third, if Trevor couldn't accept the truth, if he couldn't forgive me for what I'd done and move along the path we'd only recently reconvened on, I was going to finish what I had started out at the ravine the day Alan Kohlbrook stopped me: I would end my life, end the incessant suffering of my inadequacy, and I figured the GLOCK could only help in that case.

Kitten had already asked Trevor to give her away at her wedding. Holly already called Susan *Mom*. I, like Paul, could lift right out of the scene, and maybe everyone would be better for it.

Paul opened his arms for a hug when he saw me enter the bar. But I sat without touching him and got right down to business:

"Is it true?" I asked. "You can't have children?"

"So Susan finally told you." Paul smirked and brought his drink to his lips.

"Why would you let me think the baby was yours?"

"You said you were going to give her away. The decision was made."

"That's not *exactly* how it happened, but I may have made a different decision had I known she was my husband's baby. Instead, I was wondering how I would make things work. I couldn't ask Trev to support a kid that wasn't his, and I had trouble raising the one I had with his help. I couldn't do it on my own."

Paul shrugged. "C'est la vie, my friend. C'est la vie." He threw back the drink and promptly ordered another.

"Explain yourself, will you? I've come all this way."

"You want to know why I gave you the money. Why I lied to you. Why I misled you." He shakes his head, as if he can't believe he has to spell it out for me.

"Please."

"Because it all got out of hand, that's why. It started so easily. With your laugh."

"My laugh?"

He swallowed a shot of bourbon.

"Paul, you're drunk."

"I fell for you, Ceci." He grabbed my hand. "Fell for you hard. Susan didn't need me anymore. Her business was doing well, and she was good at juggling work and the house and kids. She really could do it all on her own. Why did she need a deadbeat gambler around? But you . . . you needed me. You leaned on me, and I liked being there for you."

"We commiserated with each other. Our spouses had an affair. It was only natural for us to band together."

He sighed. "Did they have an affair?"

"You said you hired an investigator. I split the bill with you."

"Yeah."

"You said you had pictures, and you said it made you sick to look at them."

"I hired Kohlbrook to spy on you. All your talk about revenge and getting even . . . I had to know if you were getting back at Trevor by sleeping with someone else, because by then I was so in love with you that I . . . I had to know. So Kohlbrook followed you around for a week.

The only pictures in that envelope were of you and your daughter. I gave them back to him after we talked about it that day."

My jaw dropped, and my brows came together in a painful knot. "The pictures the cops found in a shoebox under his bed? The pictures that helped to convict him of Holly's abduction? He took them for you? But you told me the photos in that envelope were of Trevor and Susan." I brought the bourbon to my lips and mindlessly sipped. It was all too much to grasp.

"You have to understand. I realized you needed me even more. I didn't have to show you proof of what we already knew was going on between Susan and Trevor."

"You just admitted we don't know what was going on."

"We both knew it would happen eventually," Paul said. "With me out of the picture, they were bound to get together."

"They didn't. Once you left, and after I drove myself to the hospital to deliver a baby I'd managed to conceal from my husband, *nothing happened*."

"Like I said, it got out of hand. I'd just bought the lake property, and I got it cheap. Really cheap because there was some tragedy that occurred there a few years before. And the guy had a son. A good kid that used to take a beating on the regular from this guy who, believe it or not, was a Methodist pastor. I made a deal with the kid. He could use the property, but he had to keep it mowed. Had to keep it cleaned up."

"Is that where you brought Trevor hunting? When he thought you'd find Holly in the field?"

"That's the place. I paid the kid to watch her. She wasn't supposed to be gone that long. A day or so. And I'd find her, and I'd be the hero for a change, and you'd finally see me as a hero, as someone you could love."

With tears in my eyes, I took a drink in hand.

"He was supposed to bring her to the field off Route 80. Only when we passed and saw the vultures, I feared the worst, that the kid had snapped. We searched the field, and thank god she wasn't dead. But she was supposed to be there alive, and there was no sign of her. The next day, I drove back out to the lake house to find out what happened, but the kid demanded money to keep quiet, and I didn't have what he wanted. I took everything out of Matt's college fund, but it wasn't enough. And the kid kept saying he'd kill Holly if I told anyone where she was. He'd already killed his sister, he said. He knew how to do it. And I couldn't risk that, Cecily. And I couldn't just go and get her or you'd know I knew where she was, and you were pregnant by then, and Susan was pissed about the money I kept gambling, so I gave up. I won a tournament and gave you the money to help with the baby. I gave up and disappeared."

I was speechless.

That money had put all the suspicion on me.

I looked at the money on the bar. This was Matt's college fund? And I'd been keeping it in our wall safe while he earned tuition on the GI bill?

But Paul wasn't done: "I'm the reason, okay? I'm the reason it all happened. I set it up. I hired him to distract the girls that day. Just like our plan, Ceci. We'd take from them the brightest spots in their lives. I'd bring them back. I'd be the hero. The ultimate revenge, just like we planned."

I lowered my voice. "We never talked about planning a *kidnapping.* We talked about *leaving them* and denying them custody."

"When Holly came back and Kitten started remembering, she was saying, it's William from church. And I knew that if they found William, he'd tell them what really happened, so I said, *No, Kitten. It's Al. You remember, don't you?* And she did it. She lied to the police because I confused her. I made her think it was someone else."

"If you knew Kitten was wrong—"

"Listen. Kohlbrook deserved it, all right? He peeped in windows and took little girls' pictures. A real sick guy. But William only did it for one reason: I paid him to do it. That's why Kitten said it was a friend of mine. She'd seen us together. That's why—"

"William who? What's his name?"

"It doesn't matter. They put the right man away."

It took another drink to pry the name out of him, a drink he ultimately pressured me to share with him, but once I heard the name, and the name he was going by now, my head started to ache.

"We have to go to the police," I said.

"Are you crazy?"

"Are *you*?"

"Keep the money," he suggested. "Hush."

I shoved the money toward him. "I don't want your money."

"They'll nab me, Ceci. I'm an accessory."

But I was already halfway out the door, instantly drenched in the downpour.

Paul was on my heels, gaining on me.

I picked up speed and was running by the time I reached the Explorer. I locked the doors just as he tried to grab me.

He pounded on the window as I turned the key in the ignition. "You can't! You can't do this to me! They'll think you were in on it, too!"

But I didn't care. It was time the truth came out.

I had to call the police. My phone wasn't hooked up to the Bluetooth in Holly's car. Through heaving sobs, and icy rain, I drove with Paul on my tail, rummaging through my purse for my phone.

I shouldn't have taken the shortcut. I should've taken the long way around to the police department, but I was just so anxious to get there.

Finally, I had my phone in my hand.

I had to enter my pass code three times before I got it right.

I dialed.

9.

1.

1.

I eased my foot off the gas to round the bend, but that only gave Paul the opportunity to kiss my bumper.

I don't know what happened, except to say that everything went black.

It's true what they say happens when you're about to die . . . you see flashes of the past. You remember intense emotions, you forgive.

I called out to him—*Trevor!*—and I hoped he'd hear me. I hoped he knew I loved him.

I heard him call back: *Cecily. I love you, too. Always have, always will.*

But when I reached out for Holly, there was only nothingness.

Holly?

Finally, in the back of my mind, I heard her reply: "Mom?"

CHAPTER 38

HOLLY

June 15

Every morning, I wake up expecting to see Sterling at my door, ready to retrieve his dog. Once the drama died down, and days after Sterling disappeared without a trace, I contacted the department kenneling her and offered to keep her until they tracked Sterling down. They were only too pleased to send her back to me.

"She ate her way out of the crate," the deputy who delivered her told me. "She chewed a hole the size of a softball in the back seat."

Every morning, I latch on her leash and head out the door.

I wave to Matt and Kitten, who are breakfasting on the veranda of the house Susan decided to keep. She'll have a roommate in Kitten for a while, too. But Matt will be staying at my parents' place, helping Dad renovate. I call through the wildflower field, "Up for bowling later?"

Matt gives me a thumbs-up.

I wave and head to my father's home office, where Dad and I are going to discuss options, now that Vellerman is no longer a foreman with the company. I enter through the back door, inhale the scent of my childhood home, and remember what life used to be like here. I see my father and Susan laughing in the kitchen; Matt, Kitten, and me sharing a bowl of popcorn on the floor in front of the television; and my mom on the fringes, with smudges of paint on her hands and shirt, her paintbrush drawing strokes over an old piece of furniture.

"Holly?" Dad's voice echoes through the hallway. "Is that you?"

"Yeah." I shake free from the memory, but the ache remains: I miss my mom.

I let Dog off the leash, and she follows me down the hall to my father's den, where he's sitting at his desk. A stack of papers is on the desktop; a box of what looks like unopened mail is at his feet.

"What's all this?"

"I found this in the basement studio."

"You're going through Mom's stuff?"

"If she was afraid of something, maybe I can figure what."

"And?"

"So far, just nasty notes from the peanut gallery. From when you were gone."

"They all thought she knew what happened to me."

Dad's eyes meet mine. "This isn't anything for *you* to worry about. Just concentrate on—"

"Dad. Stop. I'm not a kid anymore."

It takes a moment for him to respond: "Is there anything wrong with wanting to protect your daughter? I want you to live the best life possible."

"Help me understand, then," I say. "How is it you hired a retired cop to run my site before you'd consider giving me a shot?"

"He had credentials," Dad says. "A full-blown résumé with references before I even asked for it."

"Which should have been your first clue that it was all bullshit," I say. "What career carpenter has an attaché full of paperwork at the ready? But this isn't really about the cop. It's about *me.* Why don't you think I can handle it?"

"You can handle it, Holly. I just want to make sure you're doing it because it's what you really want to do. You have this degree—"

"It's what I thought I wanted to do while I started college. But I was eighteen when I decided that. A lot's changed. And now . . . now that I know everything that happened to me, now that I have the closure that was missing all those years . . . I feel like I helped the one person I really needed to help—me."

"What about Skyler? You don't think people like Skyler need help?"

"Who says I can't be there for Skyler and wear pouches on my belt for a living?"

Dad opens his mouth to retort, but I don't give him the chance.

"I'm registered with the county crisis center as a volunteer. I promised Skyler and her parents that I'd be as involved with her recovery as they need me to be."

"Finish your master's, take the LCSW—"

"Dad. I'm fine." I pause for a moment to let it sink in. "*I'm fine.* Ever since I came back, you've done everything in your power to help protect me. You taught me to shoot. You sent me to *jujitsu* classes, and they *work.* I practically kicked Matt's ass the other day. You raised me among some of the toughest guys in one of the toughest industries, and *I can hold my own*. I'm twenty-five. I've survived some pretty awful stuff in my time here. I can take care of myself."

His brows lift, as if he's perhaps considering the possibility for the first time. "When you go through what our family went through, you can't be too sure."

"I'm sure I'm okay. I'm sure I'm doing what I'm supposed to be doing with my life."

"Okay."

I wait, but Dad doesn't elaborate. I push on: "You're out a foreman at the concept house. Give me a shot. It's time, don't you think?"

After a breath or two, he nods. "Probably." He extends his hand. "Welcome aboard, foreman."

"Thank you, sir." I shake his hand; Dog noses in and licks Dad clean up his arm.

"You're going to need to fill a journeyman spot." Dad leans back in his chair. "We can put out an ad."

"I was thinking of offering the job to a certain US soldier," I say. "If he's interested."

"Good idea."

The question is . . . Is Matt Hershey man enough to work for his future girlfriend?

I take a walk past the ravine before heading home.

Through the trees, I imagine my mother there, rounding the bend safely. I imagine she made it home that night and that I dropped in for a visit.

In my fantasy, I lie on her lap, like I used to . . . before. And she plays with my hair, and we make plans for lunch. She'll joke about buying tarts instead of burning the ones she'd make in the kitchen herself. And I'll laugh, and I'll tell her because I don't think I ever did: *You're a good mom. You struggled, but you're beating your addiction. And I learned so much from you.*

"Are you ever going to wake up, Mom? You have to tell me what happened here. Who scared you and pushed you over the edge?"

Dog starts sniffing near the guardrail, still dented where Mom toppled over it.

Sniffing turns to barking.

I choke up on the leash but still have to get too close to the edge for comfort to coerce the dog to retreat.

But she's adamant, so I take her around to the steep path marked with a sign: **HIKE AT YOUR OWN RISK.**

She yanks on the leash, sniffing, leading me.

We're well into the woods when I see the body—mangled and washed up on the creek bed.

Derrion Sterling.

CHAPTER 39

HOLLY

July 18

The official ruling came in yesterday. William Eliot Wright was found guilty on all counts—including the murder of Sterling, who died of blunt force trauma to the head the night we gathered on the bluffs for a bonfire.

Wright described in detail how it happened: Once Kitten and Matt retired to Susan's place for the night, and after Vellerman got me home, Sterling found Eliot looking in my window. They struggled, and Eliot hit him across the back of his head. It was an accident, he said. He never meant to kill him.

He provided the same courtesy for the families of the missing girls. He led authorities to their remains, all of which were buried on properties his father once owned.

Since, the police have recovered the bodies of all the victims. The remains of each revealed a missing tooth—lower-right central incisor in every case—further suggesting that Wright indeed was responsible for each of their disappearances.

His motivation? Attempting to re-create the scene of his sister's death with a different outcome: he'd watch the coverage on the news, and he wouldn't be blamed for it.

Reporters have asked me if I'm sorry he didn't die. Others have asked if I'm sorry I shot the bastard. My answer is always the same. My life was at stake. Kitten's was, too. And I didn't aim to kill. I aimed to save us.

Alan Kohlbrook's appeal was put on the fast track, and he's been granted a full pardon. At his request, he'll be housed at a medical facility, where he can't possibly have access to little girls. Among the evidence pardoning him was a compilation of items Wright referred to as his Dash Stash: my missing tooth, a patch of gauze stained with Gretchen's blood, and a slew of items from each of his victims—including a scrap of fabric from my favorite romper. All this he kept in a box in the condo he shared with my best friend.

Today is also my mother's birthday, but I don't feel much like celebrating. She's still unresponsive. Today marks as many days in her coma as the number of days I was missing—ninety-four.

I'm heading to the hospital because my father is there, and I feel we should be celebrating together, even if Mom won't do much interacting.

I finger my mother's ring, still wrapped around my pinkie, and head toward the elevators.

Matt texts: Tacos at your place? I'll cook.

I reply: Good. It'll be edible.

Text you when I'm on my way home.

He texts again: I have a surprise for you.

A photo pops up. It's a dog tag, but not the kind Matt wears around his neck.

This one is for the dog I inherited when Sterling died. Her new name makes me smile: **COMISKEY**.

And I think Sterling would have understood. A Sox fan just can't have a dog named Wrigley.

"Excuse me."

“Sorry.” I step aside and look up from my phone to see I’m face-to-face with a girl I’ve seen once before. High ponytail. Blonde. Blue eyes.

She enters the elevator next to me and offers her hand. “Avery,” she says.

“Holly,” I say. “Nice to meet you.”

“Same.”

The elevator stops to let me out, and Avery follows. She takes a seat in the chairs outside my mother’s room, opens a book, and begins to read. I look at her one last time before I enter.

My father is seated at Mom’s bedside, gripping one of her hands, crying.

“Dad? What’s going on?”

Dad turns toward me.

His tears are joyful.

My mother’s eyes are open. “Holly, I have something to tell you.” Her voice is gravelly. “I’ll tell you everything.”

“Shh.” I pat her hand. “You should rest, Mom.”

“I’ve been asleep for ninety-four days. I’m not tired.”

I laugh through my tears. Mom smiles.

“You asked me what happened at the ravine. You asked if I knew about the scar on your arm . . .”

“I asked you a lot of things.”

“It all started when you were gone.”

And she tells me everything: about Paul Hershey, whom the cops picked up this morning, and how he’ll pay for deceiving her and putting me in danger.

She tells me about my little sister, who wants to be part of our lives.

I look toward the girl in the hallway, lean to Mom, and kiss her cheek. “I think we need to add another birthstone to this ring.” I twist the ring from my pinkie finger and slide it onto hers.

“I know what you must be thinking . . . I’m barely Mom enough for you, and now you have to share me.”

"Actually, I was thinking . . . what lucky girls we are . . . to have a mom like you. A mom who keeps fighting even when others would have quit. A mom who keeps up her quest for the truth, even when the whole world tells her she's crazy."

Tears brighten her eyes. "Holly."

"You fought for me, Mom. You gave me my strength."

"That came from your father."

"No. He helped me to be physically strong, but my inner strength, Mom, the strength that makes me a survivor? That came from you. I know that, Mom. I've always known it. I love you."

"I love you, too."

ACKNOWLEDGMENTS

Writing a book about serial kidnapping took me to dark places. Research was often difficult to conduct. It's not nice knowing these things occur—and often. However, something unexpected happened when I began to sift through stories of survival—I saw new hope. I thank survivors, whom I've never met, for sharing with the world stories of their strength. I appreciate the outreach of the parents and families of the missing and lost, who keep these cases at the forefront of their lives, however difficult it may be to do so. Thank you to survivors, victims, and their families, to journalists who cover the cases, to law enforcement and investigators who dig through decades of evidence, to technicians who process and preserve it. Innumerable hugs to the mothers of the missing. No one should have to endure what you have survived.

Infinite and additional thanks to (in no particular order) . . .

Readers: whether you're *my* readers or just readers in general, you're my people.

My team at Lake Union, especially Jodi Warshaw, Caitlin Alexander, Gabe, and Erin Mooney: You're always team players. With all of you, writing feels like less of a solitary process.

Frank Weimann of Folio Lit: here's to the launch of great endeavors!

Patrick W. Picciarelli: It's always a pleasure discussing our craft and police procedure. I can't wait to finish that collaboration.

Mary, Muffin, Margaret, Jonathan, and Caroline, my second family: I'm so glad we have each other!

My girlfriends, Mary, Kaaryn, Angela, Nikki, Kelly, Wendy, Jessica, Lainey, Jillicious, Melissa, et al.: You're all my Kittens.

My mom, aunts, sisters, brothers, cousins, and nana: enormous hugs in exchange for your support.

My uncle Jimmy: now that you're retired, you should spend more time reading books and less time making large canvas prints and JibJabs.

The real Holly Adryenne and her mother: I miss you! And thanks for letting me borrow your kick-ass name.

Joshua: you know why you're important . . . and it's not just because you entertained my plans for our very own chusky, who is systematically dismantling (and eating) our home.

My daughters, whether biological or honorary: I'm proud of you all! Now that you're almost grown, I thought I'd worry less. I was wrong. Momming is an eternal occupation, but I wouldn't trade it for the world on a silver platter. You have made me what I am. LOVE LOVE!

ABOUT THE AUTHOR

Photo © 2017 Bella Vie Photography

Brandi Reeds is the Amazon Charts bestselling author of *Trespassing* and *Third Party*. Under the pseudonym Sasha Dawn, she writes critically acclaimed young adult novels of psychological suspense, including *Panic*; *Blink*, an Edgar Award nominee; and *Oblivion*, which was chosen as one of the New York Public Library's Best Books for Teens, recommended by the *School Library Journal*, endorsed by the American Library Association, and selected by the 2016 Illinois Reading Council as a featured book.

Reeds earned her BA in history and English from Northern Illinois University, followed by an MA in writing from Seton Hill University. When not working on her next book, she heads a home-renovation company as a kitchen-design consultant and cabinetry specialist. She's also an avid traveler, reader, and dance enthusiast. Reeds is a Chicago native (Go, White Sox!) and currently lives in the northern suburbs with her husband, daughters, and four puppies. Visit her at www.sashadawnbooks.com.

Made in the USA
Monee, IL
25 July 2024

62650383R00184